Veil of Justice

J.J. Miller

Innkeeper Publishing

© 2022 Innkeeper Publishing

All rights reserved. No part of this book may be reproduced or transmitted in any form or by any means, electronic or mechanical, including photocopying, recording, or by any information storage and retrieval system, without permission in writing from the copyright owner.

This is a work of fiction. Names, characters, places and incidents either are the product of the author's imagination or are used fictitiously, and any resemblance to any actual persons, living or dead, events, or locales is entirely coincidental.

Books by J.J. Miller

BRAD MADISON SERIES

Force of Justice

Divine Justice

Game of Justice

Blood and Justice

Veil of Justice

CADENCE ELLIOTT SERIES

I Swear To Tell

The Lawyer's Truth

Contents

PART I	1
Chapter 1	2
Chapter 2	16
Chapter 3	22
Chapter 4	29
Chapter 5	38
Chapter 6	45
Chapter 7	53
Chapter 8	61
Chapter 9	68
Chapter 10	77
Chapter 11	85
Chapter 12	90
Chapter 13	96
Chapter 14	103
Chapter 15	109

Chapter 16	112
Chapter 17	121
Chapter 18	127
Chapter 19	136
Chapter 20	142
Chapter 21	149
Chapter 22	154
PART II	160
Chapter 23	161
Chapter 24	175
Chapter 25	191
Chapter 26	199
Chapter 27	203
Chapter 28	208
Chapter 29	211
Chapter 30	215
Chapter 31	224
Chapter 32	231
Chapter 33	239
Chapter 34	253
Chapter 35	261
Chapter 36	268
Chapter 37	274

Chapter 38	282
Chapter 39	289
Chapter 40	293
Chapter 41	300
Afterword	306
Books by J.J. Miller	307

PART I

Chapter 1

I don't know what came over me. Actually, that's a lie. I do know. It just took a long time for reality to sink into my thick skull. Only then was I able to admit that my emotions got the better of me, that I mistook vengeance for justice, which is never good for a defense attorney. Things got way too personal and I let my heart control my head. Naturally, I only understood what was what when it was too late. By then the damage was done.

It all started with grief, which, I'd wager, is the emperor of all emotions. A bad emperor. It's true that grief can be powerfully transformative, but not before the hard labor of desolation has been endured. And in those darkest of days, grief can bring out our worst, the deep injury pushing self-righteousness to steroid induced levels. It can turn Joe Blow Average into a megalomaniac, sweet Aunt Selma into Lady Macbeth. Grief has ripped families apart, pitched clans into blood feuds, hurtled nations into war.

As for me, it kept me in a rage. So much so I struggled to keep my shit together. I had a deep burning inside of me that I fought hard not to show. For my daughter's sake, mainly. It was bad enough for a 12-year-old girl to see her mother on her death bed. The least I could do was spare Bella the spectacle of me venting my fury on anyone in this world who couldn't help end our nightmare. I had to play it cool even though my blood boiled.

I wasn't comfortable being so angry. It's true when they say anger is like a drug. It gives you a rush of righteousness and power, but if a man never learns the error of giving that sentiment its head, he pretty much lacks the wherewithal to acquire wisdom. Prisons are full of such men.

I may not have understood why I was so angry, but I did know who I was angry at. Claire. My ex-wife. The mother of my child. The woman who once was, I can say with absolute clarity, the love of my life. And I was angry at her husband Marty.

It was like I actually believed none of this would have happened on my watch.

See? If you want an example of grief turning a man maniacal, there you have it.

But, like I said, I kept a lid on my rage. Everyone was doing their best. Even Marty, I suppose. Still, it was hard not to keep him in my sights.

Claire's accident was a month ago. A speeding car had crashed into her as she pulled out of her garage in Venice Beach. The offending car disappeared into the night and even now the cops were none the wiser about who was behind the wheel. They'd fallen back to play the averages, settling on the theory that the culprit was either a drunk or a joyrider. Either way, it was a needle in a haystack job for the LAPD. And, yes, I was deeply pissed at them. Add them to the pile.

Claire was barely alive when they got her to the hospital. Just about every rib on her left side was fractured, as well as her left scapula and ankle. But the critical injury was the blow she took to the head. Her brain had smashed violently against the inside of her skull. There were contusions. There were hematomas. She endured hours of neurosurgery. They actually lost her once.

While Bella and I were on a flight back from Hawaii after I'd gotten the news, Claire had flat-lined on the operating table. They managed to bring her back to life but she'd been in a coma ever since. The doctors believed there was brain function but it was so marginal they were careful not to fan false hope.

So the storm of grief centered on Claire wasn't for the dead but the slow dying. It seemed just a matter of time before her life support would be switched off, and for the end of her life to become official.

After the crash, Bella moved straight in with me. She and Marty got on well enough but she wanted to be with me. As a result, I was more closely involved in Claire's day-to-day situation than an ex would typically be.

Witnessing my daughter's ordeal was horrific. About the only positive thing to come out of it all was that Bella never shut me out. We'd always had a strong bond but we'd gotten even closer.

The hospital had rules for the loved ones of coma patients. Medical staff would only deal with one designated person for day-to-day updates on Claire's progress. Naturally, Marty assumed this role, and it was up to him to pass on the details. The email updates he sent to me and Claire's immediate family were sporadic and brief. Every week, though, the medical staff offered briefings to family members, which I attended for Bella's benefit, along with Claire's parents and sisters. Marty was never at these meetings.

Bella wanted to sleep in the ICU with Claire but this, of course, wasn't allowed. Her next best option was to maintain a vigil by her mother's bed for as long as possible. The problem was that only the designated spokesperson for the patient's loved ones, Marty, was allowed to be bedside in the morning between eight and twelve.

On top of that, Bella was just starting a new year of school. Grade 8, her last year of Middle School. Her world was in turmoil.

The way she responded made me proud. In a matter of days, her grief became selfless, her outlook mature beyond her years. She spoke calmly and compassionately about not wanting her mother to die alone. In a sense, she became her mother's guardian. She bore a soft fierceness about working with the "stupid" rules that stood between her and her mother.

We had to find a compromise, and so we transitioned into a surreal routine. We split the day. In the mornings, I'd go to work and Bella went to school. Then I'd pick her up at eleven-thirty to reach Claire by 12 on the dot. It was normalcy built on an undercurrent of dread. Claire had already died once, and it seemed only a matter of time before her condition exhausted all the neurosurgical might of the UCLA Medical Center once and for all.

Every moment I spent with Bella seemed all the more precious. I did what I could in the office for a couple of hours and my secretary, Megan, managed my time around the hospital visits. I'd return to the office for a couple of hours with Bella, get some more work done, and then we'd go home.

One morning, on the drive to the hospital, I noticed Bella lifting something carefully from her bag.

"What's that you've got?"

In my peripheral vision I could see her hand rise almost to the roof of the car.

"Something I made for Mom," she said.

I looked across and saw she was holding a dreamcatcher. A blue jewel hung in the center of the woven hoop and hanging beneath were strings of beads, seashells and turquoise feathers.

"It's beautiful, sweetheart," I said. "You've obviously inherited my creative brilliance."

"Dad!" Bella laughed softly at my joke. Claire was a jewelry designer who had founded a wildly successful business. Her daughter's artistic flair was obvious. Her laughter then faded, as a somber thought came to her.

"I should have made one earlier," she said. "They're supposed to stop you from having bad dreams."

"Your Mom's going to love it."

"Does she have dreams, Dad?"

"I'm sure she does. And if I know your mother, she would be dreaming of you and how much she loves you, and how blessed she is to have you as her daughter."

"You think?"

"Yes. I do."

I hadn't given it any thought until now, but Bella's gift reminded me of a nightmare I'd had since Claire's accident. To be honest, it was not just the one. I'd had a few and each time I'd shoved them to the back of my mind as soon as I'd woken up, glad for them to be over. Now, though, I was struck by a powerful déjà vu moment. The whole-body dread those nightmares instilled was back. In them, Claire was either dead or trapped, and I was desperate to reach her. I could hear her voice through a wall, or a door, she was calling for help and I had nothing but bare hands and numb arms. I could see but not move, I could think but not do anything of use. All I could do was stand there, on the other side, hearing Claire cry out for help while my mind was frantic and my body paralyzed.

I didn't want to say it, but I could use one of those dreamcatchers.

I tried to think of something funny to say to distract us both from our thoughts but nothing came. So I turned to practical matters.

"Have you heard from Marty?"

For the first week of our routine, we'd effectively done a handover with Marty. But over the past couple of weeks we'd seen no sign of him.

"Yes, we've been texting," Bella said with a glum tone to her voice.

"He's still coming in the morning, isn't he?"

I turned to Bella and saw her shrug her shoulders. "I guess. I sure hope so. Maybe he's been leaving earlier."

I kept my mouth shut, not wanting to air negative assumptions and stoke any kind of antipathy in Bella towards Marty. Things were hard enough already. But Marty, as Claire's husband, had a four-hour block of Claire time set aside for him and him alone. Bella would love to have every minute of that time instead of us having to come for a couple of hours, leave, and then come back again. If he wasn't coming every day, Bella would be more than a little upset. Just thinking about it got me hot under the collar. But as I said, anger was my new norm. Actually, hiding my anger was my new norm. I decided to let it go.

After parking the car, we made our way to the ICU. The whole process was all too familiar now, like commuting to a hated job. I felt like I was tagging along whereas Bella always had a sense of purpose.

She walked ahead of me with the dreamcatcher held out to the side. When we got to Claire's room, Bella put her things down and went to her mother.

"Hi Mom," she said softly and brightly as she carefully stretched over to kiss Claire's cheek. She then rested an arm across her mother's chest and laid her head upon her. She stayed like that for a minute. Then she straightened and began looking for a place to hang the dreamcatcher. She was rolling something in the fingers of her left hand and I saw that she'd brought along a ball of Scotch mounting putty. She tried stretching up to stick the dreamcatcher on the wall above Claire's head but couldn't reach.

"Let me do that," I said.

Bella handed me her gift and bent down to give Claire a kiss and hug. I backed away to leave Bella alone with her mother. She liked to talk to Claire, telling her about what was happening at school, and how she was getting along with her classmates. Thankfully, Bella had some great friends, and although I sought to include them in things we did together, most times Bella only wanted to hang out with me, or else to have time alone. She had her own phone now and was in constant contact with her buddies but I would not let her take it into her bedroom. If she was going to get any kind of cruel comments, she was not going to be dealing with them alone in her room at night. Her real-life friends were solid. It was the Facebook "friends" that worried me.

Bella took her phone out to show Claire some photos, saying that she should have seen this or that she'd have loved this or that. It killed me to watch. It was very sweet and heartbreaking all at once. Never far from my mind was the fear that this was Claire's long goodbye. The brightness in Bella's voice killed me. If I closed my eyes, Bella could have been chatting to Claire over the phone. A powerful wave of sadness rose up in me. I stepped out to the main corridor of the ward.

As I checked my phone, a nurse who I recognized approached me. She was in her mid-thirties and I knew her to be kind and thorough.

"Excuse me, Catherine," I said and she stopped. "I'm just wondering, has Marty been in today? I think we might have just missed him and I can't get him on the phone."

She looked at me like there was a sub-text to my question. She chose her words carefully.

"I haven't seen him this morning, but I've been doing my rounds, so I could have missed him."

"But you've been checking in on Claire?"

"Yes. Three times so far today."

"And you haven't seen him?"

She shook her head. "No."

"Have you been on morning shift this week?"

"This is my sixth day straight," she said, raising her eyebrows. "All mornings."

"But he's been here on other days, hasn't he?"

Catherine looked trapped.

"I'm not sure. Like I said, I'm not always here."

My blood was getting warm. "Have you seen him at all over those days?"

Catherine looked uncomfortable but she shook her head. "I can't say that I have." She clearly wanted to keep her mouth shut but her eyes told me she didn't approve.

That made two of us.

"Interesting. Thank you."

The nurse continued on.

Where the hell was Marty? His wife is in here, unlikely to recover. What gives?

As much as I was inclined to call him and ask directly I felt it wasn't my place. If I questioned his loyalty he'd no doubt tell me to butt out. And to be honest, that's exactly what I was struggling with. I felt like I was in no man's land.

I heard footsteps behind me and saw Bella enter the corridor, her eyes red and swollen from crying. She dabbed a tissue at her nose and fell into me, wrapping her arms around my waist. She then pulled away.

"I need the bathroom," she said. "And I might grab a snack from the cafeteria."

"Sure thing, honey. You need some money?"

"No, thanks. You want anything?"

I took both her hands in mine. We stood there silently for a moment before Bella spoke.

"Daddy, can you go and sit with Mom, please? While we're here, she can't be alone."

"Sure."

"Talk to her," she said, jiggling my hands. "It's really good for coma patients to hear their loved ones' voices."

I took a deep breath in. "Honey, I think your mother got pretty tired of the sound of my voice a long time ago."

"Daddy."

"Of course, I will. Maybe I'll tell her a few jokes. She always said I sucked at that. But maybe annoying her could be a good thing."

I was smiling at my daughter but my heart was shattered. As Bella walked away, I had to think twice about how old my daughter was. I had one of those moments when I felt proud of the young woman she was becoming yet mortified she was leaving the chrysalis of childhood under these conditions. I dreaded to think how she would cope with losing her mother.

I went back to sit with Claire. Her mouth was agape and her breathing loud. The machines around her were like perverse clocks, all beeping and glowing to the various rhythms of her vitals. I began telling her about Bella and how proud she would be of her. I then talked about myself, saying how my work was basically on hold and how Megan was such a trooper holding everything together. I soon ran out of my superficial news. I realized I hadn't told Claire about our trip to Hawaii, so I did that. This gave me the opportunity to steer the one-way conversation back to Bella. Then I stumbled into that horrible moment of receiving the call that turned our world upside down. The thought that Bella would have to go on without Claire tore me open.

I couldn't help it, but guilt seeped into my mind. Guilt about our marriage failing. Guilt about me being the cliche of the soldier who brought the war home. Guilt about my PTSD-induced flashbacks and the fear they put in Claire and Bella. Guilt over the look on my petrified daughter's face when I'd shot a live round into the wall during an episode in which I was convinced I was in a Taliban compound instead of my marital bedroom. Guilt over the determined protection in

Claire's eyes, and how she knew once and for all that she and Bella were not safe with me. All the shame and self-blame came back in full force. And on their heels the anger swooped in. All my anger at the world, I realized, was nothing compared to the anger I could aim at myself.

I took my ex-wife's hand.

"Claire, I don't know if you can hear me but you need to listen," I laughed ruefully at my words. Claire didn't have to listen to me anymore. She did not have to endure me anymore. She was right to divorce me, but I spent years trying to prove her wrong. I took my PTSD seriously. I quit drinking. At least I quit drinking like I used to. I got help. I became a better man. My practice thrived. And while I accepted Claire's decision, I knew that I still loved her. But that's not what I'd intended to say.

"I'm sorry I let you down. I know you were ashamed to get divorced but I gave you no choice. You did what was best for Bella and yourself. I want you to know Bella is staying with me at the moment. She's okay. She's safe. Believe me. Things are different. I'm different."

I considered how Claire had gotten on with her life after our divorce. And what a success she had made of it. Successful jewelry business, a house on the Venice canals and a new husband. A guy who was so unlike me that I was conceited enough to think I'd pushed Claire into the safe harbor of a boring man. As with the way she dealt with our divorce, I always believed, or assumed, that Claire had remarried with similar practicality, rebuilding certainty around her life and her daughter.

I felt so proud of her. I hope she knew that. I wasn't sure if I'd ever said that to her.

The thought that this would be the end hit me hard. I leaned forward and held her hand with both of mine.

"Claire, you can't go. You can't leave."

I bowed my head, lifting her hand to my forehead. I wanted to pull her back.

"You can't leave Bella. You can't. For God's sake, Claire. You can't leave me."

I felt hot tears run down my cheeks. I felt ashamed but in a way relieved by speaking the truth.

"I always thought we would get back together. I know that's not what you wanted. But deep down, did you really stop loving me, Claire?"

I wiped my eyes with my shirtsleeve, trying to collect myself and looked over my shoulder to check that no one was at the door. I sucked in some air and leaned back a little.

"Sorry, Claire. Sorry you had to hear that shit. I don't know what came over me. Pretend you never heard a thing and ignore my sappy behavior. But seriously, Claire. You need to wake the fuck up."

I leaned forward again. "Come on, this is not your time. I know it.

"I don't want to say goodbye… Jesus, Claire. You know I still…"

I hated what I was saying. I felt so weak, so pathetic. It was like I was begging Claire to save me, putting all the load on her. I shuddered, shaking the self-loathing out of me.

What happened next so surprised me that I immediately thought I was imagining things. But if I didn't know better, I thought I felt Claire's fingers move.

I held my breath, certain that I'd felt a slight pressure on my hand. I lifted my eyes to Claire's face, then my eyes darted from one screen to the next, looking for some kind of spike in the graphs.

Two of her fingers twitched in my hands. The movement was ever so slight but I was sure of it.

I stood up and leaned over Claire, my face directly over hers, looking for any sign of hope.

Her head then turned a little to the side, then back again.

I could see there was movement behind her eyelids.

I was jolted by simultaneous joy and self-awareness. If Claire was waking up, should I be here? Bella should be here. Marty should be here. I felt like an intruder.

When her eyelids opened slightly, I began to believe that our prayers had been answered.

I felt a stronger squeeze on my hands.

Her lips began to move. I leaned closer.

"Claire. Claire. Are you there?"

Her mouth parted.

"Marty. Marty. Is that you?"

I placed Claire's hand on her stomach and straightened myself. I felt like I had to leave before she saw me, my presence now seemed totally inappropriate.

"I'll go see if I can find the prick," I said quietly to myself.

Before I reached the doorway, Catherine, the nurse, rushed in.

"I think she's…" I said, as she brushed past me and went to Claire, checking all the monitors.

A moment later, she reached for the phone.

"I need Dr. Creasy here ASAP," she said into the mouthpiece.

The nurse looked at me as she spoke, smiling and shaking her head with wonder.

I had to find Bella. I went out to the hallway. As soon as I broke into a jog, Bella rounded the corner up ahead.

"Bella," I hissed at her excitedly, beckoning her to come quickly.

From the look on my face she knew it could only be one thing. She burst into a sprint, and as she got to me I gave her shoulder a quick squeeze.

"Mom's awake, honey."

CHAPTER 2

Through my office window I watched pedestrians amble up and down the Third Street Promenade. It was a beautiful clear morning, and across the way the Pacific Ocean shone blue through a gap between two buildings. I felt good about my lot in life and I savored the moment. With my practice in the heart of Santa Monica and my condo just a ten-minute walk away, life was suiting me just fine.

Since Claire's revival, I'd seen the joy return to Bella's soul. Her mother's progress was slow and the medical staff couldn't yet say if she'd make a complete mental recovery, but we were no longer faced with the worst prospect and that had lightened our days. My time with Bella became peppered with levity and laughter, and I was ready to throw all my energy back into work.

I checked my watch. It was approaching twenty past ten. My client Eddie Mawson was late, as usual.

A gentle tap on the door roused me from my thoughts.

"Eddie Mawson is here to see you," Megan said with a glowing smile. She knew I was back in mind, body and spirit, and was glad for Bella and me both.

"Thanks, Megan. Send him in."

Megan turned and called Eddie in. A moment later he entered my office looking as he always did—like one of the most harmless twenty-somethings I'd ever laid eyes on. Five ten and rake thin, I felt I could grab him with one hand and throw him like a spear. He was well dressed in his usual preppy kind of way with Ray-Ban prescription glasses, navy pea coat, and a striped buttoned-down shirt tucked into chinos with rolled-up cuffs. Every time I laid eyes on this guy it seemed so weird that he was up on a sexual assault charge. Not that such a crime has a type. I guess in some people's minds he looked the part—a computer nerd socially malformed by years of sexual exclusion.

I knew better than to offer my hand to Eddie. It was always an afterthought with him as well as being an inconvenience since his phone was practically welded to his right palm.

He gave me a quick smile as we greeted each other and I offered him a seat. The moment I did so, I could tell he was struggling not to switch his attention back to his phone. This was more than just the habit of someone who finds looking at screens more comfortable than people. Eddie Mawson was not just any computer geek. He was one of the hottest video game developers in America. His compulsion to "play" with his phone was a lot more than a Facebook-feed addiction. He had a thriving business to run.

Five years ago, at the age of twenty-one, Eddie had launched a video game company called Adrenal from the bedroom of his mother's rented apartment. He found quick success with a couple of rudimentary, app-based games. The success allowed him to ramp up the development of a fully-fledged action video game. After two years, he launched *Out There*, a haunting, post-apocalyptic adventure that just about every gamer in the world wanted for their computer, PlayStation, Xbox or Nintendo. Eddie became the latest darling of an industry that generated more than the movie and music businesses combined.

"So, how's it all going?" Eddie said, like he was checking on an underling's project that didn't concern him too deeply. I'd grown somewhat accustomed to Eddie's detachment, not that it didn't bug me a lot. On what level didn't he grasp the depth of shit he was in?

"Not so great, Eddie. Listen—"

"Just a sec," said Eddie raising a finger up at me with one hand and lifting his phone into view.

"Put that away now or get out of my office."

Eddie looked at me like I'd just stumped him with a cryptic riddle. Seeing I was serious, he looked down at the ground guiltily and he shoved the phone into his pocket. "I'm sorry, Brad. Things are crazy. I'm working remotely, and my phone is my lifeline."

Eddie had told me that in light of the charges against him he'd made himself scarce at the Adrenal offices. He knew the media would be staking out his workplace, and he wanted to keep staff distractions to a minimum.

"Actually, Eddie. I'm your lifeline. If you don't take this case seriously you won't have a company to run, and you'll have all the time in the world to look at your phone. Once you get out of prison."

Eddie swallowed and laughed nervously. "Okay."

"Right, let's get started. Now, there's no plea deal yet from the DA but I don't think we'll be waiting much longer. He'll be convinced we won't want this case getting anywhere near a courtroom."

The DA was a cheerless piece of work named Elliott Goodwin. He'd told me over the phone that I'd receive a plea offer when he was good and ready. I'd not had much to do with Goodwin before, but from our brief conversations it was clear he was willing to bet the house that an Eddie Mawson trial would go his way. This was unusual for sexual assault cases, to say the least, given how hard it is to get a conviction.

"I can't go to jail, Brad."

"Eddie, just being honest with you, I doubt we'll get a plea deal that doesn't include time served."

"So I'm going to go to jail?"

"Not if I can help it," I said flatly. "But in case you didn't know, there's a climate right now about this sort of case which increases the likelihood of conviction. The consensus seems to be that men have been getting away with this kind of crap for far too long, and the DA is no doubt itching to make an example of you."

"I didn't rape her, Brad. I swear. I did nothing to her."

"I know, Eddie. You've told me. I'm just trying to be real here."

I tapped a file folder on my desk. It was a pile of witness statements Goodwin had handed over in discovery. "There's no shortage of people ready to paint you in a bad light. By that, I mean what people saw that night and what goes on at your company."

Eddie shifted in his chair. "Brad. How could I have raped her? We were in a public bar."

"Correction. You were in a private karaoke booth in a public bar. You and Jenna Lewis. And you were alone for at least ten minutes. That's plenty of time for someone to do what she alleges you did."

Every time Eddie had come to see me, I'd have him recount the events of that fateful night, keeping an ear out for any variations in his story that indicated he was lying to me. I was satisfied that there were hardly any deviations in the details. The staff members of Adrenal were celebrating after a successful awards night. They had gathered at a karaoke bar named Blackjacks and were joined by other members of the gaming industry as well as clients. Eddie was the man of the hour and opened a tab for everyone there. At some point, he went into a karaoke booth with two girls. One of them left for the bathroom, leaving Eddie alone with a girl named Jenna Lewis. Lewis was a visual artist who worked for Eddie up until a few months ago when she got a better offer at another publisher. Eddie said she left on good terms. So at the bar that night, he said she was very friendly with him and seemed to really like him. In the booth, they took turns singing and then did a duet. She excused herself and left the booth, saying she'd come back. Eddie waited fifteen minutes. He returned to the bar and he was told Lewis had left. He stayed at the bar, even though he was already extremely drunk, and continued to drink cocktails until three in the morning. He woke to the sound of cops pounding on his door at midday.

"She could say anything."

"She says you put your hand up her dress and digitally raped her."

Eddie shook his head. "I did no such thing."

"She claims you spiked her drink."

"I've got no idea where that's coming from but that's not what happened."

"Playing the devil's advocate here, Eddie, why would she lie?"

"I thought you were on my side."

"I am on your side. I'm your defense attorney. And to do my job, I need to think like the enemy, to see you through their eyes. Okay?"

Eddie nodded. "I don't know why she would lie. Maybe she hates me."

"You found Jenna Lewis attractive, didn't you?"

"Yes," he said, somewhat sheepishly.

"Did anyone else know that?"

"Yes. I told a few people that I thought she was hot. I'd rate her a solid eight."

Eddie smirked. It was an awkward reaction but one that had me doubting his innocence. I couldn't help but think how such a display would damn him in a jury's eyes.

"Don't you ever say that again," I said firmly. "Don't you ever mutter a flip word about Jenna or the charges against you to anyone. Not to me. Not to your friends. Not to your goddamn pillow. Do you understand?"

Eddie, his mouth ajar, nodded.

"Good. Now let's go over these witness statements."

We spent the next two hours doing just that. By the time Eddie left my office, I believed the message had finally been driven home that his life was on the line.

Chapter 3

A few moments after Eddie left, Jack Briggs marched into my office unannounced. If it was anybody else on the planet, they'd never have gotten past Megan. But as my best friend, my go-to investigator, and just about the most charismatic mofo in LA—and that's saying something—the normal rules don't apply to Jack Briggs.

Most times he swans into my office and takes a seat like it's a club lounge. And he usually carries with him an air of infectious verve, and I know for sure that in his wake he's left Megan all aglow with his easy flattery. The two of them are thick as thieves, particularly since a few years ago, Megan introduced Jack to the woman who became his wife.

This time, though. There was none of Jack's usual levity. He shut the door behind him and parked his butt in the chesterfield chair across the desk from me.

"What gives, Jack? You look like you've been to a funeral."

"We need to talk."

I resisted the urge to make a quip.

"Sounds serious," I said, shutting my laptop and leaning back.

"It's about Claire."

The shock of hearing unexpected bad news shot through me. In a split-second of thought, though, I reasoned that Claire must surely be okay and wondered what could possibly be wrong. She had a lot of mental and physical recovery to go through, but she was doing well. Her brain function was hazy but doctors were confident she'd recover though they were not prepared to say she'd ever be back to normal. They simply weren't sure about the long-term mental prognosis. The stress had eased to the point that Bella didn't feel compelled to spend as much time in the hospital, and she was doing full days of school and embracing the blessing of relative normalcy. Surely, things hadn't turned for the worse? It was possible the doctors missed something. But why would Jack be the one delivering such news to me?

"Last time I checked," I said, "Claire was doing well. Slow but steady. Has something changed?"

"I'm not talking about her health," said Jack shaking his head. "It's about the crash."

"What about it?"

Jack held up a thumb drive. "Something's not right."

"What do you mean?"

He leaned forward, placed the thumb drive on my desk in front of me and sat back down.

"I think someone tried to kill Claire."

I was inclined to ask Jack to repeat what he said, but I heard him crystal clear. And I didn't have to ask him if he was serious. Of that I was certain. I held my tongue, picked up the thumb drive and put it into the USB port of my laptop.

Jack got up and stood beside me so we could view the screen together.

"You asked me to investigate the accident."

"Yes, I did." As soon as I'd gotten Bella and me onto the next flight back to LA from Hawaii, I'd called Jack. I was armed with scant details about what had happened so I asked him to get to the crash scene to find out as much as he could. I did this for two reasons. I didn't have the utmost faith in the thoroughness of the LAPD. And I thought Jack was a brilliant investigator—I wanted his take on things regardless of how well the cops did their job.

"Well, the more I looked at the evidence, the less it looked like an accident."

Jack bent down and pointed at the folders contained on the external drive.

"Start here," he said.

The folder contained Jack's photos of the crash scene.

"I've already seen your photos," I said looking up at Jack with a raised eyebrow as the files opened in quick succession. Jack had taken photos from every possible angle and distance—from the ground with his DSLR and from the air with his drone. "You went over every inch of the scene, which is more than I can say for the cops."

"Do you know where they're at with their investigation?"

"They're losing interest fast. I called one of the investigators the other day—Mark Fielding—to get an update. He said they didn't have anything new. And you can bet he was relieved when I told him Claire had come out of her coma."

"Because he's off the hook?"

"Yeah. It's no longer on him to find a killer. All he's looking for is a reckless driver. The heat's off and it's all going to fade away in a couple of weeks unless something falls into his lap."

"Well, I think I've got something to throw at him."

"Go on."

Jack took control of the touchpad and clicked on an aerial photo.

"Look at this drone shot. Claire's car is here. The driver's coming down this way." Jack ran his finger along Strongs Drive. "He's going pretty quick. From the impact, forensics estimate the car was doing at least sixty. This is a narrow side street. Not many people would push it like that. It's not the Indy 500. It's a quiet, narrow suburban street."

I nodded. "I've seen cars go faster down narrower streets than that."

"I'm not saying it's not possible. I'm just pointing out that the driver had to be particularly reckless."

"So far, this sounds exactly like what the cops are saying. The guy was most likely drunk or high, which added to the thrill to put his foot down and make like *Grand Theft Auto*."

"Yeah, I get that," said Jack. "But look at this."

Jack opened another document. It was the crash investigation report.

"This was completed two weeks ago," he said.

"Fielding mentioned it to me. Said they got no fresh leads off it."

"What else would he say? He's had it for two weeks and has done nothing. I only got my hands on it yesterday."

"How? It's not filed yet."

"I pulled a couple of strings." Jack scrolled down through the pages of the report. "No fresh leads, my ass."

"What do you mean?"

He tapped the screen.

"This section of the report details where Claire's car was positioned when it was hit and where it ended up after impact. It describes the damage done."

"Which helped them estimate the car's speed."

"That's right," said Jack. "They don't have a make but they do have a color."

"Right. Black. And?"

"They missed something."

"What?"

Jack pointed at a brief entry in one of the columns.

"Says here Claire's car was in reverse."

I read the text, frowning. "Right. Okay, so she was struck backing into her garage, maybe. But we know she was heading out, not coming home. She was heading out to meet Marty."

The story was that Marty had called Claire at about nine o'clock to coax her away from work. He said he'd meet her at a bar for cocktails and that he'd booked a table at one of her favorite restaurants. She'd been burning the midnight oil on the launch of her new collection. She apparently accepted Marty's offer, but didn't get into her car until just after ten.

"Right," Jack said. "We know for certain that she was leaving the house. Now, look at this photo here. There's a big ding on the rear fender of her car. And here is a photo I took of Claire's house. The damage to this garage column matches the damage to her car."

"So she backed into the column," I said.

Jack moved the cursor to another file and double-clicked. "Ah," he said. "Move over. I need to drive. You don't have the software to run the document I want to show you."

I stood up and Jack took my place and began to download an app onto my PC. A couple of minutes later he was done.

"I took all the images and information that I had and fed them into a 3D rendering program, and this is the result," he said as a sophisticated reproduction of the crash scene popped up on my screen. I leaned in over Jack's shoulder. The crash scene was now movie-like but it could be played and viewed from any angle.

"Look," he said, as he began to replay the event, manipulating it back and forth to suit his commentary. "This is where Claire's car was at the point of impact. The other car is speeding down here. Look, there are cars parked on either side of the street for its entire length. Like I said, it's a pretty tight channel to be doing sixty miles an hour. To hit Claire's car, this car had to swerve off course. And as you can see, it's not a swerve. It's not a correction. It had to be a pronounced swing."

I nodded with a growing sense of disquiet.

"Yes?"

"After impact, the other car reverses out fast, which explains these tire marks. Given that this vehicle was drivable after impact suggests it was a pickup. And my guess is that it was fitted with a bull bar."

"Jesus," I muttered. The cops hadn't even narrowed the wanted vehicle down to that. They only said that it was possibly a pickup, but could have been a van. No mention of a bull bar.

"Then it continues down the street," Jack continued. "And not once did it trade paint with another vehicle. Didn't scrape a door. Didn't take out one side mirror. This thing threaded that street at 60 mph as clean as a whistle except for one spot—Claire's driveway. You see what I'm getting at?"

I nodded, my mouth getting dry. "Yes. The driver sure as hell wasn't drunk. He was very much in control."

Jack stood up.

"Exactly. I think Claire saw that truck coming. I think she jammed her car into reverse and put her foot down to get out of the way. The garage door was probably still open at this stage, but in her panic she swung the car too hard and collided with the center column. She did manage to get most of her car out of the street, just her nose was sticking out, but she still got hit. No skid marks from the truck going in. No brakes. Just wham—straight into her."

"So it was deliberate," I said. Stating the obvious was just about all my dazed and furious mind could muster.

"That's right."

I remained staring at the screen as Jack replayed the collision again and again. "It wasn't an accident," I said quietly.

"Nope," Jack shook his head. "Whoever was behind the wheel wanted Claire dead."

CHAPTER 4

Marty Cosgrove's office was just a few blocks away from mine, so I made the trip on foot. Beacon Capital was one of California's top venture capital firms, occupying the top floor of a white Mediterranean complex on Arizona Avenue. It looked modest enough from the outside but when the elevator doors opened on the fourth floor, I was struck by the sight that appeared before me. Clearly, Beacon Capital was big on first impressions and they laid it on with a trowel. The bright, clean and shiny lobby was dominated by a huge image that occupied the entire wall behind the reception desk. It was a dazzling picture of a lighthouse on a white-cliffed headland with a carpet of vivid green pasture on one side and pounding surf on the other. Sea spray rose up to the foot of the lighthouse, which stood undaunted, its valiant beam reaching out to the distant horizon. In the high-risk, turbulent world of venture capital, this was a rock-solid place to put your money. The message could not be any clearer.

In recent years, Santa Monica had become known as Silicon Beach owing to the number of tech companies that had relocated there. And just about every aspiring start-up among them would need venture capital if and when the time came for them to get big, fast. Beacon Capital had positioned itself in the beating heart of a $200-billion phenomenon.

My shoes clicked on the tiles as I approached the front desk. The two receptionists were both right out of game-show casting—you know, all lip-sticked up and ready to sweep their painted nails over microwaves and stand mixers and do the magic wave as the parting curtain revealed a brand-new Chevy Trailblazer. The brunette was on a call but the blond had grabbed me with her smile the moment I'd stepped out of the elevator.

"Good morning, sir," she said as I got within comfortable earshot. "How can I help you today?"

"I'm here to see Marty Cosgrove."

Her forehead creased slightly. She cut a glance at her computer screen and ran a finger over her touchpad.

"Do you have an appointment?" she asked, even though she was sure I didn't.

"No."

"I'm sorry, Mr. Cosgrove is extremely busy. I can't possibly get you in without an appointment."

"I'm sure he is. He practically lives here, from what I gather."

The thought of all that time Claire had spent lying there alone with an empty chair reserved solely for her husband still got me hot under the collar. Things were looking up, I reminded myself. And that was certainly true. But the crisis had passed with Marty barely standing a post.

"It would be best if we could schedule a time for him to see you. Where did you say you were from?"

"I didn't. Could you please tell him Brad Madison is here to see him? Tell him it's urgent."

"Does he know you're coming?"

"No. That's what happens when matters are urgent. They need to be addressed immediately. Tell him I've got some news about Claire."

The receptionist's composure slackened at the mention of Claire's name. "I hear she's doing great. Isn't it wonderful?" Then she recoiled as she realized I might be the bearer of bad news. "She's okay, isn't she?"

"Yes. Yes. She's fine. Apart from multiple fractures and possible brain damage. But I do need to see Marty. Trust me. He'll want to deal with this immediately."

The receptionist picked up the phone at half speed. Not all her trepidation about disturbing her boss had dissipated.

"Mr. Cosgrove, there's a Brad Madison here to see you—
"Yes. Here—
"I'm so sorry, Mr. Cosgrove, but he insists that it's urgent—
"He says it's about Claire."

The receptionist set the phone down and extended a game-show hand to the waiting room. "Please, take a seat, Mr. Madison. Mr. Cosgrove will be with you shortly."

I walked over and sat down on a couch. I was there only a few seconds before I heard a man's footsteps approach from behind.

"Brad?"

It was Marty Cosgrove, greeting me with forced cordiality, a flat smile, and a demeanor that made it loud and clear he had better things to do than to respond to the demands of his wife's ex. The only light coming from his eyes were the reflections off his frameless glasses. Every time I'd seen him over the years, which was not often, I couldn't help wondering what Claire saw in him. Then I remembered Claire had given me a not-so-subtle hint. Marty was nothing like me, she said. Safe, was what she meant, I believe. But I'm sure there were other qualities on the list. To me, though, Marty seemed so straight he made Phil Mickelson look like a Hells Angel.

Speaking of Mickelson, I knew two main things about Marty Cosgrove: he was in some kind of finance game and he played a lot of golf, so much so that he could pass the fairways off as an extension of his office. Aged a little over forty, there was a boyishness to his appearance. His brown hair was short and wavy, his skin smooth and his cheeks flushed. Physique-wise, he looked like he mostly favored using a cart rather than his legs on the courses but he wasn't exactly fat. A spare tire hung over his belt, hugged by a brand-new red Ralph Lauren polo shirt, and there was a hint of a double chin. All in all, he struck me as a guy for whom things had come a bit too easy. Which was why I was particularly surprised to hear he was a very busy man. But since that came from his secretary, I was inclined to take it with a grain of salt.

"Sorry to just turn up like this, Marty," I said as we shook hands. Eye to eye, we were about the same height—six-two. "But I need to talk to you about something."

Marty looked intrigued. "It's about Claire, I'm told. I'm in almost constant contact with the hospital, Brad. If there was something wrong I'd be the first to hear it."

"This is not about her current condition."

"What's it about then?"

"Look, can we talk in your office?"

Marty hesitated for a moment, clearly disinclined to consent. He looked at his watch and shook his head to convey that this intrusion was bound to put him off schedule. "Sure. Come through."

I followed Marty through to his office. He walked quickly, and as he went he told the receptionist to hold his calls. When we got to his office he rounded his desk without delay, offered me a seat and sat forward with a straight back and an eagerness for me to get to it.

"Okay, so what's so urgent?" he said.

"It's about Claire's accident."

"What about it?"

"I believe there's a good chance it wasn't actually an accident."

Marty's head recoiled as his face scrunched into a puzzled expression. He gave his head a shake as though it would clear away his confusion. "What are you saying?"

"I think someone rammed her car."

"On purpose? Why would anyone do that?"

"Well, that's what I want to talk to you about."

My words put Marty on the defensive right away. His eyes narrowed skeptically. "Well, that's certainly not what the police think, for whatever that's worth. They're trying to find a drunk driver or a hood."

"They're ready to move on, Marty, which means there'll be close to no chance anyone's going to be held accountable for putting Claire in a coma."

"So where's this coming from?"

"My investigator. Jack Briggs. He's put together a detailed analysis of the scene, and with the latest evidence it looks like Claire saw a car speeding toward her and she tried to back out of the way."

Marty didn't offer a word. He rested a thumb under his bottom lip. "It doesn't make sense. Why would anyone do that?"

"I can't give you an explanation. But that truck—we are sure it was a pickup—went out of its way to hit Claire. That much we now know."

"You mean, that's what you think."

"That's what the evidence tells me."

"Have you run your theory past the police?"

"Marty, they have the exact same evidence. Their take's not going to change. Now that Claire is recovering, this isn't a felony with a death involved anymore. To them, the whole thing amounts to little more than a traffic offense."

Marty leaned back in his chair digesting the news.

"I don't know what to say," he said.

"Look, Claire is obviously in no state to answer questions. But I can't waste any more time trying to find answers. Which is why I'm here."

Marty looked mildly offended. "What kind of answers do you expect me to give you?"

"Well, the most obvious one is can you think of anyone who would want to kill Claire?"

"Are you out of your mind?" Marty scoffed. "Don't be ridiculous. There's no one who would want to kill her. Why the hell are you doing this?"

"Why am I doing what? I think someone tried to kill your wife."

"Your ex-wife."

"Yes, my ex-wife. Someone needs to—"

"To what, Brad? Stand up for her? Save her? Boy, you've got a lot of nerve. You just can't let her go, can you?"

"That's not the way it is."

I sensed the moment had come to give this guy a piece of my mind once and for all. All the anger I'd stored up during Claire's time in the hospital, taking Bella every day and wondering where the hell Marty was. Wondering what could be so important to keep him away from his wife's bedside. I wasn't the most objective observer, I admit, but I'd come to believe that Marty wasn't quite the great guy Claire believed he was. I wondered how she'd feel to know he simply had better things to do than maintain a vigil by her hospital bed. During those awful weeks, I'd seen no sign of anything that Marty had done for Claire. Nothing to make her suite homier. No photos of them together. And it wasn't just me. Her friend Nina Lindstrom, the one who'd called me in Hawaii with the terrible news, was not happy with Marty's apparent cursory devotion. When she inquired, he claimed he was incredibly busy with work, that there was some hugely important deal going on that demanded his presence at the office.

"Really? Are you seriously telling me you don't still love Claire?" he said, going red in the face, a face that I now badly wanted to rearrange.

"Well, where the fuck were you? You were never at the hospital. The mornings were set aside just for you and you never showed."

"I did show. I just couldn't be there every minute. Sorry, but I'm in the middle of something that is of vital importance to this company's future. You don't have all the facts. You have no right to judge me. Didn't they teach you something about that in law school?"

"Bella desperately wanted to be with Claire during those morning hours. You knew that but you never offered to swap."

"You have no idea what I thought. You have no idea what I've done. And you have no idea what I'm dealing with here at work."

"The nursing staff said you were hardly ever there, so don't try and paint yourself as the devoted husband."

"Really? Well, they told me you were holding her hand," he sneered. "So don't try and deny your feelings for Claire. It's pathetic."

How did they know that? Catherine must have seen me before she entered. God knows why she told Marty. Maybe it slipped out.

My anger was doused by shame. Marty's words made me step back from the brink. I'd anticipated some friction with him but I'd resolved to be clinical in my action on Jack's findings. I took a deep breath.

"Listen," I said. "I care for Claire only as a friend. That's all. And that's why I came here. To ask for your help. I want to find out what really happened that night. I thought you would too. Maybe I was wrong about that."

Marty's countenance eased. He dropped his hands to his lap and leaned back "What do you want to know?"

"Was there any bad blood between Claire and someone else? Did she piss anyone off recently?"

"She's a jewelry designer, not a mobster. She has tiffs with plenty of people but they're not psycho."

"There's no one you can think of?"

Marty gave a wry smile as he ran a finger under his mouth.

"Well, there was an incident with a photographer," he said. "He came to the house and confronted Claire after she fired him from a gig. He went ape-shit. You know, threw a couple of potted plants her way."

"You were there?"

"I was upstairs. I heard a crash, called out and went down. The photographer made a run for it."

"What's his name?"

"Come on, Brad. He's nothing more than a disgruntled hipster. An artistic type who got into a huff. He wasn't threatening to kill her."

"What's his name?"

"Adam Fletcher."

I got up. "If you think of anything else, let me know. I'll let you get back to work."

"Okay."

When I got onto Arizona Avenue, I called Jack.

"You got something?" he asked.

"Yeah, a photographer named Adam Fletcher. He's got a temper, apparently. Didn't take kindly to Claire firing him from a job."

"Okay. I'll get on it."

"Thanks. Oh, and there's someone else I want you to look into."

"Sure thing. Who's that?"

"Marty Cosgrove."

Chapter 5

Donna Amerson stood and gave me a quick smile as we shook hands over her desk. It was clear she had a lot on her plate, an unfortunate indication of how much she was needed. Amerson was an advocate at Mather House, a rape treatment center in Santa Monica. We'd met when Bella and her son Harry were in preschool together. She never failed to impress me when she spoke of her work with such passion and her office reflected her staunch dedication. There were piles of documents, two computers, two phones, and two white boards, each divided into columns and crammed with notes in four different colors.

There was no question I was going to defend Eddie Mawson, but the truth was that I wasn't sure he was innocent. And while as a lawyer that made no difference to how thoroughly I managed his case, as a father of a young girl on the cusp of womanhood, I'd find it hard at some moral level to help a rapist walk free. As a defense attorney, I was accustomed to being despised by some people, cops and prosecutors in particular. I chose this career to ensure that innocent people were not wrongfully punished by the justice system. But this was my first rape case, and I had no problem admitting that the merits of my role weighed on me heavily.

That's why I went to see Amerson. I'd called her and was told she was very familiar with the Jenna Lewis case. She agreed to speak to me, while making it clear that whatever she had to tell me was never going to breach Lewis's privacy.

"Thanks for seeing me, Donna," I said as I sat down. "You clearly have your hands full."

"No problem," she said. "Glad to help."

Amerson was late-thirties with an attractive face and auburn hair she had pulled back into a ponytail. Her bio on the center's website told me that she was a survivor of sexual assault herself, and the vital help she'd received in recovering from her ordeal prompted her to help others.

"Donna, like I said on the phone, I've got a few witnesses to interview for this case but I wanted to touch base with you first."

"I take it this is an informal chat rather than an interview?"

"Of course. I just want to get your take on the case."

"Okay to begin with, it's my understanding that the LAPD Sexual Assault Unit has a significant amount of evidence against your client."

"This won't surprise you but those witness statements don't bear much resemblance to my client's version of events."

"From what I hear, his recollection of events is rather hazy."

"Yes, which makes him vulnerable."

"Excuse me?"

Amerson's eyes drilled right into me.

"I mean from my side of things," I said, holding up my hands. "Look, Mawson's my client and I have to be able to advocate for him without adding a disclaimer that I'm not seeking to discredit or demean his accuser to every sentence."

"Right. But let's not confuse things here. Jenna Lewis is the victim of this crime."

"Yes, I'm most certainly aware that's the view held by many people now. But Donna, from a legal perspective, whether a crime has been committed here is yet to be proved."

"Okay, Brad. I get it. Presumed innocence and all that. You've got to do what's best for your client. I don't need you to champion the victim in the same breath. Let's just proceed."

"The fact that there are significant discrepancies between the witness statements and my client's recollections concerns me."

"Who'd have thought they'd be different? Look, let's just start from a wider angle and drill down. I take it you're aware that the video game industry is one of the worst work environments for women? This goes beyond the game development and the publishers—it extends into the online gaming world."

"I'm aware of that."

"I work closely with the LAPD Sexual Assault Unit. Several cases have landed on my desk from that industry. Most went nowhere because of a variety of reasons but the anecdotal evidence shows that misogyny is rife. It runs the whole spectrum, from casual sexist behavior in the workplace to toxic attacks on women online. Female players—we're talking girls here, Brad—are routinely targeted with heinous abuse and sexual threats. People assume older men are the most sexist in our society but I'm seeing some of the most regressive attitudes in the younger generations. And nowhere is it more prevalent than in the tech sphere in general and video games in particular."

"How do you mean?"

"This is a world inhabited by few adults over thirty-five. The industry is overwhelmingly male and it's operated behind closed doors."

"Because no one but the nerds understands it?"

"That's right. It's impenetrable to the rest of us. I mean, we all want the apps and devices but we have no interest in understanding their provenance. People always mention how we don't seem to care that tech companies exploit third-world workers. But we seem to care even less about the conditions under which some tech industries operate here in America."

"The social conditions."

"Yes. Here you don't just have sweatshops, you have a work culture in which sexual bullying and harassment are the norm. And your client Eddie Mawson is part of the problem. Guys like him grew up with their faces glued to a screen. They had sand kicked in their faces. They never got the girl. But in the world of technology, which they built for themselves, they can be kings. It's an enclave, a refuge where they feel at home. And it's a realm that's been shaped out of teenage rejection."

"I understand that," I said. "Facebook's roots lie in an act of revenge against women after Mark Zuckerberg was rejected by a girl."

"Exactly. But we are seeing a lot of sexual assault cases coming out of the gaming industry in particular. The problem is it's very hard to make a case stick. Just recently, there was a case up in San Francisco where the cops were on the cusp of a conviction but the victim withdrew her claims. My colleagues up there say she was intimidated out of going through with the case."

"Well, so far Jenna Lewis seems to be standing firm."

"Yes, so far."

"But coming at it from my client's angle—"

"As you would."

"He's heading up a fast-growing company that's making him a fortune. Why would he do something so stupid like this?"

Amerson's mouth went slack and she let out a short sarcastic laugh. "Right you are, Brad. Success and money have never spurred a young man into acting entitled."

"Okay, I see your point but—"

"Hang on, let me finish. Since we're on the subject of what a case like this costs. Setting aside for a moment the fact that this young woman was sexually violated, there's very little on the upside for her in coming forward. Her ordeal will be played out publicly. It will be recounted, challenged and dissected in minute detail. A lot of people are going to think, and say out loud, that she's lying. Some will be convinced that she's conniving, that she's just out to get money off this guy. She faces public humiliation whether she wins or loses. The only thing she has going for her is the support of other women who are proud of her standing up for herself. Like that case in San Francisco I mentioned, most women don't go through with it. Sexual assault is one of the most unreported crimes in this country because the process of getting justice is almost as violating as the offense itself."

"Which is why the justice system puts a lot of faith in victim statements. I understand the importance of that, but we're still looking at a he-said-she-said argument here."

"Well, that's just the nature of it."

"Donna, are you convinced Jenna Lewis was raped?"

"I've spoken with Jenna but I'm not going to tell you what I think."

"You talked about the price Jenna will have to pay. Even if Eddie is proved innocent, he'll be just about ruined."

"Brad, I'm sorry but there's only one person in this room who feels for your client."

"I get it."

"Look, a false accusation is the last thing I want. That would do immense damage to other cases where the survivor has had the courage to come forward. It would piss me off no end, not just because it wasted my time but because the fallout would be devastating to our cause. That said, if you ever find compelling evidence to prove your client is innocent then I'll look at it."

"I'll keep you to that. I just need to find that evidence before this goes to trial. No small task."

"Brad. How's Bella doing?"

I didn't want to go into what had happened to Claire. "She's doing great. Loves school."

"She's twelve now, right? Same as my Harry?"

"Yes."

"Well, I hope to God she never suffers anything like what we deal with here. You know the figures, right? You know there's a one-in-five chance someone will try to rape her at some point and that there's an eighty percent chance she'll be sexually harassed."

"It's beyond shocking," I said, shaking my head grimly.

"You seem like a good man, Brad. You're probably a good father. But what do I know? What I'm getting at is if you have a conscience, how can you defend a man charged with sexual assault?"

"As much as I want my client to be innocent, my job is not about believing he is. It's about ensuring he gets fair treatment by the justice system. It's what every citizen deserves, Donna. Defending people is not a whim, it's my professional obligation."

"Fair enough. I understand. We're both busy people. Now if that's all, I need to get back to work."

"Sure. Thanks for your time."

I walked out with an unpleasant feeling in my gut. Despite what I said, I wanted more than ever to believe Eddie Mawson was innocent. Given the thoughts about Bella that Amerson had put into my head, the idea that he might well be guilty sickened me.

CHAPTER 6

Bella was now spending two weekday mornings with her mother, Wednesdays and Fridays. Although Claire was awake, her head was far from clear. She was fatigued and unable to speak more than a few basic words. This didn't upset Bella one bit. She was overjoyed to see a glimmer of joy in her mother's eyes, and she was a willing helper in Claire's physical rehab.

Marty had offered to take Bella this morning, which I'd appreciated as I was throwing myself into the Mawson case. At the last minute, though, he said he couldn't. So Megan offered to drive Bella. She then returned to work before going back to pick her up again.

Ten minutes after Megan left to pick up Bella Abby Hatfield's name lit up my phone. The sight of her name sent a pleasant rush through me, as we hadn't seen each other for months. You couldn't say the two of us were an item. We'd gotten together a few years back, right after Claire filed for divorce. It was a difficult time for me and, given that I wasn't the most stable of men, Abby moved on. She then got married and divorced. As an A-list Hollywood actor, it turned out she wasn't the most stable person on the planet either. She was in and out of LA like a yo-yo, shooting movies in Europe, Australia and even South

America. Her globe-trotting life had made it hard for her to hold down a steady relationship but she seemed to like my company a hell of a lot, and the feeling was more than mutual. Over the past weeks, we'd been trading emails. She'd been shooting in Scotland and Italy before heading down to Africa to do some charity work in Somalia.

After Claire's accident, I wouldn't say I confided in Abby, but I filled her in on what had happened and how Bella was coping, without sharing my own somewhat conflicted feelings. She picked up on my reticence and, while expressing her concern, she kept herself a little distant in terms of affection.

With Claire's prospects at least positive now, my heart felt a lot lighter and I took Abby's call with a flush of joy.

"Hey there, Mother Teresa. You back from fixing Africa, are you?"

"Look, I don't want to brag, but child poverty? Solved."

"Wow. Look at you the miracle worker."

I detected relief in her voice, like she was pleased I sounded unguarded. Happy, even. I heard her take a deep breath, then relax. I could almost hear her thinking she could talk to me about anything. Talk for hours. That us at our best was still in play.

"Seriously, Brad. It was an amazing experience. Upsetting, disturbing, frustrating but ultimately profoundly eye-opening."

"In a good way, I take it?"

"Yes and no. I mean, can you talk right now?"

"For sure, I'm just waiting for Bella. I'm all yours."

"Now that's a pleasant thought. Now where was I? That's right. Africa. I know this sounds so Hollywood fake and flaky, but helping out these communities that had so little, I felt like I was doing something with real purpose, even though the whole problem seems insurmountable."

"I take it that's a big change from acting?"

"Yeah. Look I love acting and I won't knock the thrill and challenge and fun of making movies. But you know the downsides of the whole stardom deal. And not just your life being public property but how the currency of fame leaves you empty."

"I can hear violins."

There was a pause.

"Look, I'm sorry," I said. "I was kidding. No offense. You know, Mike Tyson said the happiest he'd ever felt during his whole career was after he'd lost all his money. And you know why? Because no one wanted anything from him anymore."

"Okay, Iron Mike isn't actually my go-to guy for life wisdom but I get his point. Nothing I do outside of acting is taken seriously. No, seriously is the wrong word. It's just like whatever I do in public, everyone thinks I only do it to feed my fame. And this is when I can't set foot in the real world without the paparazzi looking on. Yet the way it's reported, it's like I hired them to follow me."

"I take it your motives for being in Somalia were questioned."

"Yep. I was just an Angelina Jolie wannabe. You know—another self-absorbed movie star playing the saint. There were some hateful write-ups. They really savored it."

"Of course they did. But you did good, right? You said so in your emails."

"It was a start. A first step for me to offer genuine help. It's inspired me to do more. I met someone over there from the UNDP."

"UNDP?"

"United Nations Development Program. I said I didn't just want to be the face of their efforts. It just seems so token."

"But that's why they get you on board. That's how they bring attention to the issues. Are you going to start your own charity?"

"Not quite. What I've decided to do is raise money to fund innovative projects that address problems in developing countries. You know, get some high-tech brainpower directed at solving issues surrounding poverty."

"You should talk to…" I was going to say Marty Cosgrove but I checked myself.

"Who?"

"Don't worry. I was off track. Forget it."

"How's Claire doing?" Abby asked.

"She's okay. Improving. Not fully lucid yet but the consensus seems to be that it's only a matter of time before she's recovered her full mental function. She's still in the hospital. Got a lot of physical therapy to do."

"I bet she has. Bella must be so happy."

"She's walking on air. I'm about to take her for lunch."

"Nice. I'd like to see you. Could you fit in dinner together any time soon?"

"I'd love to but right now I can't do nights. I don't want to leave Bella alone, nor with a babysitter."

"What about her step-father—Marty, isn't it?"

"Well, he's kind of working all hours. He's in the middle of some big work project, and it seems that's all he's got the headspace for."

"That and taking care of Claire, right?"

"Of course," I said unconvincingly.

There was a pause before Abby spoke. "Brad, is there something you're not telling me?"

"No, I'm just not comfortable leaving Bella with Marty, like I said. That's all."

"You're a good father, Brad."

"Some days, yeah. Others, not so much. But I do want to see you."

"Tell you what. I'm planning a fund-raising event in a couple of weeks. It will be a lunch. I'd love you to come."

"Sounds perfect," I said.

Once our call ended, I spun around to look out the window. Hearing Abby's voice stoked a powerful desire to be with her. Yet this simple, heady passion was clouded by the complications going on in my life. I kicked myself for shifting our conversation onto Marty. I'm sure Abby heard the tightness in my voice when I spoke about him.

I heard voices from behind me. Megan and Bella had arrived. I spun around and saw Bella walking toward me, her beautiful face lit up to see me. Her eyes were full of kindness, and her steps buoyant. She was the embodiment of everything good in the world, and a tonic for my inner turmoil. Thank God Claire had pulled through. I extended my arms and she fell into me.

"How's Mom?" I asked when I released her.

"Better. She's tired still but her speech is improving."

"I thought we'd go out for Lebanese today. How about it?"

"Awesome. You read my mind, Daddy."

We left the office and headed north along the promenade. Bella reached to take my hand. As she did, I saw two teenage boys approaching, checking her out, one nudging the other and both smiling.

"You're so pretty," one of them said, as they got close.

I gave them a look. "Just keep walking, boys."

I shook my head at their nerve yet wondered if I overreacted. But after discussing the Eddie Mawson case with Donna, I found myself a little more protective of Bella than perhaps I needed to be.

"I'm sorry, Bella."

"That's okay, Daddy. No harm done."

"Do you get that much, darling?"

"No, not really," she said but I know she was not being entirely truthful.

"Has anyone ever—"

"No, Daddy. I'm fine. No one's done anything I can't handle, okay?"

I leaned over her head and gently pulled her close.

"Please, tell me if there's any kind of problem. You'll do that, won't you? At least talk to me? I won't overreact. I promise."

"I will, Daddy. But it's not an issue. Okay?"

"Okay."

It wasn't that I wanted to prevent my child from growing up. I just didn't want her hurt or disrespected. I knew there was little I could actually do about it unless I sought to physically shield her from negative encounters, which was absurd. Bella was beginning to enter the wider world, getting into areas that were beyond my reach. I took comfort in knowing she had healthy self-esteem, confidence and a good deal of common sense. To me, these were the fundamental tools I'd always wanted to equip her with. Claire and I had done something right.

We took an outside table at the bright Byblos Café and ordered.

As we waited, Bella filled me in on school and how the new year was going. She'd always loved school and this year was no different.

The waiter brought us our food, which was the picture of healthy eating—brightly colored salad with falafel and pita bread.

As we started eating, there was something on my mind I couldn't shake.

"Hey, honey. Did Marty tell you why he couldn't take you to see your mom today?"

"He just said sorry and that he was busy. As usual."

"Bella, how's he been? I mean, how was he before Claire's accident?"

"Busy. Like crazy work hours. He was hardly ever at home. And when he was…"

Bella trailed off, stopping herself from completing her sentence.

"He was what?"

"I don't know, Dad. I don't know if I should say."

"It's okay, sweetheart. I'm not trying to pry but I'm a little concerned that Marty has seemed pretty distant throughout this whole thing. I don't know how much time he's actually spent with your mom."

Bella frowned a little, reflecting her concern and her doubts about what she should say. "Before the accident, they were arguing a lot. When Marty was around, that is."

"Arguing a lot? About work stuff? Your mom's a workaholic too."

"True. But it wasn't that. It was more about money."

"How do you know?"

"I've got ears, Daddy. It wasn't like they were whispering. They were shouting, sometimes."

"About money? They've both got plenty of cash."

"I think Marty wanted Mom to lend him money or to give him some. Something like that."

"What for?"

Bella shrugged her shoulders. "I don't know."

"And Claire didn't want to?"

Bella shook her head. "No."

This made no sense to me. I always thought Marty cruised through life with cash to burn.

"Why are you asking about this, Daddy?"

"I don't know," I said. "I'm just concerned about your mother, I guess. I think she would have expected Marty to be around more since she's been in the hospital. Not that she'd have known until recently."

"He does love her, Dad."

I nodded. "Yes, I'm sure he does."

"It's like you said. Some people don't handle hospitals that well. Marty must be one of those people."

"Yeah," I said. "I guess you're right."

I didn't believe that for a second.

Chapter 7

A man holding an AR-15 stood in my way. He was not a soldier but a civilian in thick black boots, ripped jeans and a tattered t-shirt. He'd been through hell and back, clearly. His weapon was slung in low-ready position—muzzle pointing to the ground, right finger across the pistol grip, left hand gripping the muzzle guard. He could put six rounds into me before I moved an inch.

I stepped around this life-sized figure of Daniel "Danny" Tench, the main character of *Out There,* and over to Adrenal Gaming's front desk. I told the receptionist that Alex Herron, Eddie Mawson's second-in-command, was expecting me. The short, blond and perky receptionist, who had introduced herself as Taylor, got up and invited me to follow her. With quick steps she led me through a side door that opened onto a huge space that looked like no other workplace I'd ever seen.

At least thirty staff, no one under thirty-five, were clearly busy working yet the place was silent save for the clatter of keyboards. All the employees wore headphones. Some were at conventional desks with banks of computer screens while others occupied arcade-game chairs holding controllers and staring intently at the dynamic screen in front of them.

"That's our testing pod," Taylor said of her game-playing colleagues. "Doesn't look like work, but it is."

All around the space, the walls featured huge blown-up posters of Danny Tench and other *Out There* characters in action. As a *Call of Duty* fan, I was fascinated to get a first-hand look at how these rich and complex pieces of entertainment were put together. In between the posters, the walls were covered in what appeared to be schedules. At the far end of the room was a huge red digital clock.

"That's for deadlines, like the launch of *Out There*," Taylor said.

"Everyone seems to be in the zone."

"It's pretty intense but they get the job done."

"Is this all of Adrenal's staff?"

"It is for now. When we get closer to deadline, we'll fill the whole floor above us with developers."

"How many?"

Taylor deferred to her boss to demonstrate she knew her place. "I'll let Alex answer that."

I nodded and continued to scan the room. I'd planned my visit with Eddie's help. There were a few employees I wanted to speak to and he'd called ahead to line it up. He'd insisted that I sign a confidentiality contract before going. I thought he was joking. He wasn't.

"It's a must," he insisted. "Not that I don't trust you."

"I'm your goddamn lawyer, Eddie," I said.

"Brad, I wouldn't let the President of the United States into my office without signing one. If you don't want to do that then you'll have to do your interviews off site."

I'd signed the form in front of Eddie and emailed a scan of it through to Herron.

Taylor had waited silently for a few moments to allow me to take everything in.

"Alex is in the conference room through this way," Taylor said, tilting her head to the right.

We entered a short, dark corridor that brought us to a large room where a guy in his late twenties sat with his face buried in a laptop.

"Hi Alex," said Taylor as she entered. "Mr. Madison is here. Do you want me to bring some coffee?"

Herron did not look up from his screen. "Great. A double espresso."

Taylor looked at me.

"I'm good, thanks," I said.

"Okay then," she said. "I'll leave you to it."

Herron's eyes lifted briefly. "Have a seat, Brad. I've just got to finish this one small thing. There. Done." He then turned to me with a smile and closed the lid of his laptop. "Sorry, it's just crazy busy here."

He was a cheery faced kid—which was what I was all too inclined to call anyone under thirty-five these days—with bright eyes and a narrow face. His blond hair, which was thinning and receding, was kept short at the sides and longish on top. He ran a hand through it, leaving a couple of thin wisps stranded. His eyebrows were thick and arched in a pronounced way that lent a degree of pleasant surprise to his expression.

"Eddie tells me you're running things here," I said.

"Let's not kid ourselves," Herron laughed. "Eddie is very much running the show. He thought it was in everyone's best interests for him not to be here until the case is over. He wants everyone to stay focused."

"It must be hard for him to stay away."

"He may be physically absent but he's very present spiritually. And digitally. He's everywhere. He's online twenty-four-seven. There are video chats, message apps, phone calls. He's looking over everyone's shoulder, that's for sure. But what do you expect? He's the boss. I'm just the lieutenant."

"Isn't it a bit odd for everything here to be business as usual while your boss is facing work-related sexual assault charges?"

"He'll get through it," Herron said cheerfully. "Adrenal will go from strength to strength."

"You sure about that?"

Herron nodded confidently. "I wouldn't say this company is too hot to fail but there's still such huge momentum behind this project and the sequel to *Out There* is going to be massive. Once Eddie decides on the best strategy going forward."

"Well, Eddie's got something more important on his plate."

"I know. Running your own gaming company is tough. And this investment deal he's doing is critical for—"

I held up a palm, confused by Herron's words.

"I'm not talking about some business deal. I'm talking about the charges he's facing."

"Of course," Herron said, realizing we had our wires crossed. "How's he doing? I mean, I know you're his lawyer and you probably can't say anything because of attorney-client privilege and all that, but do you think you can get him off?"

I shook my head. "I'm not here to talk about Eddie's prospects, Alex. I'm here to gather information."

"Yes, of course," Herron said, lifting the lid of his laptop and running his finger over the touchpad. "Who do you want to start with?"

I pulled out my notepad and pen.

"Why don't we start with you?"

In reply to a series of questions, Herron told me he'd had various jobs in the gaming industry and that, like many tech workers, he had migrated south from Silicon Valley to Silicon Beach about nine months ago. He said he loved everything about the industry—the creativity, the teamwork, the games themselves and the thrill of bringing these incredibly rich worlds to life. He found a place to rent in Pacific Palisades and, soon after, a job at Adrenal. When he spoke about the gaming industry his face lit up. He said he'd been obsessed with computer games since he was about seven and that his current life was a dream come true.

"Alex, I want to address the night of the alleged rape," I said. "You were there at the Blackjacks party, weren't you?"

"Yes, I was."

"Were you drinking with Eddie?"

"When we first got there I was but I mostly hung out with other people."

"I see. And you saw Eddie drinking with Jenna."

"Yes."

"Anyone else?"

"Polly was with them."

I looked at my list. "Polly Gould, right?"

"That's right."

"And from what you saw, the three of them were having a good time?"

"I guess. I wasn't keeping an eye on them or anything. But, you know, Eddie's the boss and you know how girls are with the boss."

Herron was smiling, his eyebrows perched up like there was something unsaid about his words that I should, as a man, understand.

"What do you mean?"

"I mean, like a lot of bosses Eddie has a pretty healthy ego. And why wouldn't he? The guy's a genius, and he owns a multi-million-dollar company. He's a star in one of the fastest-growing industries in the world. He's on frickin' fire, man. And that king-of-the-world feeling rubs off on the girls. Or at least they smile and say yes when he's buying rounds of drinks."

There was a light in Alex's eyes. I couldn't tell if it was reverence or envy. Maybe it was both.

"Alex, was Eddie doing drugs with the girls?"

Alex's smile froze. "Drugs? Like coke, you mean?"

"Yes. Like coke."

He looked a bit shocked and shook his head resolutely. "No, not that I knew about, anyhow. I wouldn't know if Eddie was into coke or not. As for the girls, you know, it's not like they couldn't afford coke if they wanted it. They get paid pretty well here."

"So Jenna is some kind of designer, right?"

"Yes, video game artist. She creates the designs for characters and locations that then get actualized by programmers. She was at Adrenal for a few months before moving on to another company."

"Were you working here when she was?"

"Yes, I was."

"How did she and Eddie get along at work?"

Herron shrugged. "Okay, I guess. I don't really know."

"At the bar, did you see Eddie do anything suspicious that night with regards to Jenna?"

"No."

"Let me ask you this: do you think Eddie would drug a girl and rape her?"

I was hoping for a fast denial but Herron bit his bottom lip and gave the question a few moments' thought.

"Look, and I'm trying to be honest here, I'd like to say no. But the truth is I've only known Eddie for less than a year. I can't claim to know what goes on in his head, and what he's capable of."

My gut tightened. This kind of conditional support for Eddie would damn him. I'd read the statement Herron had given to the police. There was so little in it that I doubted the prosecution would call him as a witness. But if they did, he could do some damage talking about Eddie like this.

"Is that what you intend to say on the stand, if you're called, Alex?"

Herron got flustered by my tone. "No, Mr. Madison. I was just saying, like, how well do you really know someone? Of course, I don't think Eddie did that. No."

"Did you see Eddie and Jenna after they came out of the karaoke booth?"

"Um, yeah. I saw Jenna and she was upset but she didn't stay long. Then I saw Eddie and asked him what was up with Jenna. He said he had no idea. We had a couple more drinks and forgot about it."

"Okay, thanks Alex. Can I speak to Polly now?"
"Sure, I'll message her for you."

CHAPTER 8

Polly Gould entered the room and extended her arm straight out with her elbow locked. The rather officious gesture added to her overall eccentric, geekish appearance, her look was too curated to be unintentional. Her straight black hair fell to her shoulders and was held back off her forehead by a pink hair band. Her hazel eyes cordially peered at me through a pair of glasses that looked straight out of the Bill Gates' 1980s collection. A brown cardigan, tartan skirt, white socks pulled up high and back Converse sneakers completed the look. I shook her hand and said hello. She brushed the back of her skirt to sit and then clasped her hands in her lap while sitting up with a straight back.

"Thanks for agreeing to see me, Polly. And relax, this isn't a job interview. I just want to get your take on a few things."

"I know. And I'm not nervous," she said, pushing her glasses up the bridge of her nose. "I just don't do relaxed that well. At least, that's how it seems. I understand what's going on."

Herron had left the room before Polly entered so it was just the two of us. Still, I cast my eyes around to see if any cameras were present. I saw the door had been left slightly ajar. I got up and closed it.

"That's right," I said as I moved behind Polly and then retook my seat. "I want to hear your account of the night of the alleged assault, but first I have some questions, if that's okay."

"This isn't a deposition, is it?"

"No. For that I'd be recording our discussion with a video camera, you'd be sworn in and you'd have your own lawyer, if you were smart, that is. And I'm willing to bet you're sharp as a tack."

"The geek-factor-ten look gives it away?"

Polly smiled at her self-deprecating remark.

"Kind of," I laughed. "Can we start with your relationship with Jenna Lewis? Are you two friends?"

Polly tilted her head to give the question a moment's thought. "I wouldn't say we're close but we're friends. We worked together here for a few months before she left to join Ubivision."

"Ubivision?" I asked, jotting the name down. It was the first I'd heard of it.

"Yes." Polly nodded. "They're huge and she loves it there."

Polly went on to tell me that she and Jenna were the only two females in Adrenal's core programming team. They worked on *Out There* together. The experience bonded them as coworkers but they hadn't seen each other much since Jenna left.

"But you were hanging out with Jenna at Blackjacks that night?"

"Yes, I was."

"Were you two with Eddie most of that time?"

"Pretty much. Eddie was on a high after the awards night and he really wanted to party. We kind of took over the bar."

"Did you see Eddie and Jenna interact at the awards night?"

"No. I was at Eddie's table and I didn't see Jenna until we got to the bar, I don't think. No, I saw her earlier but we didn't meet until Blackjacks."

"But at Blackjacks the three of you were drinking together?"

"Yes."

"And there was a lot of alcohol being consumed?"

Polly nodded with a knowing smile. "The gaming industry is pretty intense work-wise, so we do tend to let our hair down when we get the chance."

"How much did you drink?"

"Do you mean was I getting shit-faced, too?"

It kind of took me by surprise to hear Polly swear but the more I heard her talk the more I came to believe there was a charismatic edge to this girl.

"Yes."

"I was," she said with a look of defiance as though I'd thought geeks don't get smashed.

"What about drugs?"

"What about them?"

"Was anyone hitting the party drugs?"

Polly paused and bit her lip, weighing how much to tell me.

"I guess you could say that it goes without saying."

"Who exactly are we talking about here?"

"Everyone. Just about."

"Did Jenna like drugs?"

"I don't know about drugs in general but she liked cocaine. And Eddie tended to have plenty of coke on hand when he wanted to celebrate."

"Do you know if he supplied Jenna with coke?"

"He shared with both of us."

"What about GHB? Did you know of anyone who had GHB that night?"

"No, not at all. That really surprised me. When I heard that, you know, Jenna was drugged with GHB. She wouldn't be into that, I don't think."

"You don't think or do you know that for sure?"

Polly shrugged. "Who knows?"

"Polly, do you think Eddie raped Jenna?"

"Again, who knows?"

"Don't you know Eddie well enough to form an opinion of whether he'd do such a thing?"

"You mean, is it out of character? Well, if you want to put rape in the ballpark of general sexual cluelessness, then maybe it's not out of character."

"What do you mean by that?"

Again she paused. "How much do you know about the gaming industry?"

"A little. I'm into *Call of Duty*. That's about it. I don't play online—just me at home. Today is my first glimpse behind the scenes at how video games are made. So in answer to your question, let's assume for the sake of conversation that I pretty much have no idea."

I kept what Donna Amerson had told me to myself, and just let Polly talk. As it turned out, Polly echoed Donna's words.

"Mr. Madison, I work in arguably the most sexist, the most misogynistic industry on the planet. The guys running these companies are the type who have next to no idea about how to relate to girls. Tech companies like this attract like-minded men. Young men with a truckload of sexual repression that manifests in many ways."

"I was briefed by someone about the workplace culture in gaming. It's as bad as I've heard, it seems."

"Worse, probably."

Polly had relaxed somewhat but she still sat straight-backed in her chair with her hands resting in her lap. There was something almost Victorian about her comportment.

"What kind of sexual abuse have you experienced, Polly?"

This seemed to be a question that hadn't been asked of her often, if at all. She warmed to the chance to address it, launching into a catalog of incidents at her desk, during meetings, out drinking, while playing online games. All of them made me feel embarrassed to be a man. The offenses ranged from being lame to downright vicious and vile. She said nothing had daunted her love for game development, but she never revealed her gender in online games. To do so would only invite a nasty pile-on from the male players. What was most disturbing was that she knew that some of her anonymous attackers—she'd managed to out a few—were boys as young as eleven.

"Polly, why do you continue to work in these conditions? Doesn't it make your life miserable?"

"I wouldn't say miserable. Just difficult. I'm working towards the day when I can go out on my own. Maybe even start an all-girls gaming company. That was something Jenna and I talked about when she was here but I'm not sure she's too committed to the idea. Ubivision hires a higher percentage of girls so it's less pent-up than here."

"Is the misogyny at Adrenal a reflection of Eddie's character?"

"Of course, it is."

"How does Eddie behave towards women?"

"He has no idea, not that he'd ever admit that. I'm not saying he's a bad person and that he was the type of guy to force himself on a girl, but, like I said, with these guys you never know. If you ask me, he's on that tragically clueless spectrum when it comes to women."

"What do you mean?"

"He's one of those guys who girls were never interested in. He probably had crushes on the prettiest girls at school who never gave him a second look. Jenna is pretty and arty and, you know, a very feminine sort of girl. I think she was probably Eddie's ideal woman."

"Was she interested in him?"

Polly shook her head.

"Not at all. She used to make fun of him at work. She used to tell me how his breath stank or that he was such a dork."

"Was she mean to him?"

"No. Never. This was all behind his back, of course."

"So she had no sexual interest in him?"

"No. No way."

"Then why was she hanging out with him at the bar? Why were you? The three of you were drinking together and then went to one of the booths to sing karaoke. That doesn't make it sound like either of you find Eddie repulsive."

Polly bowed her head briefly and took a breath. "Look, he was getting us cocktails and he had plenty of coke. And just because we don't want to sleep with Eddie, it doesn't mean we find him repulsive."

"Why did you leave Eddie and Jenna alone in the karaoke booth?"

"I needed the bathroom, and I just didn't feel the urge to go back in there."

"I take it that you didn't think Jenna was in any kind of danger, being left with Eddie?"

"No. That didn't cross my mind."

"Okay. Do you think Eddie might have misunderstood Jenna's feelings towards him?"

"You mean, did he think she was attracted to him?"

I nodded.

"I wouldn't be surprised. I mean, she wasn't flirting with him or touching him or hanging on him. Not from what I saw. She was just being friendly and social."

"But he was giving her coke that night?"

"Yes."

"How can you be sure?"

"Because she came and got me when he gave her a bag. We went to the bathroom to do some."

"Polly. What do you think happened between Eddie and Jenna that night?"

"I don't know. All I know is that he did something that really upset Jenna. So I'd have to go with her version of events."

"You believe he drugged her and sexually assaulted her?"

Polly nodded. "You asked for my opinion and that's it."

From everything I'd just heard, that's precisely what a jury was going to think, I was sure of it. Maybe a plea offer was the best Eddie Mawson could hope for. Which, like I told him, would mean he'd have to brace himself for the prospect of going to prison.

CHAPTER 9

I grabbed two bottles of beer from the fridge, took them out to my deck and handed one to Jack. The air was warm and the dusk sky over the Pacific was rich and purple. Jack had called earlier saying he had something to show me, and since I wasn't venturing out at night I told him to come over and I'd throw some steaks on the grill.

A swig of chilled Sierra Nevada went down easy, and looking out over the view from my condo, I took quick stock of my blessings.

"You're not doing too bad for yourself, buddy," said Jack, reading my mind as he too admired the view.

A few years ago, after my divorce, I was desperate to leave LA. The only thing tying me to the city was Bella, and I never wanted to be a flight away from her. When she finished school and went to college that was a different story. I liked the idea of heading back to my hometown of Boise, Idaho and hanging my shingle up there. Whether I did that alone or with company I didn't really care. A big part of me was done with this city a long time ago but for now everything was okay. More than okay.

"I'm pretty happy with my lot in life," I said as I lifted the lid of the grill. It was preheated, so I turned down the burners, grabbed the tongs and placed three steaks onto the hot rack.

"Good job, Brad. You've got the meat on. Probably best I take it from here," said Jack, casting a worried eye at the steaks then at me. "They look kind of pricey. Hate to see you ruin them."

"Hilarious," I said. "They'll be done to perfection."

Jack winced and turned away. "Don't know if I can. Just let me know when it's over, and I'll order pizza for me and Bella while you chew on charcoal."

I waved the tongs ruefully at Jack. "You'll be eating your words soon."

Jack laughed and took a swig. "We'll see, Gordon Ramsey." He turned to me and kept his voice low. "So how's it going with Bella?"

"It's been awesome," I said. "She'll go back and live with Claire when her mom is up to it, but I don't really want her to go. It's been the best."

"Look at you," he was about to make a joke but changed his mind. "I think having her here has done you the world of good."

"I'd have to agree."

Jack looked over his shoulder into the condo. Bella was on the couch watching Netflix. "So we can talk shop out here?"

"Sure. Let me bring you up to speed on the Eddie Mawson case first."

"Okay. Shoot."

I ran Jack through the latest developments and recounted the conversation I'd had with Polly. I said a jury would believe every word she said, which was fine from her point of view—she was a young woman of integrity. The problem was that any shade she threw at Eddie would stick. And it was clear she thought Eddie was most likely guilty.

"Okay, that's her take," said Jack. "What's yours?"

I shook my head. "I just don't know. But I've got a case of Jack Briggs about it all at the moment."

Jack's chin jerked back. "What do you mean?"

"You know," I said. "You always tell me you never want to help a guilty person get off. And I've never had a problem standing up for a person's right to a defense, but for the first time in my life I have serious misgivings about that. I mean, I have a professional obligation to defend my client to the hilt. And I will. But I will do so feeling so shitty if I think he's guilty."

"How can you ever know for sure?"

"That's it. I don't know. And maybe I'll never know. It's just getting to me. I need to shake all this emotional bullshit out of my head and focus on the law."

"Yeah, you're normally pretty good at that. And you wonder why people think defense attorneys are such assholes."

Jack laughed and stepped out of arm's reach as I clenched my right fist and faked a punch. I shook my head and turned my attention back to the steaks. "So how'd it go with the photographer?"

"Spoke to him over the phone. It was a pretty interesting conversation."

"He told you about his run-in with Claire?"

"Yes. He said he was just letting off some steam. Said he was a bit of a hothead, that it was nothing serious. By that, he meant he wasn't out to get Claire at all. He said his piece, had his tantrum and that was it."

"Did he tell you what their argument was about?"

"Claire knew he was cheating on his wife, and she called him out on it and axed him from a job. He said he was humiliated and extremely pissed off."

"Pissed off enough to ram his car into her?"

"No," Jack said, shaking his head. "It wasn't him."

"You sound pretty certain about that."

"I am, because at the time of the crash, he was in London, holding the hand of his wife as she was giving birth to their first child."

I thought about Claire and how she wouldn't have spoken out unless she was sure. "So she was right. He was cheating on his wife?"

"Oh, yeah for sure. He was guilty of that, that much I know. I could feel the fear in his voice over the phone. His wife was in the room when I called. He was shitting himself. You'd better turn those steaks."

If the photographer had nothing to do with Claire's accident, then why would Marty throw his name at me? To get rid of me or to throw me off the scent?

I turned the steaks once more and pressed the meat with my tongs. "Watch and learn, buddy. Watch and learn."

"More like scorch and burn."

"Ha ha. Perfect medium-rare," I said as I moved the steaks onto a plate and covered them with foil to rest. "Call that pizza in now if you want."

Jack shook his head and said nothing. He knew I'd nailed the steaks. "You got lucky, Madison. And right now seems like a good time to change the subject. Has Eddie Mawson told you much about what's going on business-wise at Adrenal?"

I shook my head. "Nope. Well, only that he's trying to take the company to the next level. His latest game was a huge success and getting the sequel out ASAP is critical. So having to face these charges isn't great timing, he said."

"Adrenal's had a lot of press lately. Did you know that? Mostly business press coverage."

"I'm not like you, Jack. The business pages bore me to tears. To me, it's all a pea soup of numbers and baloney."

"Not to me," said Jack.

He would say that. Jack had studied IT at college and had made a fortune parlaying his passion for technology into a large stock portfolio. He was by looks and nature the antithesis of the IT geek. He was once a gifted quarterback at college who was marked for a big NFL career before a horrific elbow fracture sidelined him for good. Once he'd made his fortune on the NASDAQ, he started working as a private investigator. He liked the way it took brainpower, street smarts and a bit of spy work. He always liked to give the impression that it was all a game, but deep down he was driven by a desire for justice. His elder sister Nora was murdered in Australia and her body was never found, and even though he was a kid when it happened, Jack always felt he let her down. Working for the likes of me, Jack was helping to right the world in some small way. But he was only willing to work for me on the presumption of innocence. If at any stage of a case he became convinced a client of mine was guilty he would stop helping. His commitment was to only help the innocent. That was why I told him about my reservations about Eddie Mawson. And the truth was that Eddie's case was affecting me personally, so much so that I was beginning to see things Jack's way.

"What has Eddie Mawson told you exactly?" Jack asked.

"About his work?"

"Yes."

"He said he's been negotiating a big deal. Something about Adrenal's future hanging on it. He said the sexual assault case had come at the worst possible time. He's stressed beyond belief, worrying that right when everything was going brilliantly he finds himself struggling to hang on to his company."

"So he gave you no specifics then?"

"I'm his defense attorney on a sexual assault case, not his business adviser. What are you getting at?"

"Right now Eddie Mawson is in the middle of a huge deal. He's negotiating with Beacon Capital."

"What? Marty Cosgrove's company?"

"Yes."

"Let me get this straight. Marty Cosgrove is in the middle of a business deal with my client Eddie Mawson?"

"Yes."

I thought on this for a few moments, wondering why Eddie hadn't told me or why Marty hadn't mentioned it. Then again, how would Eddie know that Marty was married to my ex-wife? Marty, on the other hand, must know I'm defending Eddie Mawson.

"Why didn't Marty bring it up when I went to his office?"

"Because it's highly confidential."

"Then how do you know?"

"Let's call it a calculated guess. Looking at Adrenal, I know what they need to take the next step. And this is the kind of opportunity Beacon Capital seizes on."

"So you're guessing."

"No, I'm not. My sources tell me Eddie and Marty are in the thick of negotiations. And my sources are never wrong."

"Marty has been saying he was crazy busy," I said, thinking aloud. "So this is what kept him from being beside his wife's hospital bed? Investing in a video game company?"

Jack shook his head. "It's a little more complicated than that."

"How so?"

"Beacon Capital has been sniffing around Adrenal for months now. You know it's a venture capital firm, right?"

"That much I do know."

"Well, what they mostly do is step in to help burgeoning companies expand. They find the funds to grow these ventures at the speed the market demands. And right now the market wants Adrenal to scale up tenfold, and fast. That's a lot for a young executive like Eddie Mawson. A deal with Beacon would allow his company to reach its potential in a year as opposed to a decade."

"Are the returns for Beacon good?"

"Stellar. Video game up-and-comers like Adrenal offer some of the best returns out there."

"So long as you back the right horse."

"Exactly."

"Is Adrenal such a horse?"

"It's about as good as it gets."

"So if it's such a win-win, why are both Eddie and Marty acting like their fricking ships are sinking?"

"Well, there are two big problems from what I can see. One they share and one that's Marty's alone."

"I'm listening."

"Their mutual problem is that another company is trying to muscle in and squeeze Beacon out of the deal."

"Really? Which company?"

"It's called Crestway Enterprises. They've been busy investing in gaming too, but who actually runs it is a mystery."

"What? No website? No phone number?"

Jack shook his head. "See? This is why I'm the investigator and you're the suit. I've thrown more at this than a Google search. It's not very often I come up cold but the only name I can connect to it is that of a lawyer named Cobus Lombard. He works for a law firm called Summerfields."

Jack showed me his phone. On the screen was the photo of a grim-faced man in his late fifties. His eyes were fierce, his head was bald and his cheeks were a little sunken. First impressions were that he was the type of guy whose idea of fun was enduring torture. The serial marathon runner type or the high-voltage-nipple-clamp-loving type. Maybe both. Either way, Cobus Lombard's photo didn't scream life of the party.

I knew of Summerfields. Every lawyer in Los Angeles knew of Summerfields. They were a big private firm with a long list of corporate clients. It was a millionaire factory of a firm, the kind that makes law grads drool. "They handle a lot of blue-chip corporations. So this other company is trying to steal Marty's lunch?"

"That's what it looks like."

"Okay, so Eddie has a couple of suitors. What's the problem?"

"I don't know yet, but this kind of interest in Adrenal must be making Eddie's head spin. He'd have a full-time job making sure he didn't get screwed. Maybe you should ask him for some specifics."

"I will, believe me. Okay, so that's the mutual problem. What about the problem that's Marty's alone?"

Jack drained the last of his beer. "Like I said, Beacon's been moving on a few video game companies. They provide seed capital for some to fast-track an undeveloped idea. Then for others they step in to, you know, help realize the target company's potential."

"Okay."

"The thing with Beacon is that they got burned recently. They raided a bunch of start-ups in San Francisco. You know, zero in on some fledgling enterprise that has promise, take it over and then spit out its founders. They did a string of them up there but then they hit a speed bump."

"What kind of speed bump?"

"It was a hot prospect, just like Adrenal, that needed to scale up fast. They seemed to be locked into a deal when all of a sudden the company went with another party, leaving Beacon high and dry."

"Why is that a problem?"

"Well, Beacon had been struggling and was using these churn-and-burns to recoup some of their capital. But when they got cut out of that deal, they were suddenly left without the $20m in projected earnings. Their investors were not happy."

"When you say struggling, how bad?"

"Critically bad. The way I see it, if Beacon loses out on Eddie's deal, they're done."

"You mean they'll go under?"

Jack nodded. "No wonder your ex-wife's husband is shitting himself. If he blows this deal, he's as good as broke."

Chapter 10

I left a message with Eddie Mawson first thing in the morning, telling him I needed to see him urgently. He texted me back to say his day was full. It never ceased to amaze me how wealthy clients who faced serious charges expected their lives to continue as normal. They seemed to think staying out of prison was just a matter of whipping out the checkbook. I replied to Eddie that if he wasn't in my office at three o'clock sharp he could get himself another lawyer. His next text said he'd see me at three.

That done, I got myself dressed, walked Bella to school and then headed into the office. The plan was to get a little work done before going out to speak with a prosecution witness or two. When I checked my inbox I found something that added extra urgency to my meeting with Mawson. It was an email from Assistant District Attorney Elliott Goodwin. The plea deal was in.

I spent some time fleshing out all the implications to present to Eddie later then turned my attention to the witnesses. At the top of the list of people I wanted to grill was a twenty-two-year-old barback named Oscar Guzman who'd told the cops he saw Eddie groping Jenna Lewis in the karaoke booth. He said he was certain he saw Eddie shove his hand up Lewis's dress. Naturally, I wanted to hear this from the horse's mouth but Guzman was proving hard to pin down. His cell number was dead, and when I visited his address a few days ago—a run-down apartment block in Boyle Heights—the place was vacant.

Number two on my list was Matt Tirado, the Blackjacks bartender on shift the night of the alleged assault. I got his details off his police statement, figured he wouldn't be up at the crack of dawn given he was a cocktail bartender, and so knocked on his front door at a pretty reasonable eleven-thirty.

At first, there was no answer and no sound of movement inside. For a moment I wondered if I had another Oscar Guzman on my hands.

I banged on the door harder, gave it a few seconds, then pounded again.

"Okay! Keep your shirt on!" shouted a disgruntled voice.

Footsteps approached the door and the peephole went dark. I smiled and waved.

"Mr. Tirado. I just want to have a quick chat about your work at Blackjacks."

There was a moment's pause as Tirado tried to process how this stranger knew he worked at Blackjacks.

"Doug said I should speak to you," I continued. "He's thinking about changing things up."

Doug was the owner of Blackjacks, according to my Google search. I'd never spoken to Doug in my life.

The door swung open to reveal a mid-twenties guy who looked straight out of Hollywood casting. It was clear in an instant that his bar job paid the rent while he tried to land something that might lead to his dream gig—which by the looks of him could have been a rock star, actor or model. Standing six feet tall in a white wifebeater with chains hanging down his chest, tattoos up his arms and lank black hair swept off an anvil-jawed face, Tirado looked for all money like he wasn't going to be stuck in a bar for long. Then again, this was LA, and there were hundreds of good-looking, fame-hungry dudes who never graduated from mixing drinks and doling out advice to barflies.

"What are you talking about? I told Doug I can't commit to more shifts. He was okay with that." Then Tirado checked himself. "Who the hell are you, anyway?"

"Matt, I need to level with you. But before I do can I just ask you not to slam the door in my face? It might get ugly if you do."

The veiled threat woke Tirado up pronto. He stood taller and physically readied himself. He didn't look the least bit intimidated.

"Okay."

"I'm a lawyer, Matt. My name is Brad Madison." I handed him a card. "I represent Eddie Mawson. He was in your bar a few weeks ago. You gave a statement to the police about an incident that involved him."

Tirado's brow furrowed as he panned his brain for the memory. "Yeah, he raped that girl in the booth."

I held up a hand. "Allegedly. He is *alleged* to have sexually assaulted Jenna Lewis. There's a big difference."

"Whatever. What do you want?"

"I want to ask you a few questions, get your take on events."

"What? Now?"

"Yeah. Look, I'm sorry to just show up like this, but to be honest once I tell people I'm a defense attorney they tend to hang up on me or refuse to open the door."

Tirado was non-plussed. "You said it would get ugly if I slammed the door in your face. What's that supposed to mean?"

"It means I'll have to do things formally. You'll get a subpoena for a deposition and you'll have no choice but to answer my questions under oath with a video camera rolling."

Tirado shrugged his shoulders. "I don't know what else I can tell you that I didn't tell the cops. Anyway, shouldn't I get a lawyer before talking to you?"

"Okay, maybe I'm the wrong guy to ask, but I swear, this will be just an informal conversation. It's not a deposition. We're just talking. I'm just trying to get a complete picture of what went down that night. It won't take more than thirty minutes."

"What the hell. I'm up now. Come in and take a seat. I'll get dressed."

As Tirado walked straight for his bedroom, I scanned the living room. There were posters of rock legends like Jimmy Page and Hendrix on the walls, a well-worn Fender Telecaster leaning up against an amp in one corner and an old-school hi-fi stereo positioned in the other corner, replete with a turntable and a bank of vinyl albums. Music was clearly Tirado's first love. A black and white cowhide rug lay between two red couches. As soon as I sat down, Tirado came out buttoning up his shirt.

"What's going on, babe?" a girl's voice called from the bedroom. "Come back to bed."

"Can't right now, babe. Go back to sleep."

Tirado walked into the kitchen. "I need coffee. You want some?"

"Sure. Why not?"

"How you take it?"

"Black will do."

I heard the sound of banging as Tirado emptied the cup of his espresso machine before refilling it. Within seconds the smell of freshly ground coffee beans reached my nostrils. I guess it was no surprise for a bartender to be particular about his coffee. "So, this is off the record. Is that what you're saying?" Tirado said over his shoulder as the thrum of the machine's pump kicked in.

"Look, I'm not recording it but I am taking mental notes."

"Right," Tirado said. He finished preparing the coffees and walked over sipping one cup and offering me the other.

"Thanks for your hospitality," I said, taking the cup. "It's not exactly what I'm used to in my line of work."

Tirado was alert now. Wide awake and looking eager to talk. "So you defend drug dealers? Murderers? Rapists? That must be a fascinating way to make a living."

I gave a wry smile. "Well, at least you said defending them as opposed to keeping them out of jail. Not all my clients are guilty. Not all are innocent. But what they all have in common is a right to a staunch defense."

"No, it's cool, man. I was just thinking it'd be great to hang out with you if I was ever going to go for a part as a lawyer."

"So you're an actor. I thought you were a musician."

"Actor slash rocker slash model slash writer. I've got a few irons in the fire. I've actually got a screenplay that's kind of a legal thriller. I'm a big John Grisham fan. Maybe you could read it? You know, for authenticity."

"Sure," I said hesitantly. "But not until this case is done. But if you get it written, by all means, hit me up."

"You serious?"

"Yes. I am. Now, about my client, Eddie Mawson."

"Cool," he said enthusiastically, amped by my offer. "Now, Eddie is it? What do you want to know?"

"Had you seen him at Blackjacks before?"

"No, that was the first time I ever laid eyes on him. I'm sure about that."

"Does that mean he left a strong impression on you?"

"You could say that."

"How so?" I asked, knowing it would be for the wrong reasons.

"Look, I'm not going to lie. Guys like him stand out. You know, they're cashed-up dorks who've suddenly found that they've got it all. But they don't know how to handle it, and they've still got a lot to learn when it comes to chicks."

"That's what you thought when you saw Eddie?"

"Yeah, I mean he spent most of the night trying to impress these two girls."

"Did you see him behave disrespectfully towards them?"

"Not to their faces but when he was at the bar I heard him talking to one of his friends. It was a little off but it didn't surprise me."

"What did he say?"

"He said they were gagging for it, like they were hot for him. And he said something like these bitches would do anything for some blow. That's right, he also said Cosmopolitans were great leg openers. It was a sad joke, this fool trying to convince his buddy that he was a player. So I offered him a little advice."

"What did you say?"

"I said those girls are never going to go to bed with you. You know why? Because your attitude sucks."

"What did he say?"

"Nothing. He just shut his mouth and went off with his drinks. I didn't think anything of it until the cops came around."

"Did you see him use drugs?"

"No. I would have kicked him out if I did."

"Did you see the girls use drugs?"

"No," he said shrugging his shoulders.

"You mean, you think you know what the girls were up to but you don't want to say?"

"If two girls go to the bathroom together who knows what they're up to? I didn't see them do drugs."

"How was Jenna Lewis treating Eddie?"

"Which one was Jenna?"

I showed him a photo.

"Ah, yeah. It was like she was kind of flattering him with her company. She smiled to his face but looked kind of disengaged otherwise."

"She wasn't flirting with him?"

"Didn't look like that to me."

"But they got pretty drunk together."

"Yeah, God knows how many rounds of drinks he bought. Cosmopolitans, mostly. But there was champagne early on."

"So you paid attention to them?"

"I like to watch what goes on in the bar. It's good for doing character studies. And he caught my eye from the start. He was like a kid who becomes king of the world but doesn't know shit. Well apart from coding apps, or whatever he does."

"Eddie did a lot more than code an app. He founded a hugely successful video game business."

"Well, good for him. But he may have blown it, yeah?"

"That remains to be seen. Did you see him or anyone else interfere with the girls' drinks?"

"No, that kind of thing would be easy to miss, though. It was a pretty busy night."

"Okay, I get that Eddie was awkward and a bit of a dick, but did you see him do anything sexually inappropriate to either of those girls?"

"I don't know whether this is what you'd call inappropriate. But I saw them head to the karaoke booth. He put his arm around that Jenna girl and he gave me this smug look and a thumbs up."

"What kind of a look?"

"You know. That look that says, 'I'm in.'"

Chapter 11

Eddie Mawson strolled into my office twenty minutes late while talking on his phone. Tempted as I was to bark at him while he was still on his phone, I'd waited for the end of the call. He stood there for half a minute before signing off. Only then did he lay eyes upon me and saw how pissed off I was.

"Next time you're late, I'm billing you triple my rate for a minimum three-hours," I said. "And you come in here on the phone like that again and it will be the last call you make with that thing. I'll take it and shove it where the sun doesn't shine. Got it?"

Eddie went white as a sheet and began removing his AirPods from his ears. "Yes," he stammered. "I'm sorry."

The uncomfortable truth was that I was just about sick of the sight of Eddie Mawson. Never before had I seriously considered dropping a client but I was beginning to feel I could fire Eddie with relish. What I'd been told about him only added to my misgivings. It now seemed plausible, if not highly likely, that he was the kind of maladjusted jerk who'd think it was funny to diss women, heap sexist scorn on them, and, yes, even drug and rape them. Who knows? Not me. I felt like I didn't know Eddie at all. It was now only too apparent that I'd have a tough time convincing a jury he wasn't a maladjusted tool.

But as much as I enjoyed the thought of letting Eddie go, there was no way I was going to turn my back on him.

"I'm sorry, Brad. It's just that work is... No, I'm just sorry, that's all. I shouldn't have done that. And feel free to bill me accordingly. You can do it for today."

"Take a seat, Eddie," I said wearily. "As I've said before. If you go to jail, the only work you'll have is making license plates. This case needs to be your priority."

He nodded. "Yes, sir. I mean, Brad."

"I don't know what I have to say to get you to take this seriously but—"

"I am taking this seriously."

"Really? Then why the hell did I find out from somewhere else that you're in the middle of a war with millions of dollars at stake?"

"You mean—?"

"You know what I mean but I want you to explain to me exactly what's going on between your company and both Beacon Capital and Crestway Enterprises."

Mawson had his elbows on the arm rests of the chair and his hands clasped together. He was initially at a loss for words.

"How do you know about...? The first thing is that this business deal is confidential. I can't believe you know about it. Who told you?"

"Never mind how I know. I need you to explain it to me."

"Brad, it's confidential. And it's got nothing to do with my sexual assault case."

"Let me be the judge of that."

"What do you mean?"

"Start talking, Eddie."

Mawson took a deep breath. "Okay, here's what I can tell you. For months I'd been in talks with Beacon Capital about them investing in my company. With the success of *Out There* I need a bigger and better sequel and I need it fast. I don't have the money to fund such a rapid expansion. The only answer was venture capital. It was just a question of who I'd team up with."

Mawson explained that Marty had approached him when gushing user reviews of *Out There* had begun to drive sales up the charts. He said Beacon had some solid experience in the gaming sector. He was adamant that he'd never let go of his controlling stake and Beacon was okay with that.

"So you've been dealing with Marty Cosgrove," I said studying Eddie's face.

"Yes," said Eddie, studying mine, which obviously displayed some consternation. "Is there a problem?"

I shook my head, wondering why I was surprised to learn my client was involved with Marty.

"Eddie, has my name ever come up in conversation between you and Marty?"

Eddie shook his head. "No, never."

"I see. When you needed a defense lawyer, why did you come to me?"

"I found you on Google."

"No one recommended you?"

"No. There are a lot of stories online about your cases. A lot of praise. You're one of the best defense attorneys in Los Angeles. One news article actually said that. So do the testimonials on your website."

"My website?"

I'd almost forgotten I had one. I'd tasked Megan with putting it together and had paid scant attention to it after it went live.

"And when I read that you dated Abby Hatfield," Eddie said with a big smile, "I knew you were definitely the man."

Eddie said this with a semi-guffaw that made him look even more like an undersexed undergrad. His words made me feel uncomfortable, grubby even.

"Jesus, Eddie," I said, shaking my head.

"Well, that's how I found you. Why?"

"Never mind. Okay, you've been offered a deal by Beacon. Where does Crestway Enterprises fit into the picture?"

Eddie looked at me somewhat indignantly.

"I can't believe you know about Crestway? Who told you?"

"What do I look like, Eddie? A bumbling idiot? It's called due diligence. Everything that's going on in your life might have a bearing on your case. Everything. I thought that would be obvious. A multi-million-dollar business deal is not something you should be hiding from me."

"Like I said, that part of my business is highly confidential."

"Correction. It's an aspect of your life that could be integral to you going to jail. Tell me about Crestway."

Eddie shook his head. "I'm sorry but there's not a lot I can tell you. I deal with them via a lawyer named Cobus Lombard. I've never met anyone from the company itself."

Eddie said this Lombard character was very intimidating. He just appeared out of the blue insisting that it would be in Eddie's best interests to go with Crestway instead of Beacon. The way he talked it sounded more like a threat than good advice. Lombard's sudden arrival on the scene meant Eddie was facing a tough choice about who to go with. Then he was hit with sexual assault charges which made his decision all the more urgent. The deal had to be signed off on before his case went to trial to minimize the damage to Adrenal. There was also a personal motive to close the deal.

"I want to make sure my mom and sister will be financially secure, if my case goes, you know south," said Eddie.

I shook my head. "So you have been taking this case seriously."

Mawson nodded. "Much more than I've been letting on. It's like if I let myself think about it, I gravitate to how bad it could be and that's so unbearable I just shut it out of my mind."

Maybe Eddie Mawson was someone I could believe after all, and believe in.

I leaned forward, resting my arms on my desk. "Eddie. Let me ask you this. If you are truly innocent as you claim to be, who would benefit most from seeing you convicted of these charges?"

Eddie took a deep breath and nodded, like it was a salient point to mull over. He shook his head and declined to offer up an answer.

"That was a question, Eddie," I said. "Who would benefit from you going to jail?"

"Seriously?"

"I couldn't be more serious."

"Well, I'd have to say Beacon or Crestway. Whoever gets the deal."

Chapter 12

After Eddie relayed everything he was prepared to tell me about Crestway, I had to admit I was impressed with how he was keeping it all together. Here he was, not even thirty and he was handling a multi-million-dollar business and had two very big sharks circling. He'd have to be razor sharp to ensure he didn't get screwed. On top of that, he now had a plea deal to consider, and it wasn't pretty.

I took a piece of paper from my desk and handed it to Eddie. "What's this?"

"It's a plea offer. The prosecutor sent it through this morning. Take a moment to read it."

I stood up and walked out of my office to get us some water. When I got back I placed one glass in front of Eddie. He reached out and drained it. I waited for him to speak. He leaned forward and placed the paper back on my desk.

"So they want me to plead guilty to assault and drug possession?"

"Does that mean I'd go to jail if I take it?"

I nodded my head.

"Yes. For two years. But this is just the opening bid, so to speak. This is where the negotiating starts. If you want me to negotiate, that is. And I might be able to get the DA to drop the drug charge. But there's more to this than the threat of jail time."

Goodwin had offered to reduce the severity of the sexual assault down from a tier-one offense to a tier-three. This was a big concession in that it meant Eddie wouldn't be facing the prospect of eight years in prison. The charge he wanted Mawson to plead guilty to was felony sexual battery and that meant a solid two years if Goodwin wasn't willing to budge. It seemed pretty clear that he was gunning for a conviction with jail time served. Under normal circumstances I'd have felt confident about completely removing jail time from the deal, or at least securing a suspended sentence. And if I got it down to misdemeanor sexual battery then Eddie would be looking at one year at the most. But my gut told me Goodwin wasn't going to play ball. This to me seemed like a take-it-or-leave-it offer from a prosecutor who was itching to take the case to trial.

"There is another big concern here, Eddie. Something that affects your life way beyond any time you might spend in prison."

"What's that?"

"You'll have to register as a sex offender."

Eddie picked up the plea document again. "What? Where does it say that?"

"It doesn't, Eddie. It's implicit in the penalties. It's just a question of how long you stay on the list for. For a tier-one sex offense you'd be on it for life. For a tier-three like what's been offered here, you'd be on it for ten years minimum."

Eddie looked appalled. "Ten years minimum? Is it public?"

"Yes. It's a public list, and it's national. Anyone can access it anywhere in the country. In the world, for that matter. Now here's the thing, even if Goodwin was offering misdemeanor sexual battery, you'd still have to register for at least ten years. In fact, even if he reduced the charge to just plain assault, you'd have to register for the same length of time."

"If it's common assault, then why?"

"Because your assault conviction stemmed from an alleged sex crime. It sticks. So you have to give some deep thought to whether you are prepared to be branded a sex offender for the next ten years of your life."

I knew I didn't have to spell out that there was a hefty social stigma tied to being on the sex offender register. It might trigger objections from, or even confrontations with, people in his direct community. And if he wanted to move anywhere else in the US—or even the world—he risked a hostile reception. People don't like sex offenders moving into their neighborhood. And in the business world, it wasn't hard to imagine his shame being contagious, that any company that dealt with him risked being publicly accused of supporting a sex offender. He could become an exile.

"We need to work out some parameters, Eddie."

"Such as?"

"Such as whether you're prepared to do any time served and whether you're willing to become a registered sex offender."

Eddie, his lips pressed together grimly, shook his head resolutely. "No."

"Then we'll be going to trial. Now you have to remember that nothing's guaranteed in a trial. If we win, you'll emerge with your liberty and your standing intact, save for the ignominy of having been accused of sexual assault. But if we lose, you could be locked up for eight years and put on the sex offender register for twenty."

"Jesus Christ," muttered Eddie, exhaling audibly.

"You don't have to answer now."

"What are the chances we'll win at trial?"

"Well, that's all going to come down to how strong the state's case is against you. What can they actually prove?"

Eddie looked shellshocked. "What do you think, Brad?"

"The case against you is strong but sexual assault convictions are very hard to come by. We've just got to make the prosecutor's job harder. On that note, there are a few things we need to unpack. Why don't we get started on that?"

Eddie reached for his glass but it was empty. I called Megan in to get us more water.

"Eddie, one of the biggest problems we have is that a few witnesses have painted your behavior at Blackjacks in a pretty poor light."

"Like who?"

"Like the bartender for one."

"He's a bartender. What does it matter what he says?"

I held Eddie's eye for a good few seconds, wondering how he could so quickly jump from the sober reflection of his predicament to a high-handed brush-off of a prosecution witness. This kind of reflex arrogance ruled out the possibility of ever putting him on the stand. He would be clueless about how poorly his attitude would come across to a jury and how swiftly they'd damn him. Matt Tirado, on the other hand, would present as a real and genuine character. The jury would lap up his every word.

Catching the drift of my unspoken reprimand, Eddie changed his tune. "I mean, what did he say?"

"He said he heard you speaking disrespectfully about Jenna and Polly."

"What?"

"He said he had a word with you, that he gave you some advice along the lines of 'watch your mouth.'"

Eddie looked bewildered. "That wasn't in his police statement."

"It was referenced. He told the cops that he told you to behave. But those extra details will come out in a trial. He said you were gloating about the fact that the cocktails were leg openers. What do you suppose the jury will make of that?"

A pall of shame fell over Eddie's face.

"My God, I'm such a tool."

While I was pleased to see a degree of self-awareness, I didn't want Eddie to confuse poor form with criminal behavior.

"Behaving like a jerk and being a rapist are not the same thing. But the narrative of your night from the viewpoints of others doesn't look good. It looks like you're a young, rich, white, entitled misogynist. And it doesn't really matter whether that image of you is an accurate representation of your character, it's the impression that will stick in the jury's mind."

"It's not who I am."

"I hope not, Eddie. But we're going to need to find a way to prove it."

Eddie bent down and put his head in his hands. "I'm such a dick!" he yelled. He then straightened up, looked at the ceiling and rubbed his face. He then fixed his eyes on me.

"Maybe this is what I deserve," he said with resignation.

"What are you talking about?"

"I said maybe it's what I deserve. I've said some really sexist things in the past. I've seen some real shitty things done to women and I stood by and said nothing. Worse than that, I laughed."

Eddie proceeded to tell me about a conference where one of his peers gave a talk and all the while made sexual references to a girl sitting in the front row. The guy even stood behind her touching himself, prompting a roar of laughter that left the girl humiliated. There were other similar sexist incidents that only on reflection now did he consider them to be not just unfunny but borderline sinister.

"Was that partly why Jenna left your company?"

"I don't know. It could have been."

"Eddie. I've got to be honest. You'd better hope that some of your work colleagues can sing your praises."

Eddie shook his head dejectedly. "I don't know. Like I said, maybe I deserve this. I mean, I didn't rape Jenna but maybe it's just karma coming back, you know. Maybe I deserve to go to jail."

"You only deserve to go to jail if it's been proved beyond reasonable doubt that you have committed a crime. Prison isn't a consolation prize. It's part of a direct exchange. A quid pro quo. If you didn't do the crime then you don't deserve the time. End of story."

Eddie smiled weakly, and leaned back in his chair jiggling his legs.

"Of course. You're right," he said.

That was when I found myself believing that, as imperfect as he was, Eddie Mawson might just be innocent.

Chapter 13

Claire was sitting up in bed with her head buried in her phone when I entered her room. It had been a couple of weeks since I'd seen her but I knew from Bella that her cognitive abilities had improved remarkably. Although she had no recollection of the crash, she was able to talk relatively freely. She was expected to be given the all-clear to go home in the next few days.

For better or worse, I couldn't wait that long.

Her face lit up when she saw me arrive. Her color was back, as was her lovely vibe.

"Brad," she said warmly, setting her phone on the bedside table where she ate her meals. "What a nice surprise."

She placed her hands on the mattress and pushed herself up, wincing as she did so. "Is Bella with you?" she said through gritted teeth.

"No. It's just me today. Are you okay?"

"It's just my ribs. They'll take a while to heal. Six weeks at least."

What followed was a pause long enough for Claire to detect my hesitation. Clearly, I wasn't doing a great job of pretending I wasn't apprehensive about being there.

"What's wrong?" she asked with a quizzical look.

I stepped closer, waved my hand and pulled up a chair. "Nothing's wrong," I said as I sat. "Everything's fine."

Claire hadn't taken her eyes off me for a split second. "You don't fool me, what's the matter? Is Bella okay? She's still enjoying school, isn't she? She says she's loving it but I know how that can change in a heartbeat."

"No, Bella's totally fine," I said and leaned forward. "Listen, have the police been to see you?"

"Yes, they were here a couple of days ago. They asked me a few questions but I wasn't much use to them."

"What did they ask you?"

"They wanted to know what I could remember about the crash. They hoped I might be able to give them a description of the driver."

"But you couldn't, I take it?"

Claire shook her head. "It's a total blank. I don't remember a thing. Not about the crash, nor about the hours before. I only know what Marty and the police have told me. I'm not sure I want to know anymore, to be honest. I'm just feel blessed to be alive. Bella's loving being with you, Brad, and that makes me so happy. She says you've been wonderful, that you drove her here every day and stayed for hours until she was ready to go. I can't tell you how thankful I am."

"No worries, Claire. We're all just so relieved that you pulled through."

"I've been thinking about that a lot, Brad."

"About what?"

"Well, I was thinking when I get back home maybe we should give you and Bella more time together."

"You mean I'd get her more than every other weekend?"

Claire nodded. "If that's what you and Bella want."

The gentleness and goodness in Claire's voice just about melted me. Her words struck deep. She'd obviously come to believe that she no longer had to fear Bella being around me, that I was a better man than I used to be, that my demons had faded. I'd of course told Claire as much over the years but she was naturally wary, if not skeptical, and never convinced enough to relax my access to Bella. Now she'd obviously reconsidered. I could have kissed her.

"Thank you, Claire," I said. "That means a lot. Let's wait till you get out of here, okay?"

"Okay."

I steered the conversation to Claire's work, asking how she was coping with being absent. She told me about the arrangements she'd made with her staff, how she'd shelved a whole bunch of projects. She was happy for her company just to idle until she was fully ready to get back behind the wheel. The funny thing was that Claire was obviously not in a hurry to resume her grueling work routine. Maybe the accident had given her pause to reflect on how much of her life she should devote to work.

"It feels like the person who started and ran my company was someone else entirely, not me," she said.

"What do the doctors say about your recovery?"

"They're confident my memories of my life will return but they're doubtful that details of the accident will. They said it would be pretty much normal if it stayed buried deep in my subconscious."

I put my hands together, bowed my head and twiddled my fingers.

"Brad, would you please tell me what's going on? Something's bothering you. I know it."

I wasn't sure whether or not to share what I suspected but there was no time to waste.

I leaned closer. "Claire, look I don't know if this is the right time to tell you but Jack and I have reason to believe that your accident was not actually an accident."

Claire's face contorted with confusion. "What? What are you talking about?"

I paused and took a breath and continued in a quiet, soft voice. "We've analyzed the crash scene, okay? And I mean thoroughly. You know how Jack is. He produced a 3D model of it."

"And?"

"And we think someone rammed into you on purpose."

Claire turned her eyes from me and stared ahead in bewilderment. "That doesn't make any sense at all. Why would anyone want to do that?"

"Well, that's what I'd like to know."

Claire's gaze switched back on me. "You're saying someone tried to kill me?"

I leaned back and nodded once. "You had your car in reverse. You backed it into the garage column. It looks like you saw the car coming straight towards you and you tried your best to get out of the way."

Claire spent a few moments thinking in silence. "If that were true," she said at last, "if I saw them coming and tried to get out of the way, how does that prove that the crash was deliberate?"

"That alone doesn't prove it, I know."

"The police said nothing about this. They think it was a hit and run."

"Yes, I'm well aware of that but that's what *they* think."

"But you and Jack disagree?"

I nodded.

"Why would anyone want to kill me, Brad?" Claire said and left her mouth agape.

I shrugged. I weighed whether I should push forward with my next line of inquiry. I bit the bullet and forged on. "Look Claire, I'm serious about this and so is Jack. We want to look into every possibility because if we're right you could still be in danger."

"From who?"

"I don't know yet but… look, we can't rule out anything at the moment and… Listen, you're not going to like what I'm going to say next but—"

"Just say it."

There was something very familiar returning to the manner in which she was now addressing me. Bafflement had morphed into irritation and was just a hair away from annoyance.

"Look I shouldn't have said anything. I'm sorry. Too soon."

"But now that you have mentioned it, Brad. Say it."

"Okay, look, I'm not accusing anyone of anything but I understand that there were some money issues between you and Marty."

Claire's jaw dropped and her eyes dared me to go on. She mouthed the letters W-T-F as her eyes went stone cold on me.

"It's probably nothing but I need to look at this from all angles, and I understand Marty wanted to borrow money off you and you didn't want to."

"I can't believe you're saying this. You questioned Bella about this?"

"Look, this is the last thing that I want to be saying, Claire, but I have to."

Claire knew where this was going. "You're suggesting my husband had something to do with this? Are you going to ask me about my will, Brad? Are you going to ask me who I've left my money to? Are you thinking that's how Marty planned to get money off me?"

"Claire, I'm just—"

"Are you for fucking real? My God, Brad. You just can't let go. Can you?"

Annoyance had gone straight to fury.

"I just want to find out who did this to you."

"You are so far out of line. And you have no idea. I'm not your wife anymore, Brad. That ended years ago. But you've never been able to accept that. And now this. That's how pathetic you are. But just so you know, I do have a will."

I nodded my head and stood up, knowing that it was time for me to leave. Claire's mental acuity was now back in full force. No doubt about it.

"If you must know, I've left money in a trust for Bella," Claire said, her eyes on fire. "And I've left a large amount to Marty. He's the man I love, Brad. I trust him with my life, Brad. You're the one I was scared of."

I nodded grimly. I should have kept my mouth shut but I couldn't. "So where's he been all this time you've been in the hospital? He's sure as hell hasn't been here. He left you lying here while he practically lived at his office. That's what was most important to him."

"You don't know Marty. You don't know what kind of man he is, and you certainly have no idea how much we love each other."

"Well, that's plain to see. Wild horses couldn't drag him from your side."

"Get out, you bastard," she seethed.

"I'm going."

"You know what? There is something in my will that does concern you, just to give you a heads up."

"What's that?"

"If I actually die in the next few years, I've stipulated that Marty gets equal custody of Bella."

I glared at her. "You can't be serious."

"Oh, believe me, Brad. I'm deadly serious. Now get the fuck out."

A nurse appeared looking concerned. Clearly she'd heard raised voices. Now that she was in the room, she felt tension thick in the air. "Is everything okay in here?" she asked.

"Yes, thank you," Claire said. "He was just leaving."

Chapter 14

They say there are three jokes about lawyers and the rest are true stories. Critics of defense lawyers in particular say we don't have a conscience. And I get it. I sure know a few who don't and they're among the richest attorneys in LA. But without us, who's going to try and free those hundreds of innocents rotting away in US prisons? Without us, what you've got is a police state, a country where even fake charges are a one-way ticket to jail. If you want to see what that's like, move to Russia.

I'd never met Assistant District Attorney Elliott Goodwin face to face but he'd already made it clear when we spoke on the phone that he was no fan of criminal attorneys. I'd called him as soon as I'd taken Mawson's case to introduce myself. Given the gruff reception, I said I'd forward my contact details to send me the plea offer when he had it. He cut me off, telling me he'd put an offer together when he was good and ready in a tone as even and dry as the Bonneville Salt Flats. He remained on the call long enough to indicate that he knew of me, and that I wasn't someone he particularly admired. I thanked him for his time, and said I looked forward to hearing from him. "That hard up for company, huh?" he said gruffly. "Figures." So the guy had a sense of humor.

From his voice, I'd pictured a Tommy Lee Jones type character. Big, imposing man with a bullhorn voice and an ever-percolating temper. When I arrived at his office and he stood up and stepped out from his desk to greet me with a brisk and firm handshake, my impressions went out the window. Goodwin was at most five-eight—half a foot shorter than me and, in his mid-thirties, about ten years younger. There was nothing flashy about his dress—gray suit, blue tie and button-down white shirt—but his neat-and-tidy overall appearance reflected a telling pride. His black shoes, which I caught a glimpse of when he stood, were polished to a mirror shine and his brown, thinning hair was just long enough for him to slick back with some kind of product. His face, although cleanly shaved, was rough skinned and a three-inch scar extended from his left cheek down to his mouth. Another one ran across the top of his left eye. There was a story in those old wounds, not that I was going to ask about it.

"Grab a seat, Madison," he said as he held his tie and sat. "I take it you put the offer to your client?"

"Yes. And he's not interested."

"You could have told me that in an email. What are you doing here?"

"I wanted to meet you, Elliott, and I prefer to discuss plea deals in person."

Goodwin raised a palm to cut me off. "What's there to discuss? Your client doesn't want the deal, we go to trial. If that's the way you want to proceed, fine by me. It's his ass on the line."

"That's one thing we can agree on. His ass meaning everything—career, life, prospects, reputation."

"You can't be here seeking a better deal. Tell me that's not why you're here."

"You know as well as I do that if he pleads guilty to assault his name goes on the register."

"Your point being?"

"He's marked for life as a sex offender."

"My heart bleeds. Maybe he shouldn't go around putting his hands where they don't belong. And maybe it's in society's best interest to know exactly what kind of man your client is."

"And you want him to accept jail time?"

"It's a couple of years. But maybe if you're half as good as people say you are, you can get it suspended."

"He'd still be branded for life."

"No. Ten years. That's it."

"You say it like it's nothing. It will stick to him to the grave."

"Again, if you want a shoulder to cry on I'm not your man. Was there anything else you wanted to chat about?"

Goodwin looked at me expectantly. I was sure he was about to lift his arm and show me the door.

"I emailed you about providing me with some specific discovery evidence," I said. "I assume you've got it ready?"

"I do. Here you go," said Goodwin as he grabbed a folder and lobbed it on the desk in front of me.

I picked up the folder and began flicking through it. "Where's the DNA report?"

"They're still working on it."

"What? That's BS. They've had weeks to get it done. So I guess you're not happy with the results."

"Are you accusing me of withholding evidence?"

"Not yet. But if I ever think you are, I won't hesitate to contact Judge Odell." Both Goodwin and I knew that Superior Court Judge Sean Odell, who was presiding over Eddie's case, didn't tolerate discovery stalling tactics. "I'm sure he'd be eager to hear your explanation."

"Go ahead," said Goodwin, doing his utmost to appear non-plussed. "I've got even more witnesses speaking to your client's behavior now."

I checked the witness list and saw a couple of names had been added. Both female, who said they worked with Eddie. I began scanning their testimony. None of it was good but most of it was hearsay.

"So no new evidence then?"

"That's not the end of it. I'll have more in a few days. But that plea offer you've got? I'm only keeping it alive for another forty-eight hours."

"He's not going to take it. He's not going to do time and be branded a pervert for the rest of his life."

"That's his prerogative but I'm not watering it down any more than I have already. That's as good as he's going to get. If you knew what's best for him you'd advise him to take it. If we go to trial, all his depravity will become public. Being on the sex offender register will be nothing compared to how eviscerating the court testimony will be for him."

Goodwin was expecting me to stand and leave but I wasn't done yet. "I can understand why this case is personal for you, Goodwin. I just hoped you'd be professional enough to keep your feelings out of it."

Goodwin's face froze and he stared at me with narrowed eyes. "What are you talking about?"

"Are you kidding me? Do you think I don't know anything about you? I know what happened to your mother. And that was horrific. But I say this with all due respect—go hard at your job, by all means, go hard at me, but if you think you can avenge what happened to your mother by taking my client down you've got another thing coming."

I'd looked into Goodwin, making a few calls around the legal circles, and learned that when he was in his late teens he witnessed his mother being attacked by her boyfriend. When he went to defend her he was knocked out and he woke to discover that his mother had been raped. I wouldn't wish such a horrific experience on my worst enemy, and I could understand why he was renowned to have a particular hatred of alleged sex offenders. But if he was inclined to let personal grief be the guiding light of justice, then it was my duty to oppose it.

"Spoken like a true pervert apologist," Goodwin scoffed. "I get it. So long as this guy keeps writing big checks for you he's a saint being crucified by the system. You make me puke."

"I'm sorry that my insistence on due and proper process offends you. But you don't have enough evidence to prove this case beyond a reasonable doubt and you know it. No matter what you might want to believe, it's all here in black and white. I'm going to make sure the jury looks at one thing and one thing only—evidence."

"Believe me, you'll be seeing something very strong soon. But by that time, your client's best course of action—that plea deal you find so unreasonable—will be off the table and we start putting a jury together. And I'm telling you now, at trial he's going to get ten years with eighty-five. That's what he's going to get for listening to you."

What Goodwin meant was, in his view, Mawson was going to get a ten-year sentence and would have to serve a minimum eighty-five percent of it, no matter how good a boy he was inside.

"Don't make me laugh."

"I'd never suggest it was a laughing matter, Madison. But something I will suggest is this: when you lose, your ex-wife will feel certain she was right to ditch you. What's her name again? Claire?"

My blood hit boiling point in a flash.

Goodwin laughed. "What? You think I don't know about you too, Madison?"

"You piece of shit."

"Since she left you she's done very well for herself. I'm happy she's recovering well. At least that's what I hear. Comas can mess with the memory. But that could be a good thing. If she's lucky she might forget she was married to you."

I got up. "You're lucky you're behind that desk. Keep talking like that and I'll rip your throat out."

Goodwin laughed. "Ah, there it is. The old Brad Madison composure. What was that sage advice you just offered me about letting your emotions get the better of you?"

"Get me that evidence and the DNA report by close of business tomorrow or I'm going to Judge Odell."

Chapter 15

On my way back to the office Jack called. I still had steam coming out of my ears from my meeting with Goodwin.

"Why do prosecutors have to be such dicks?" I snapped.

There was a pause on the line.

"Er, tough day, sweetheart?"

I pounded my fist on the steering wheel, not exactly picturing it land on Elliott Goodwin's nose but just about. "Yeah, you could say that. What's up?"

"So I've been looking into Marty like you asked."

"And?"

"And I just came across something interesting."

"What's that?"

"You know how I said he was involved in a string of deals up in San Francisco?"

"Yep."

"Well, there was one deal that kind of sticks out from the rest."

"How so?"

"Beacon targeted a gaming company run by a guy named Aldo Roche. And Roche ended up getting squeezed out."

"That sounds familiar."

"Yeah, but you haven't heard the most interesting part."

"Which is?"

"Right when Aldo Roche's company became a takeover target he had sexual assault charges filed against him."

"You're kidding! Jesus, crazy coincidence or what?"

"Maybe, but what are the odds?"

"Given the sexist reputation of the gaming industry, the odds might be rather high."

"Okay, but for argument's sake, if it's not a coincidence then—"

"It's a pattern."

"Right," said Jack. "Now you know the fundamental goal of investment is to buy low and sell high, right?"

"Right."

"Well, what if there's a company you want but it's selling high? What if you decide to try and get it low?"

"By compromising the company," I said. "Or at least the guy running it."

"Exactly."

"You're saying this could be a tactic, a type of market manipulation?"

"Sure. A pretty ruthless one, but I wouldn't put it past a high-street banker let alone an aggressive venture capitalist."

"And these gaming company founders aren't exactly veterans of the cut and thrust of high-stakes business. They'd be soft targets."

"That's right," said Jack. "These are young owners, guys who got started in their bedrooms living off nothing but air, soda and pizza while mom foots the broadband bill. Five years later they've got a start-up worth millions. There's blood in the water and the sharks are circling."

"Who's this guy in San Francisco again?"

"Aldo Roche."

"Let's track him down."

"Way ahead of you. I know where to find him. We should go pay him a visit."

"I'll get Megan to book the flights. You good for tomorrow morning?"

"As long as you're paying. No problemo."

"Done. Nice work, Jack."

Chapter 16

I steered the rental car, a late model Chevy Impala, south along the 101 from San Francisco Airport. We were heading for the heart of Silicon Valley, where tech titans like Apple, Google and Facebook were headquartered. Jack knew a lot about these companies, in that he got in early enough on all three to make a fortune in stocks. And he'd spent enough time in the area to be able to direct me straight to where we wanted to go, which was a coffee shop in East Palo Alto called Java Joint. Jack had had no problem tracking down and keeping tabs on Aldo Roche. The guy did social media check-ins just about everywhere he went. And there was one place he spent so much time that Jack figured he either worked there or just liked to use the free Wi-Fi. Either way, Jack figured if we got ourselves there it would not be long before Roche showed his face. And given Roche's face was all over his social media accounts, we knew who to look for.

Java Joint was one of those places where they roast their own beans. The air was thick with the aroma of good coffee and the sound of clattering cups and cutlery. We scanned the floor and couldn't see Roche at any of the tables. There was a very Silicon Valley feel to the place. Just like you couldn't swing a cat in a Sunset Strip restaurant without hitting a wannabe screenwriter, this place was a conspiracy of nerds. Not loser nerds but enterprising ones, sitting here with their compact laptops probably riffing on a crunch project that would become the next NASDAQ darling. Barely anyone under thirty, all wearing clean sneakers, Apple watches and at least one item of active wear. Jack might have felt somewhat at home here. I felt somewhat like a misfit.

"There he is," said Jack pointing at an apron-wearing guy behind the counter who was inviting a customer to tap a white credit card reader. Roche was a pleasant looking late-twenty-something with dark hair that fell straight and hung just over his ears. We joined the line and waited our turn.

"What can I get you, guys?" Roche asked when the customer in front of me stepped away.

I leaned forward a little and kept my voice low and my tone friendly. "You're Aldo Roche, right?"

Roche knitted his forehead. "Um, yeah. Have we met?"

"No, Aldo. We haven't met. I'm a lawyer from LA. Brad Madison," I handed him my card. He read it with purpose and turned it over in his hand. There was nothing to see on the back. "I'm defending a client whose story sounds a whole lot like yours."

Roche's instant discomfort was clear. I could practically see the sweat beads growing on that confounded brow of his. "Look, I'm busy—"

"His company's being targeted by Beacon Capital. Actually he's in a three-way with Beacon and another outfit. And he's been accused of sexual assault. Sound familiar?"

Roche cut a few quick, wary glances around the room. "Look, I can't talk to you. I'm working, for one. And for another, I've got nothing to say to you. Please leave."

"I can hold the fort," said the barista two yards away. He'd obviously caught some of our conversation and none of Roche's fear. Roche glared at his colleague.

"This won't take long, Aldo," I said. "Ten minutes tops, I promise."

"Please keep your voice down," Roche said as quietly and forcefully as he could. "There's a park across the street. I'll meet you there in ten."

"Sounds good," I said, rapping my hands on the counter. "We'll get two flat whites to go."

Roche looked at me like I was pushing my luck before putting the order through and getting me to tap my card.

Armed with our coffees, Jack and I crossed the street to the park and found a bench.

"Were you ever tempted to come here to start something of your own, Jack?"

Jack shook his head. "Working on a start-up only to see it fail—which is what happens to most start-ups—wasn't what I considered the best use of my time. I didn't want to chain myself to a computer. I like to have the tech industry work for me, not the other way around. My tech stock portfolio keeps me in tune with what's going on."

"Yeah, well thanks for letting me in on those tips. Not."

"Hey, you never asked. Next time I find something hot I'll let you know and you can drop what you can afford to lose on it. That'd be about ten bucks, wouldn't it?"

"Hilarious."

Jack proceeded to detail a few of the tech companies he'd bought stock in lately. None of their names sounded familiar to me and Jack found that sad. For my own sanity, I switched the conversation to football.

I'd just drained the last of my coffee when Roche crossed the street and walked briskly toward us. He looked very troubled and, clearly not used to much exercise, was breathing hard as he approached. Rather than stop, though, he walked straight past us.

"Not here," he said under his breath. "It's too exposed."

We got up and followed him past a fountain and over to a playground that had a shelter beside it. He stopped at the shelter, looked around and then took a seat.

"What's with the cloak-and-dagger act?" I asked as we joined him. "What are you worried about?"

"Look," he said. "Tell me again what you're doing."

I repeated what I'd told him in the cafe with a few added details.

"And who's this guy?" asked Roche, nodding in Jack's direction.

"This guy here is Jack Briggs. He's an investigator. He's the one that found you."

"And you came up from Los Angeles to see me?"

"That's right. I want to know about your sexual assault case. And I was hoping you could shed some light on your dealings with Beacon Capital, and why you decided not to go with them in the end."

"You make it sound like we're just talking about the weather."

Aldo was jittery, scanning our surroundings and rubbing his hands together.

"Aldo, what's the problem? Who are you afraid of?"

"I'm afraid of all of them. I got screwed out of my company and almost went to prison on some bullshit charge." Roche was breathing hard, almost reaching panic levels. I raised my palms in front of me to reassure him.

"Okay, take a breath. Calm down. No one's out to get you. Why don't you just run me through what happened, starting from when you were first approached by Beacon. Who from Beacon approached your first?"

"Marty Cosgrove. You know him?"

"Yes. I know him."

"It was exciting at first. My company had started making waves and now here was this guy saying they'd been watching me and thought that they could help take Aldoron to the next level."

Roche said he met Marty a few times but was reluctant to deal with Beacon at first. He'd heard they had churned and burned a few start-ups but Marty denied that Beacon was a predator. He insisted they were looking for partnerships, not takeovers. Eventually, Marty got Roche to listen. Time was short because Roche had to ramp up Aldoron quickly and so Beacon became more and more attractive. But then the police turned up at Roche's office saying there'd been a sexual harassment complaint made against him. He denied it and got on with his work. A week or so later the cops returned, took him downtown and booked him for sexual assault. The girl was a co-worker who claimed he'd groped her on a team bonding trip to a Napa Valley vineyard. Roche said the accusation was baseless but felt he'd been trapped. His attention to the deal with Beacon strayed. There were stories in the media about the charges and his position at work became untenable. Roche became a pariah fast. Backers pulled out. Right when everything should have been booming, it went pear shaped. He said Beacon remained interested, saying they weren't put off by the accusations leveled at him. It was at this point that Roche got a visit from a lawyer. At first he thought the lawyer was representing the young woman who'd made the accusations against him. As it happened, this lawyer was making a rival pitch for Aldoron. Roche said this guy was very intimidating. He wasn't going to take no for an answer. He refused to tell Roche who his boss was, but promised huge rewards if Roche went with them.

"He offered you a bribe?" I asked.

Roche nodded.

"What was this lawyer's name?"

"Cobus Lombard."

Jack and I looked at each other.

"Then it got weird," said Roche. "After Lombard's visit, I got an anonymous text message saying the charges would disappear if I took the deal."

"From Lombard?"

"That's the thing. I never knew. I decided to go with Lombard but I never asked him about the message. I was too scared to. And he never said anything about it, but the cops told me a few weeks later that the charges were dropped. The girl disappeared."

"What was the girl's name?" asked Jack.

"Sara. Sara Briseno."

"And why aren't you still at your company?" I asked.

Roche shrugged. "They forced me out. It was all a big con."

"How do you mean?"

"They only wanted to use Aldoron for their own shady purposes."

Roche clearly didn't want to keep talking. I had to urge him to continue.

"Aldo, this is just between us. But I really need to know what happened."

"I can't. They'll kill me."

"Just give me the gist. You don't have to go into specifics."

Roche nodded and began talking. He tried to choose his words carefully but once he got started it all came out. He said that under the new management Aldoron was being transformed. The new game was released and was doing well but there had been a massive ramp up in in-game purchases. These were goods that players could buy to advance more quickly in the game. Items like armor, first aid, and power-ups. The massive popularity of online gaming meant that huge digital economies existed inside the games. He said a game like *Fortnite* had 350 million registered users, more than the population of the US. He said that these in-game buys were a goldmine for publishers. He said some games had virtual credit cards that served as in-game currency. For about a hundred dollars in real money, these cards made you better equipped to thrive in the virtual world. He said serious players would spend hundreds if not thousands of dollars on these cards.

"Okay," I said. "But that sounds to me like a legitimate arm of the business. If someone wants to pay that kind of money to get an edge in a game, it's not against the law."

Roche shook his head. "No, that's not the issue. That's not the problem."

"What's the problem?"

"You can buy into these virtual economies without leaving a trace. And then you can trade or sell the cards, points and goods to other players. These virtual economies are being flooded with dirty money."

"Are you saying your company was taken over to be used as a money laundering vehicle?" I asked.

Roche nodded.

"So the video game industry has become some kind of new version of Vegas?"

"That's about it in a nutshell. Games offer these guys—criminal organizations—the opportunity to launder more money that you can imagine. That was the main reason they wanted my company."

I could hardly believe my ears. I pressed Roche a little more, asking him how he was sure that this was happening at Aldoron. He said some friends who still worked there kept him posted, despite having signed confidentiality agreements.

"So now my company is little more than a laundromat for dirty money. That's all these companies want."

"You mean Lombard's client?"

"Yes. And Beacon too. They're all the same. If you ask me, they're all predators who serve organized crime. That's what I think. Why else would they be doing it? Why else would they be zeroing in on this new, relatively unregulated industry? It allows them to launder millions of dollars, that's why."

Roche's words raised a few questions, such as if Beacon was into this kind of activity, who were they laundering money for? And it suggested that not only was my client, Eddie Mawson innocent, but that he was being played in exactly the same way as Aldo Roche had been. I thanked Roche for his time and again assured him that everything he told us was in confidence. I don't think he took much solace in my words. I think he made his way back to the coffee shop feeling like he'd said way too much. Jack and I headed for the car.

"We need to find out exactly who this Cobus Lombard represents," I said to Jack over the roof of the Impala.

"Most likely it's Crestway," said Jack.

"Yes, but what we really need to know is who's running Crestway?"

"I'll dig deeper."

"And we need to find out what happened to that girl. I want you to stick around a while and see what you can find."

"Sure thing. I'll get on it."

I didn't think I needed to spell it out that Jack needed to be careful. From what Roche had said, the guys we were dealing with were ruthless. Jack knew as well as I did that the more we pushed into this case, the more we'd be putting ourselves in grave danger.

Chapter 17

At the airport, I pulled the Impala into the drop-ff lane. "She's all yours," I said to Jack and went to get out but Jack didn't move. He'd been silent for most of the drive back from East Palo Alto and now he was staring ahead at the cab in front of us, his mind off somewhere in the distance. "Jack?"

"You know, buddy, someone's got to say it and it's going to have to be me."

I took my hand off the door handle. "Say what?"

Jack turned to me. "You just seem to be looking for ways to gun for Marty. That's what. And I don't know but—"

"What? You worried about me?"

Jack let out a quick, dry laugh. "No. But maybe I should be."

"Meaning?"

"I don't know. The way you're acting, I'm worried you might be fixated on the guy."

"I'm not gunning for Marty Cosgrove," I said.

I was inclined to continue but Jack held up a hand. "I'll be straight with you. I'm wondering if your head's in the right place. I think you may not be operating under the best of circumstances, mentally speaking."

"Are you saying—"

"You know exactly what I'm saying."

He let his words hang there.

"Your visit to the hospital," he said.

To say I was surprised was an understatement. To say my anger switch just got tripped again was not. The burning in me was not just fury, it was embarrassment.

"Claire told you? She actually called and told you?"

Jack nodded. "She's worried about you. Actually, she's more pissed off with you. She's wondering what the hell you think you're doing running around with her husband in your cross hairs."

The idea that both Claire and Jack had concerns about my mental welfare was of no comfort to me. It felt like an insult. I felt indignant and small. Which was not very big of me, I had to admit. Still, I tried to park my resentment and lay out some logic that maybe Jack had missed.

I was about to speak when a loud blare of a car horn came from behind. I looked in the rear-view mirror and saw some guy gesticulating wildly, suggesting I move up ahead into the empty space or else get the hell out of the drop-off lane. I ignored him.

The distraction left the door open for Jack to continue.

"Maybe you need to step back a bit and take stock.""

Through my indignation, I knew Jack didn't want to have this conversation any more than I did.

"I'm going to keep my mouth shut and let you keep talking for a bit," I said.

"Look," said Jack. "I'm still convinced someone tried to kill Claire, okay? We're on the same page there. But I think it's a stretch to point the finger at her husband. You don't seem to have any doubt. You're locked in on this guy, your ex-wife's husband, as a suspect."

I stared ahead. "Go on."

"And now I see where your head is with the sexual assault case. You think he's involved in that, too. Right?"

I shook my head.

"Jack, my mind isn't made up on any of it. I'm just following my leads and looking for clues. I'm trying to figure this shit out. I hear what you're saying, but you know as well as I do that our investigations have brought us here. I'm not out to destroy Claire's husband. I've only ever tried to—"

Again, the horn behind us sounded. Longer this time. I cursed and reached for the door handle again. Jack quickly put his hand on my shoulder.

"Dude, leave it to me. I don't want to see what you'd do to this guy."

With that, Jack got out of the car. I watched him walk back. I saw the driver behind us—a middle-aged fat guy with a goatee and a Giants cap on—mouth off at Jack as he approached. Jack kept his hands in his jeans pockets and bent down. I could see apprehension on the face of the driver. Then he nodded as Jack spoke. And nodded again. Jack tapped the roof of the car in a friendly type of way then started walking back.

"What did you say to him?" I asked when he got back in the car.

"I told him my friend was having a nervous breakdown and threatening to shoot everyone else around him, and that him sitting on his horn wasn't really helping."

The driver behind us pulled out and took off fast. I watched him go by to give him a wave but he kept his head dead straight, not wanting to make eye contact.

"Jack, you know we now have a precedent of sexual assault being used to leverage a business deal. You said it yourself. This could be a tactic. I don't know who's guilty here but Marty's involved in both cases."

"As is this lawyer guy, Cobus Lombard."

"Exactly. There's a lot we do know, I admit. But we don't know who sent that message to Aldo Roche saying the sexual assault case would disappear if he took the deal."

"It had to be Lombard."

"We don't know that. It could have been Marty. He could have just been offering an incentive, one that could never be traced back to him."

"Look," said Jack. "I have to bring it back to the fact that it's clear that for you this is all very personal."

"I can't help that."

"If it's too frickin personal, you should think about dropping the case. Let someone else do it who can be objective."

"I am being objective."

"Are you? Tell me you're not trying to save Claire."

"Save her? What the hell are you talking about?"

"Dude, this is me here. I'm not going to say I know exactly what's going on with you but one thing I can say is that Claire doesn't need saving. And even if she did, she doesn't need you to do it."

I took in an audible breath and shook my head. Now it was me who was staring ahead through the windshield, casting my thoughts way off into the distance.

"It's hard to tell what's right," I said. "Hell, Jack, my daughter's in the thick of it all. I don't see myself as Claire's knight in shining armor but there are serious questions to be answered, both about her accident and about my case. And her husband isn't... Jesus, man. He's not right. He's just not..."

"What? Good enough? As good as you?"

I turned to Jack. "I'll be happy to give that prick my very best wishes when I'm convinced he had nothing to do with any of this. But no. I admit it. I don't like him. I don't know what the fuck Claire sees in him. His behavior during her hospital stint was distant to the point of disinterest. He's in a shitty financial position and has hit Claire up for money. And, as you told me, if this Adrenal deal doesn't go through, then he's going bust."

"You didn't tell Claire that, did you?"

"No, of course not. Jack, I didn't ask for this. I didn't ask for these two to come in and take over my life. But I, we, need to find out what happened to Claire. No one else is going to."

"True, and I'll do everything I can to help find out who's responsible."

"What if I miss something?"

"You tell me. What if you do miss something? What happens then?"

"If I miss something, then next time Claire won't survive. And whatever happens to Claire affects Bella. I've seen what my daughter's gone through and I won't let that happen again. I'd only have myself to blame if someone takes her mother away for good. I'm not trying to get Claire back. I'm trying to do what's right."

Jack shook his head. "I don't know, buddy. You've just got to keep your emotions in check. It's all getting too close, too personal. And that's going to mess with your judgment. That's when you'll miss something. That's when you'll make a mistake."

I nodded in silent agreement. Jack was right.

But as for dropping the case? Not a chance in hell.

Chapter 18

The foyer of Mesa, a five-star restaurant in Malibu, was crammed with people bathed in the late morning sunlight captured by floor-to-ceiling windows. A sweeping view extended from Escondido Beach down the Pacific coastline and all the way back to Los Angeles. Abby had told me the owner had offered her the space for free without hesitation. No doubt it was good PR for the owner to host a charity event hosted by *the* Abby Hatfield. I weaved through the throng in search of Abby and I spotted her off to the side, holding court with three people who were hanging on her every word. Even for someone who is accustomed to blockbuster movie launches, this was her big day. It was her brainchild, her idea, her initiative. She'd wanted investors to back tech projects that could solve problems in the developing world, and now here it was. Her fundraiser was ready to go and there was a room full of money to kick it off.

My spirits were high due to the fact that I was getting some me time and I was going to spend it with Abby. I hadn't felt like that for a while, a long while. It was that freedom and excitement of being out on a date. Just the sight of Abby made me walk lighter, feel that much more alive. She was wearing a sleek blue dress that showed off her figure and heels that accented legs that were—I kid you not—ranked by some website as being the fifth most beautiful in the world. With her auburn hair pinned up, a few silky strands delectably loose at the back, she was stunning to behold. I hadn't laid eyes on her for months and I'd almost forgotten how powerfully she could take my breath away. I wanted everyone out of the room there and then. I didn't want to share her with anyone.

Her eyes flicked sideways as she talked to her companions, noticing my arrival with a gorgeous smile.

"Hello there," she said as I joined her and kissed her cheek. She then directed her attention back to her companions—three young twenty-somethings whose projects were the centerpiece of the event, effectively being put up for auction.

"Let me introduce you to the stars of the show," Abby said to me. "These guys are doing some amazing stuff. Seth here has an idea to improve irrigation efficiency with an app that, if we find the right backer, can be available for free. Camilla and her team have an ingenious, cheap way to boost internet speeds in remote areas, with huge health and education benefits for isolated communities. And David here has developed low-cost solar-powered pumps for well water."

"Very impressive," I said.

"And what do you do?" David asked me.

"I'm a lawyer."

Abby would allow no modesty on my part. She assured the others that I was exceptionally talented before giving them a run-down of my most high-profile cases.

"What are you working on now?" asked Camilla.

"A sexual assault case."

If Camilla actually tried to hide her distaste, she failed. "You're defending someone charged with sexual assault?" she asked, her moral outrage locked and loaded.

"As it happens, yes."

I was just about to roll out the standard defense of my profession when Abby stepped in and changed the subject, reminding the others of how the event was going to run. She asked them to go and give their presentations one last check—the last thing they needed was a technical hitch disrupting the show. After the three had trotted off, Abby hooked her arm into mine and led me away.

"I think I deeply offended her," I laughed.

"Don't worry. They'll forget about you in a minute," she said with a nudge to my ribs.

"I'm that impressive, huh?"

"You got that right. Now let's get you a drink. Ah, here's some champagne. How's that?"

"Suits me fine."

She took two glasses off a waiter's tray and handed me one. We clinked glasses.

"I'm no expert but this already looks like a winner," I said.

"Not yet, it isn't." Abby took a sip and then found a spot to set her glass down. "I don't want to drink any more before I get up there."

"It's going to be a huge success," I said. "You've done an amazing job."

She looked into my eyes, and that Abby Hatfield effect hit me. She was drinking me in like this whole damn thing was put together for my benefit.

"You are incredible," I said. "A few weeks ago, you say you wanted to make a real difference to the world and now you're doing exactly that."

She beamed. "I have to admit, it's pretty exciting."

"Not as exciting as seeing your face fill up a thirty-foot movie screen, I bet."

"God, no," she scoffed. "Doesn't come close." She then let loose her glorious husky laugh.

"You actually look happy doing things for others. Just don't hog the spotlight tonight, okay. Those kids? It's their time to shine. It's not all about you. They're the stars of the show. Remember that."

She slapped my shoulder lightly. "You dick," she said, glaring at me with mock offense.

Abby checked her watch. "Okay, I need to get the ball rolling. If it all goes as planned, we'll be done here in a little over an hour. We can grab a bite at the restaurant. I've reserved a table."

"Sounds good," I said. "Knock 'em dead."

Abby stepped up to the microphone and soon had the crowd eating out of her hand. She then passed the baton to the start-ups, who each gave a presentation followed by a pitch. Once they were done, the auction began with guests bidding via a phone app. Each project had a hidden target unknown to the bidders. Whichever bidder reached that amount first got to be that start-up's "angel investor." The escalating bids appeared on three giant screens that displayed the bid amount and the bidder's name. This crowd couldn't get their names up there fast enough. It was a battle between celebrities, companies and suits.

Suddenly, there was a loud cheer as one screen showed that Camilla's internet project was the first to reach its target. I joined in the applause but when I saw the name of the bidder, I almost spat my drink.

Crestway.

As the hooting and applause continued, I scanned the crowd, sick to my stomach. And there he was. Cobus Lombard in the flesh and exactly how I'd imagined he'd be from his photo—a monument of stern joylessness. He was standing by himself, tapping at his phone. He was the only person in the room besides me not caught up in the excitement of the moment, as Camilla climbed up to the stage to receive Abby's embrace.

I moved through the crowd towards Lombard, watching him as I went. As I neared him, he turned his back to me and put in an earpiece before turning to face the stage. He then spoke a few words, presumably to a caller on his phone before hanging up.

I was a few feet away when he saw me. His eyes, locked on mine, moved only slightly, but he stood dead still and unsmiling. His shaved head and rigid countenance gave him a menacing look. He was not a big man but he looked fit—the tailored suit showing off his lean physique. His lean face suggested he was a runner but whatever he did to keep himself fit, he clearly did so with unvarnished discipline. He looked like one of those ex-commandos who never stopped being physically ready to leap from a plane in combat gear, despite getting their discharge papers decades ago.

Even in the dim light of the gallery, Lombard's eyes were piercing. As I stopped a couple of feet in front of him, I could see that they were gray. And dead cold. I could see what kind of power he could wield over the likes of Aldo Roche and Eddie Mawson.

"Good evening, Madison," he said. "I did not expect to see you here."

Lombard didn't look unpleasantly surprised or otherwise but I had no idea how he knew who I was.

Standing opposite each other, it seemed mutually obvious that shaking hands was out of the question.

"I was about to say the same thing, Lombard. Your name's come up a lot lately."

"That doesn't surprise me."

"And as Eddie Mawson's lawyer, I'd suggest now isn't the time to be trying to force him into a deal."

"No one's forcing him to do anything," said Lombard. "But you're a defense lawyer with little capacity to navigate the world of business, so forgive me if I ignore your advice."

"You couldn't care less about what's best for Eddie. Why doesn't that surprise me?"

"And you care for him, do you?"

"You know he's facing a sexual assault case. He needs to focus on that."

"Mawson's personal circumstances have next to no bearing on the proposal we've put to him."

"That's a nice way to put it. Put to him. You mean threatened him with."

Lombard held his eyes on me unblinking. "Is that why you came over here, Madison? To tell me how to go about my business?"

I ignored the question. "What are you doing here, Lombard?"

"I'd have thought that was obvious. You just saw it with your own eyes. I'm investing in worthwhile projects."

"On behalf of Crestway."

A second cheer erupted as Dave's solar-powered water pump project reached its goal.

I took a step closer to Lombard. "If you're looking for another way to whitewash your boss's profile, look elsewhere. This isn't it."

Lombard was now looking away, as calm as can be.

"I know you're laundering money through Aldoron up in San Francisco," I said. "And there's no doubt you want to use Adrenal the same way."

Lombard's eyes narrowed before he turned his face to me and cracked a reptilian smile. "Is that what Mr. Roche told you?"

He watched me closely as he saw me realize that he knew I'd spoken to Roche.

"You touch him, Lombard and—"

"And you'll what, Madison? Come at me with Mr. Briggs by your side?"

Again he enjoyed watching it dawn on me that he knows a whole lot more about me than I'd expected.

"Allow me to dissuade you of any heroics you might envision," Lombard said calmly. "You have no idea what you're dealing with and it's far more than you and Jack Briggs can handle."

"You love that air of mystery, don't you, Lombard? I'm going to find out who your boss is. You can be damned sure of that."

"It's not wise to go poking your nose where it doesn't belong."

"Thanks for the lame advice. Duly ignored."

"Suit yourself. But don't say I didn't warn you."

"What is that supposed to mean?"

"I can't put it more clearly than that. Stick to your case, Madison. Who knows, if Mr. Mawson plays ball maybe he won't have a case to answer to at all."

This was clearly both a bribe and a threat.

"Is that what you did in San Francisco where that girl disappeared?"

"I have no idea what happened to that girl but I'd suggest you have an overactive imagination."

"For you to offer to make the sexual assault case go away tells me you had a hand in setting it up."

"You may draw that conclusion, Madison but one doesn't necessarily beget the other. What I can tell you is that in this country money talks and my client would be willing to step in with an offer that Mr. Mawson's accuser could not refuse."

"You mean pay her off?"

"Your words, not mine. I'd look at it purely as a business transaction. If you won't pass this offer onto Mr. Mawson, I'm happy to do so myself. Now, I have to go."

With that, Lombard turned and headed for the exit.

After the show, Abby came up to me, brimming with excitement. I thought about Lombard getting his nefarious hooks into Abby's noble enterprise. That he could potentially pollute the entire thing sickened me. Now wasn't the moment to tell Abby, though.

"Let's go eat," I said.

As I spoke, a photographer approached us, smiling and lifting his camera to his eye. Abby held up a hand to check the photographer and he lowered his camera. She didn't want a photo of us together getting the gossip press foaming at the mouth. Clearly, Abby called the shots at her own event, a welcome respite from having no say at all in the face of the paparazzi. I knew it was my cue to leave.

"See you next door," I said.

As I left, I heard Abby telling the photographer that it would be great to get some shots with the three project leads and the winning bidders. Little did she know that her fantastically upbeat event had been tainted by Lombard's touch. I had no idea what his intentions were meddling in Abby's fundraiser but I was damned sure he and whoever he worked for were not playing good Samaritans.

I had a wretched feeling that it was me who had led them here.

Chapter 19

I waited at the table looking out over the ocean as gentle waves rolled on to the sand. There was only one surfer out there and I envied him. It didn't matter that the waves were barely ankle height, just being out there was a tonic I missed. I vowed to take Bella for a pre-school surf before she moved back in with Claire.

Abby had clearly requested a discreet table, as it was tucked around the corner of the bar out of sight from the foyer. I completely understood why Abby needed to be discreet about us being seen together. I myself had seen more than one article that had examined the hits and misses of her love life while wondering whether Abby, approaching her mid-thirties, had missed the boat. These vampires found a malicious joy in implying she'd sold her chance at motherhood for fame. With any new man she was seen with, the stories suggested Abby was desperate to get pregnant. As for us, I wasn't sure what either of us wanted this time around.

I'd asked the waiter to bring a bottle of champagne on ice, and now he'd positioned the stand next to the table. I declined his offer to open it, so he set the bottle deep in the ice and wrapped a white napkin around the neck.

As I waited, I found it hard to keep Lombard and Crestway out of my mind, weighing up whether to say anything to Abby.

When Abby came in at last, I stood up and greeted her. The chairs were positioned side by side so we could both enjoy the view. As Abby sat down she gave a shudder of excitement. "Well," she beamed giddily. "That went well."

"It was fantastic," I said. "We need to toast your success."

The waiter was already at the table and was soon filling our glasses.

"To the amazing Abby Hatfield," I said. "The hottest, smartest, and most generous soul in LA."

She laughed and we clinked glasses.

Abby took a deep breath. "You know, those projects are going to be deployed into the real world, doing great things for people who need them. I can't believe it."

"I'm impressed," I said. "You should be proud of yourself. You had a vision and look at what's happened."

"It's turned out so much better than I imagined. That's why I took so long. I was approached by a guy who said his company wants to partner with me and make this a twice-a-year event. Maybe turn it into a nation-wide competition, reaching out to all those people who want to make an immediate difference to the world. We can actually make that happen."

"Careful, you may have just created a new career for yourself. Abby Hatfield, game changer."

"I like the sound of that."

The waiter returned and we ordered food and he refilled our glasses. I was soon feeling a world away. Abby's buzz was infectious and the way she looked at me, like I was the only person she wanted to share her good news with, was a rush. I set aside any thought of discussing Crestway with her.

"So you haven't told me about this sexual assault case you're working on. A case you're obsessively devoted to, no doubt."

I laughed at her joke, knowing that there was a lot of truth to it, and began giving Abby a run-down of the Eddie Mawson case.

"Wow," Abby said, shaking her head. "I didn't know it was Eddie Mawson you were defending."

"Why? Do you know him?"

She shuddered, as if to shake off something unwanted. "He's from Adrenal, right? The video game company?"

"That's right. How'd you know?"

"I voiced one of the characters in *Out There*."

I was momentarily at a loss for words. Why didn't I know this? Suddenly, I remembered that Eddie had said he knew I'd dated Abby Hatfield. That was all he said and it was all he seemed to know, but it made me look good in his eyes. At the time, I thought it was a real undergrad comment, the kind of thing a weak man can be awed by. I recalled the way Eddie had looked at me with such admiration, and shuddered too. This was going to be a huge red flag in court. And it was going to be a huge advantage for ADA Elliott Goodwin. He'd barely have to lift a finger to paint Eddie Mawson as a nerdy incel whose sexual repression had devolved into aggression and violence.

"I'm sorry, I had no idea," I said. "But he obviously made an impression on you."

"He was almost drooling on me at the recordings. I hate to sound vain, but I had to ask that he not be present at my recordings. I made up some story about how I needed to work with as few people around as possible. Honestly, I half thought he wanted me to turn up in costume."

"Oh, that would have been his wet dream, no doubt."

"Sorry, Brad, but your client gave me the creeps."

"I get it. He did mention you to me."

"In what sense?"

"He knew you and I had dated. That was one of the reasons he hired me."

"Oh, my God. Could it be any more pathetic? And you took him on?"

Where it had happened exactly, I don't know, but the conversation had leaped from banter to something more uncomfortable and serious.

"I run a business, Abby. And his case isn't as straightforward as some people want to make out. Whatever he is, he's not a rapist."

"Fair enough," Abby said. "Look, I'm not judging. I was just surprised. But my agent told me that the *Out There* sequel was being delayed."

"Were you approached to voice the sequel?"

"Yes. A while ago now. But we'll have to wait and see, I guess. I think you'll find everyone will be reluctant to stay involved."

I waved my hands. "Okay, enough about my client," I said. "Let's talk about you."

"If you insist," said Abby, and she squeezed my thigh gently and leaned in to kiss me. She then did a quick scan of the room to make sure no one saw us. "You okay with that, Brad?"

Glad that the awkward moment passed, I held her mischievous gaze. I still hadn't lost the novelty, the idea that I was "dating" a movie star but the beautiful woman I was looking at wasn't gazing at me from a poster, not some person who I knew by way of a composite of gossip stories. She was an incredible, stunning woman who I could barely keep my hands off. In this moment, I felt a lightness of being I hadn't enjoyed since I don't know when. All the constant stress and the mental wrangling that ruled my life receded. I let go of all the puzzles I was trying to solve, the problems I was trying to fix, the work I needed to do. I just stayed present in the moment. How could I not want to have more of this woman in my life?

"I'm more than okay with that," I said, and kissed her again. She pulled away and scanned the room again.

"Sorry, I hate being so paranoid, but I can't help but feel I'm being watched. Like, all the time. I don't want to be fielding questions about us when I'm not sure I know how to answer."

We were in a discreet restaurant but anyone with a smartphone could post a video of Abby Hatfield out canoodling on a date.

"Of course," I said. "I understand."

She looked at me like she was waiting to hear more. I wondered if she was expecting me to take this opportunity to let her in on my feelings. I know she wasn't asking for a ring and that just having fun was fine, for a while. But there was a sense that it wasn't appropriate for this relationship to be just aimless and light. We weren't twenty-somethings on spring break.

I decided to go out on a limb, a little.

"Abby, I feel the same about you as the first time I met you. Standing there in an incredible dress talking about Scotch whisky. I can go back to the moment in a heartbeat. I know I'm a workaholic—"

She put a finger to my lips. "Hey, handsome. I dumped you, remember? You were unavailable. You were still struggling with your divorce. I don't know where this is going to go but I know I want you. That said, I'm going to protect myself. I'm not scared of what might happen, but I'm not going to endure a man who doesn't know where his heart's at. Let's just enjoy today. I've got something to celebrate, and I want to celebrate it with you."

"Lucky me."

As I spoke those words, my phone pinged with an incoming message.

"Oh, you're going to get even luckier. Unless you say something really stupid."

I zipped my lips.

My phone buzzed in my pocket, loud enough for Abby to hear.

"I know that's not me because I put mine on silent," Abby said. "You want to check that?"

I did, but I didn't. I shook my head.

"Good," she said. "Why don't we finish up here and go back to my place?"

"You read my mind."

Chapter 20

"Jack's here," came Megan's voice through the speakerphone. She knew better than to let Jack breeze on in this morning. I'd made it clear that I wasn't to be disturbed. On Eddie's instruction, I'd formally rejected Elliott Goodwin's plea deal. I did so with no small amount of relish. We were going to settle this matter once and for all in court, and I got a little inner charge at the thought of taking Goodwin down. Even though I'd been on Eddie's case for weeks now, it was like the yellow light had suddenly turned green. I did not need a trial date yet to feel a powerful upsurge in intensity. I had a man's life, liberty, and future in my hands. My vision and my world narrowed down to a singular point.

I pushed the talk button. "Good," I said. Jack was punctual as always. "Tell him to grab a seat in the meeting room. I'll be with him shortly."

I spent another ten minutes making notes before gathering up the case files and heading out.

In the meeting room, Jack was seated with eyes glued to his phone and his feet on another chair. "Hey," he said when I entered. He set his phone on the table, yawned and ruffled his hair.

"Did you have a big night?" I asked.

"Yeah," he said. "It was wild. Pulled an all-nighter, just about."

There was a pause as I raised a curious eyebrow at Jack. He was a married man with two young boys.

"Noah was throwing up half the night. Then I couldn't get back to sleep."

"Hell, is he okay?" Three-year-old Noah was Jack's youngest child and, like his elder brother Adam, my godson. "We could have done this another day."

Truth was, I didn't want to delay this meeting for another hour let alone a day. Jack had gotten back from San Francisco the day before and I wanted to know every detail of whatever he'd managed to dig up.

Jack waved a hand. "Noah's fine. And so am I. Let's get into it."

"Great," I said, pulling up a chair. "Listen, Eddie should be here in about half an hour, if he's on time, which I bet he won't be. There's a bit of ground I want to cover before he arrives."

"Okay."

"And I'd like you to stick around when he gets here, if that's alright. Shouldn't be more than an hour."

"No sweat," Jack said. "You want to start with San Fran?"

I nodded. Jack had sent me a couple of intriguing messages while he was away. One said Aldo Roche's accuser had skipped town hastily. The other said he thought he was being followed. After my conversation with Lombard, it seemed pretty clear who had Jack followed.

"The girl. Sara Briseno. What did you find out about her?"

Jack said he found out she'd been living in a rental in San Jose with her elder brother. The brother knew Aldo Roche, and it was he who encouraged Sara to go for a job at Aldoron. He told Jack it was the biggest regret of his life. He had no doubt that Roche sexually assaulted Sara and he encouraged her to go through with her claims against him. He said Sara was a mess and things only got worse once the police charged Roche. Her lawyer was really supportive, he said, and was telling Sara how important it was for her to see it through. He said the lawyer was confident about getting a conviction. Then one day Sara said she was going to see her lawyer, and she never came back. Her brother said she'd packed some things and fled San Jose. She later called to let him know she was okay. He told Jack he didn't know where Sara was living now. When Jack asked if someone had approached her, the brother seemed to know more than he was prepared to tell.

"That's where Lombard comes in, right?" I said. "Lombard told me he paid her off. But if you believe Sara's brother, hers wasn't a trumped-up case."

"That's right," said Jack. "He was adamant she was assaulted."

"He's her brother. Of course, he's going to support her in whatever she says. In any case, I don't think I'd try to secure her as a witness."

"You'd be putting her life in danger if you did," said Jack. "I told you I was being followed, right?"

"Yes. Any idea who?"

"Not exactly, but what I didn't tell you was they didn't keep their distance."

"Who's they?"

"Two black dudes in a black Hummer."

"They approached you?"

"Guess you could say that. They frickin' rammed me on the freeway. I knew they were following me and as I slowed down on an exit, they came up from behind and used me as their brakes. They then pulled up alongside me and made it clear it was no accident."

As Jack spoke, he made the gun gesture with his hand, lowering his thumb to fire.

"They made a hand signal?"

Jack chuckled and shook his head. "The dude was waving an Uzi."

"Were they gangbangers?"

Jack nodded. "I reckon so. I'd put money on it."

"Did you get the plates?"

"Yes. LA plates."

"Really?"

I told Jack about what Lombard had said at the fundraiser, that he knew we'd been up to see Aldo Roche.

"What the hell?" he said. "Is Lombard hiring gang members as muscle?"

"Sure looks that way."

Just then Eddie Mawson appeared at the door. Surprised by his arrival, I checked my watch. Sure enough, he was five minutes early.

"Come in, Eddie. This is my investigator, Jack Briggs. I've asked him to stick around, if that's okay with you."

"Sure it is," said Eddie as he found himself a seat at the table. I told him now that the plea deal was rejected we were in full trial preparation mode. I explained how my goal was to cast as much doubt as possible on the prosecution's version of events. Part of that was discrediting witnesses, but another part was presenting an alternative story that a jury would feel compelled to consider, if not believe.

"Have you heard of Aldoron, Eddie?"

"Yes, I have. It's a gaming company up in Silicon Valley. Cobus Lombard told me it was one of their recent investments."

"So Lombard told you it was an investment. Not an acquisition?"

Eddie shook his head. "Investment. He used Aldoron as part of his sales pitch to me. Not that he was relying on the argument to persuade me. He was more stating that when I partner with Crestway, good things will happen. He showed me the figures, and Aldoron's doing extremely well."

"How so?" I asked.

"Since Crestway got involved, profits have boomed. I know how to read the books and it was night and day."

"Eddie, did you hear about a girl named Sara Briseno?"

Eddie shook his head. "Never."

I explained that what was happening to him was almost identical to what happened to Aldoron's founder, Aldo Roche. I told him Briseno had skipped town and so the charges against Roche were dropped. I told him Lombard had boasted that he'd made that happen, that he'd paid the girl to make herself scarce.

Eddie's composure sank visibly, and a shocked expression on his face indicated he was consumed by weighty thoughts. No doubt his mind was spinning to think that the sexual assault might have been part of a plan to take over his company. I began by telling Eddie that Jack was going to keep trying to find Sara Briseno. We needed to hear directly from her why she backed off, not just take Lombard's word for it.

"How does that help my case?" Eddie said somewhat vacantly.

"On two fronts. It would be good to show there's a precedent for the nasty tricks used by both Beacon and Crestway. We need the jury to believe that you've been targeted by ruthless criminal behavior disguised as business as usual."

Eddie barely acknowledged what I said.

Jack tapped his hand on the table to get Eddie's attention. "Eddie. How did they boost the profits so quickly?"

"They had huge pre-sales for their next game, plus there was a pile-on of sponsors and advertisers. But the biggest contributing factor for the uptick was in-game buys. That was pretty phenomenal, actually."

"And he promised you the same, no doubt?" asked Jack.

"Yes, he did."

"Do you actually know how they achieved that spike in in-game purchases?"

"It's what we already offer—you know, things players can buy inside the game world like weapons, ammo, health—but these guys have taken it to another level from what I can see. I don't know what's going on at a more granular level, if that's what you're asking."

"That is what I'm asking," said Jack.

Eddie could tell Jack and I had some information to share that wasn't exactly good news. Jack looked at me, allowing me to step in. "Eddie, we believe Crestway is pumping dirty money into their games."

Eddie looked stunned and remained motionless until he felt the need for a steep intake of breath.

"They're using video games to launder money, Eddie," said Jack, trying to drive the point home. "That's why they want your company. To them, video games are the best thing since casinos for turning illegal cash into legal tender."

Eddie slumped forward and put his head in his hands. "Oh, my God," he said, drawing the words out in a tone of disbelief and fear.

"What is it, Eddie?" I asked.

Eddie lowered his head onto the table.

"You need to know about this, Eddie," I said. "You need to know who you might be getting into bed with."

Eddie raised his head and slumped back in his chair. He looked crestfallen, as though someone had stolen all his worldly possessions. He kept shaking his head.

"It's too late," he said at last.

"What's too late?" I asked.

He looked at me, his face as white as a ghost. "I signed with Crestway this morning. I'm in with them lock, stock and barrel and there's no way out."

"Jesus," I said. I was initially lost for words. I understood that Eddie wanted to get the deal done before a trial could damage the value of his company, but this still seemed hasty. That said, I can certainly imagine how hard it would have been to keep Lombard at bay.

"Have you told Marty?" I asked.

Eddie shook his head. "No. He's not going to be happy."

That was an understatement.

"You got that right, Eddie," I said. "He's going to be mighty pissed."

Chapter 21

"He's back."

The text was from Marion Platt, the neighbor of the prosecution witness Oscar Guzman. A while back, I'd made an unsuccessful attempt to speak with the Blackjacks barback. He told the police he'd seen Eddie grope Jenna Lewis. When I got no response at his apartment, I knocked on the doors of his neighbors. One of them was Marion Platt who agreed, in exchange for a hundred dollars, to let me know if and when she saw Guzman return. There was no point trying to find Guzman at the bar because he apparently never went back after the incident. The speed with which Guzman had made himself scarce had me wondering if, like Sara Briseno, he'd been persuaded to lie low somewhere until the trial. The message from Platt suggested I could have it all wrong. Maybe there was some other explanation. I wasn't about to sit around and waste time wondering.

I texted Platt immediately. "He's there right now?"
"Yes."

I sprang up out of my chair and told Megan I was heading out. Boyle Heights was about a thirty-minute drive. As I got to my car, I texted Platt again.

"Keep an eye on his door. If he leaves, let me know."

The reply took five minutes to come. It was a thumbs up emoji, but it didn't fill me with confidence. I doubted Platt would stay by her door looking through the peephole. I figured she'd have hit me up for another fifty for going the extra mile. I could only hope Guzman was planning to stick around.

When I got to his apartment, I looked over at Platt's door and saw it was slightly ajar with her face visible in the crack. She nodded when I pointed at Guzman's apartment door to indicate he was still in there as far as she knew. I listened at the door and could hear a television on inside. I knocked three times, even and firm. There was no way the occupant didn't hear that over the television. I placed my ear against the door again and heard the volume drop. There was no sound of physical movement, no footsteps. I knocked again. This time the television was muted or switched off and I heard feet tread quietly to the door. The peephole blacked out as Guzman checked me out.

"Who's that?" he called.

"Oscar, my name's Brad Madison. I'm an attorney. I just want to ask you a few questions."

Light reappeared in the peephole.

"What about?"

I took a breath. "It's about the Eddie Mawson case. I'm defending Mr. Mawson, and I just want to have a quick talk with you to get your take on the events."

"You his lawyer?"

"Yes."

"No," Guzman said resolutely.

"No, what?"

"I ain't talking to you. Leave me alone."

"Oscar, I just want to have a chat. Totally off the record."

"No way. Not interested."

"Okay, how about I come back with a subpoena? If I do that, you'd be legally obliged to speak with me. We can make it an official deposition, with a video camera and all, and that way you have to answer my questions under oath."

There was no response. Just silence.

"Oscar? I don't want to get all formal about this. I just need a few minutes of your time."

No response. I put my ear to the door again, and I just knew I'd been talking to myself. I thought I heard a noise inside Guzman's apartment. It sounded like a window being lifted open. I turned to look at Platt, who was still watching from behind her door.

"Marion," I hissed. "Is there a—?"

"A fire exit? Yes." I couldn't help but roll my eyes. "I should have told you, huh?"

I didn't reply at first because I was already bolting for the stairs. "That would have been good to know," I called out.

I charged through the door and bounded down the six flights of stairs and burst out through the entrance of the apartment building, turned left and sprinted. Another left turn brought me to a back alley, and I could see what had to be Oscar Guzman down at the far end. He had fifty yards on me and was getting away fast. There was no point in chasing him. If I wanted to speak to Oscar Guzman again, I'd have to make good on my threat to subpoena him or else wait until I cross-examined him at the trial. Given what I knew of him already, it was best to wait until the trial. I don't know why I spooked him so much but he clearly didn't want his story rigorously examined. Then again, he could just be paranoid.

Either way, I suddenly found something to especially look forward to at the trial.

As I made my way back to my car, I took out my phone and saw two new messages had arrived. They must have landed while I was chasing Guzman because I'd neither heard the pings nor felt the vibrations.

Both messages were from the same unknown number. When I opened the first, I stopped in my tracks. My blood went cold and my stomach tightened up with disgust.

It was a photo of Aldo Roche lying dead in a pool of blood. His eyes were puffy and bruised, and his throat was cut from ear to ear.

There was a caption to go with the photo: "ALDO SAYS HI"

My mind raced with thoughts about the pure hell that poor Aldo Roche's last minutes of life must have been. And I had no doubt that he was dead precisely because of me. I opened the second message with acute trepidation.

It was a photo of Abby and me leaving Mesa restaurant together.

There was no text with this photo. There didn't have to be. It was crystal clear who they'd go for next.

I looked around me, thinking for a second that they could be watching me now. There was no one in sight apart from a couple of old men coming towards me from where I last saw Guzman.

I ran a hand over my hair, wondering who the hell was behind this. I didn't have to wait long to find out, as it happened. I felt my phone buzz in my hand. It was Jack.

"Yeah?" I said flatly.

"Guess who owns Crestway?" he asked.

"I don't know, Jack. Who?"

If he'd picked up the dejection in my voice, he wasn't about to get sidetracked by it.

When Jack said the name, I almost asked him to repeat it, but I'd heard him loud and clear yet I still couldn't believe my ears.

Eddie Mawson's new partner, not to mention the bidder who'd won the first auction at Abby's fundraiser, was one of LA's most feared and powerful drug lords—Darius Tucker.

Chapter 22

Bella had her arms full with her iPad and all the books she'd brought with her to my place, so I carried her two pieces of luggage as we headed up the path to the side door of Claire's house. Bella's emotions were split between lamenting about having to leave me and the excitement of being back home with her mother. I was glad I hadn't told her about the conversation I'd had with Claire about her spending more time with me if she wanted. That was before the scene at the hospital, and I was sure Claire now had no intention of following through on that offer.

Claire had been back two days. Her broken ankle was still in a cast, but she was able to move herself around using one of those four-wheeled scooters on which she could rest her knee.

Bella knocked on the door and a few seconds later Claire's new assistant came to the door, a young guy named Tyson. As Tyson and I became acquainted, Bella swept through. The big smile Tyson wore was clearly shielding a degree of awkwardness. God knows what Claire had told him. I handed him Bella's bags. I could hear Bella and Claire greet each other warmly. I was happy for Bella, despite everything that was going on between me and her mother. I called out a goodbye to her and then turned to leave. Bella came running back and gave me a big hug and told me she loved me. I did the same as I kissed her cheek.

"See you soon, darling," I said and headed to my car.

I'd gotten a few steps away when I heard Claire call my name. I stopped and began making my way back to see Claire standing alone in the doorway gripping the handlebar of her mobility scooter.

"Next Saturday," she said matter-of-factly, projecting contained scorn. She wasn't inclined to elaborate on her words and she didn't have to. Today was Sunday. That meant I wouldn't see Bella for nearly two weeks. She was making it loud and clear that there'd be no change to the custody arrangement. It would stay right where it was, with me getting Bella every other weekend.

"Fine," I said, and walked away.

When I got behind the wheel, I found myself feeling somewhat aimless. With Bella gone, the day ahead was all my own and I had nothing to do with it. In a reflex response, I decided I'd go to the office. It was a decision made with barely a thought. The emptiness in my gut was ugly. I knew the sensation well—the loneliness and isolation, the feeling of having all the worst thoughts about myself pressed up against a door that was right in my face, so close I could feel the uncomfortable heat of their presence. I had an urge to open that door and drown in the self-hatred that would pour over and through me. It was all so tempting, but I knew if I did, all that remorse and darkness would lead me to drink.

I blocked out the ogres by switching my brain back to work. I got my phone out and dipped into my emails. One from Elliott Goodwin was near the top of the list. Sent that morning.

The subject line was: "Told you I'd have something big."

I opened it up and read it. The message was short and sweet. Goodwin had a new prosecution witness to add to his list.

That witnesses name? Marty Cosgrove.

My initial reaction was alarm. What the hell did Marty have to offer the prosecution's case? To date, Eddie had said they had met a few times to discuss business. Then I thought about my client and how he had a tendency not to tell me things I needed to know. Shaking my head, I called Eddie. He picked up after three rings.

"Hi, Brad," Eddie said tentatively, indicating that he at least had the awareness to know that if his lawyer calls on a Sunday morning, it wasn't a social call. "Is everything okay?"

"No, Eddie. Everything's not okay. I take it you told Marty Cosgrove you were going with Crestway?"

"Yes. The same day I told you. How come?"

"Well, I'd ask how he took it, but I know he didn't take it well."

"He was very upset."

"That doesn't surprise me one bit, Eddie. And guess what? I've just been informed that Marty's going to be testifying against you."

Initially, there was no verbal response from Eddie. Dead silence.

"Eddie?" I prompted.

"Yes, Brad. I'm here."

"What the hell does Marty Cosgrove have on you?"

Eddie began stammering. "I have no idea."

"Was he at the club that night?"

"I don't remember seeing him but he said he was going to drop by."

"Great," I said sarcastically. "Another piece of information you haven't told me."

The line went quiet except for the sound of Eddie's breathing. I had to feel for the kid, if I could call him that. I couldn't blame him for being overwhelmed by the events swallowing him up. I had to remind myself that I was his one and only lifeline. He was in deep trouble and he needed me more than he knew. Eddie Mawson may not have been the warmest guy on the planet, he may have no idea about how to deal with the opposite sex, he may well be guilty of thinking life was just about making and selling video games. Eddie Mawson had his faults, but he wasn't evil. There was a time when he was able to shut himself away from the real world, avoiding something he had trouble dealing with effectively. He could isolate himself with computers and the virtual realities they gave him access to. Not anymore. Whenever I entertained the thought of Eddie going to prison, I could not dwell on it for long. He would be destroyed in there, mentally and physically. I could not allow that to happen. Eddie Mawson didn't deserve to be annihilated like that.

"Eddie, I want you to get to my office right now, okay?"

"Now?"

"Yes now. I want you to think about every detail of every meeting you have had with Marty Cosgrove. And when I see you at my office, we're going to get it all down. Okay?"

"Okay."

"See you soon."

After I hung up, I sat in the car for a moment wondering if I should depose Marty. Before long, I rejected the idea. It would only throw more fuel on the fire of antagonism between Claire and me, and would definitely impact Bella. No, I'd deal with Marty in the courtroom and find a way to expose how companies like his preyed-on people like Eddie.

I looked across the street. I'd parked almost directly opposite Claire's house and found myself staring at her garage. My eyes locked onto the center column that Claire had backed into the night of her accident. It hadn't yet been repaired, and the sight of it made me recall the photos that Jack had taken. The animation he had put together began replaying in my mind. The speeding truck, coming from behind where I was parked. Her car retreating fast to get out of the way. The visualization was so vivid I could almost hear the explosive crash of impact.

Beyond the walls of the garage lived my daughter and my ex-wife. Both of them living with the man who I suspected of trying to kill Claire. What could I do about it? Kidnap Bella to remove her from a danger that only I perceived?

A powerful wave of anxiety consumed my entire body. My gut was stirring with dread, my nerves hitting the brink of panic. A part of me felt I should propel myself from the car, storm into Claire's house and get Bella out of there. The fact that I was contemplating this course of action raised alarm bells inside my brain. This hyper-vigilant state had all the hallmarks of the flashbacks that had terrified my wife and child when they lived with me.

I gripped the steering wheel tight to keep myself grounded in the car.

Maybe I was wrong about Marty. Maybe.

Maybe Jack was right. Maybe this case was getting way too personal—clouding my judgment, making me more prone to mistakes that my client might pay dearly for. Maybe.

I became aware of my breathing—it was fast and shallow. I closed my eyes and sucked air deep into my lungs. I fought to let go of all my thoughts to try and give my racing mind some peace. I focused only on my breath, keeping it steady and deep. After a minute or so, the meditation began to do its work. My state of panic was deflated. My entirely self-contained emergency passed.

I fired up the engine. I had to go spend some time with my client.

Then I had to go see Abby and break it to her that her noble charity efforts had been infiltrated by a drug lord, who in all likelihood was led to her by me.

I could just imagine how well that was going to go down.

PART II

Chapter 23

I sat at the defense table and took a small break from making notes. I had a routine of always getting to court early on the first day of a trial. The emptier the place, the better. That morning, the bailiff was my sole company when I arrived. We greeted each other, talked a little about the weather, then I sat down, arranged my materials, took out my pen and pad and jotted down the key points of my opening statement. I'd already committed them to memory. I wrote them down not so much out of necessity but as a ritual.

I wouldn't say I never felt nervous about addressing the court, but to me it encapsulated precisely what my chosen profession was all about. In this speech, if you want to call it that, my job was to get everyone to focus on what the essence of our entire legal system was about: justice. Yes, the other guy got to do that too. But that only heightens the deep and very real purpose of my mission. Most people think the law is there to protect them. It's a guardian of your humanity and rights. That's fine up to a point. What about when the law turns on you? It can be the most powerful threat to your life and liberty. If and when the law comes after you, then it's my job, my calling to see to it that all that power doesn't flow down a one-way street.

Today, I was representing a man who claimed to be innocent. He'd be going straight to jail for the best part of a decade if someone like me didn't stand up for him. He may not have been facing the electric chair, but Eddie Mawson had placed his life in my hands. And I intended to ensure he made the right call.

Slowly the court began to fill, but it soon became clear it was going to hit capacity. The media had given the case generous coverage, speculating on the guilt, character and fortune of the young, rich tech entrepreneur Eddie Mawson. It was no surprise that much of the coverage leaned heavily in Jenna Lewis's favor. Eddie's guilt, the press by and large believed, was a given. How I wished that every two-bit hack who wrote so freely and damningly about Eddie, pushing the contempt laws to the hilt, would spend a day or two in his shoes. They would change their tune pretty quickly, I'd wager. Overnight, they would become strident champions of the presumption of innocence.

I heard the gate squeak to my right and turned to see Elliott Goodwin arrive with two underlings at his heels. I observed the guy as he got himself set up and I could tell that the last thing he was going to do was turn my way. He was determined not to give me so much as a perfunctory nod by way of greeting. It was almost like he was repeating it in his head not to look my way, based on his intense focus on doing so many menial things at his desk. My feelings weren't hurt. It was actually informative. Goodwin was more tightly wound than I thought. This case was more personal to him than I'd imagined. And I knew then and there that I had to find a way to use it against him.

I wasn't so self-deluded as to forget how invested I was in this case myself. While I was pumped up with the first-day buzz, I hadn't forgotten the almost overwhelming way this case had consumed my life. Somehow the matter of a man coming to me for help had turned into a Pandora's Box that had cursed some of my most important relationships. At times I had considered taking Jack's advice and quitting, just picking up the phone and telling Eddie he'd have to get himself another lawyer, but I didn't. I always came back to the same point—I had to maintain my true north, which was justice. That was why I was here. That was why I was about to advocate for this man. If an innocent man went down on my watch, then whatever loss I incurred would be nothing compared to his.

Sitting beside me, that man, Eddie Mawson, was the image of respectability. He was clean shaven without a hair out of place and was dressed in a navy suit. He'd texted me when he'd arrived at the underground garage, and I went to meet him and usher him into court. When his right leg began jiggling nervously, I put my hand on his shoulder and offered a few words of encouragement. He nodded and his leg stopped jiggling, but I could see he was a still a bundle of nerves. His eyes followed every movement ahead of him, watching the bailiff and the stenographer. He once glanced over his shoulder but immediately swung his head back. I noticed this and turned around to see what had repelled him. I got the same treatment—a cast of people drilling me with dagger eyes.

"God help me," said Mawson with a tremulous voice. "I'm going to prison, aren't I?"

He kept staring ahead and I think he was talking more to himself than to me.

I rested my elbows on the table and leaned close to Eddie, for a moment shielding him from the gallery's judgmental eyes.

"You're not going to prison, Eddie. I've got your back. I know this is just about unbearable, but hang in there."

Journalists who write stories about court cases and the people who read those stories tend to think of prison in a single, black-and-white dimension. It's a punishment that fits the crime. They have no idea about the consummate impact it can have on a person who is sent there. They have no real understanding that prison is the last place on earth you want to be, even for a day. It's the last place on earth you should put someone—at least someone innocent. They have no idea that a six-month stint can so easily turn into two years, even ten. They don't know how prison eats men up from the inside out. Sometimes someone needs to stand in the doorway, as society bays for a man's blood, and tell them to back the hell up.

I looked over at Goodwin again. My adversary remained unmoved. And while that was something to exploit, it was also a threat. I could tell he would move heaven and earth to prevail in this trial. I couldn't help but wonder to what lengths he'd be prepared to go.

"All rise," called the bailiff loudly, and Eddie almost jumped out of his chair. Judge Sean Odell entered the courtroom and took his seat. I'd met Judge Odell a few times now and had come to know him as a man who was both rigid and convivial. Aged in his early sixties, he was a great personification of the law and his role in it, which is more than I can say for a lot of judges. Take away the robes and judges are just people—and people by nature can't help but carry their own personal biases wherever they go. Judge Odell had to date displayed an implacable neutrality which quickly won my respect. I'd tested his patience once or twice during jury selection, but nothing that was anything other than water under the bridge.

On Judge Odell's request, the bailiff let the jury in. The twelve members filed in to occupy two rows to our far right. I kept my eyes on them as they settled and noticed a few took it upon themselves to glare at Eddie. This was exactly what I expected from these particular jurors. I wasn't able to get them excluded during voir dire because my misgivings were more gut feelings than any bias I could expose. From my first impressions of them in court, my gut instincts were right on—jurors six, nine and eleven were going to be a problem.

I needed to give them something to challenge their preconceptions immediately. I looked over my left shoulder and was pleased to see Eddie's mother and sister had taken their seats directly behind us. They looked at me, unsure whether they should greet their loved one.

"Your family's here, Eddie," I said.

Hearing my words, Eddie's back straightened and he spun around. His mother stretched her hand out to touch Eddie's face. She was in tears and told her son that she loved him. I wasn't so crass as to turn and check, but I knew the jury members were watching. I couldn't have scripted it better. That may sound cynical, but given the beating Eddie had taken from the press, any chance to humanize him was vital.

Eddie took comfort in his mother's presence, but I could see the shame quickly spread over him. I stepped in to counter his negative thoughts, reminding him that I had a good strategy, and that I was ready to handle anything Elliott Goodwin threw at us.

"Are you sure I won't be taking the stand? Maybe I should."

We'd discussed this at length, but Eddie's mind was spinning, the fact that we were now in court and the trial was about to start was sending him nearly into panic mode. This kind of reaction often prompts a client to question everything at the last minute. It was like his mind was searching for a quick way out, a way for him to convince everyone present that he was innocent.

In short, Eddie Mawson just wanted to go home.

"For now the plan is to keep you off the stand, Eddie. Let's stick to that. Down the road things might change. In some circumstances it might make sense to get you up there. But you know the risk—Goodwin over there will come at you with every tactic at his disposal. If you're up on the stand, every minor flaw can get blown up and turned against you."

I'd explained in detail to Eddie that the accused is not like other witnesses on the stand. Other witnesses may be judged by jurors as liars or hotheads or just plain unpleasant. Such perceptions are but one link in the chain, though. They don't make up a juror's mind. It's different for the accused. Just one twitch, one disagreeable inflection on the accused's face, can turn the juror's perception against them for good, proving to be the spur of justification they needed to feel okay about finding the accused guilty. I'd gotten to know Eddie Mawson well enough to know that he irritated me. It would be a piece of cake for Goodwin to get Eddie to offend the jury and it would be game over.

"Counselors, are we ready for opening statements?" asked Judge Odell after he'd addressed the jury.

"Yes, Your Honor," Goodwin and I replied in unison.

"Let's get started, shall we?" said Judge Odell. "Over to you, Mr. Goodwin."

Goodwin stood up and went to the lectern. He placed a file on the top and opened it. He put his hands on either side of the lectern and looked for all the world like he was about to read a passage from the King James Bible. He then lifted his eyes from the lectern and turned to the jury, still maintaining his grip. I could only see his face in profile but the faces of the jury all went still as they instantly respected the gravity of his mood. They were almost as solemn as funeral mourners.

"Ladies and gentlemen of the jury, I think I can speak for the people of California when I say how grateful we are for your service. As a group, you play the most important role in this case. You have a tremendous duty to see that justice is done here in this courtroom. Effectively, the buck stops with the common sense, firmness of character and goodness of heart that each and every one of you possesses. So, I humbly thank you.

"The pursuit of justice is what we're engaged with here. Justice does not just happen automatically. It is not dispensed naturally in this world. And this case is about finding justice for the vulnerable. Justice for the less powerful. Justice for the exploited. Justice for the defenseless. That is the basis for this trial. It's about a fine young woman who was preyed upon.

"Jenna Lewis is the kind of girl our society wants more of. She's smart, talented, ambitious, and she's brave. Why brave? Because her choice of career for one. She decided to forge a career in one of America's most sexist industries—the video game production industry. In exchange for her efforts, she experienced sexual harassment at work and sexual assault at an after-work celebration. For most of her working life, she was picked on and preyed upon for being a female. And then she was raped by her former boss, Eddie Mawson, the man sitting right over there.

"As a society, we like to think we've come a long way in terms of workplace equality, but the truth is that we are kidding ourselves. What goes on within the walls of some businesses in this day and age is shocking. In one of the most modern workplaces, a high-tech, cutting-edge firm, Jenna Lewis endured months of humiliation. As one of the few female staff members she was subjected to sexist and demeaning remarks on a daily basis. This pathetic, sick and ultimately dangerous culture was overseen by the man who owned and ran that company—the defendant, Eddie Mawson.

"Jenna Lewis left that company to escape the misogyny that thrived there. She found a better, fairer place to work, a place where she wasn't sexually objectified, humiliated, abused or targeted simply because she was female. At her new company, she could focus on her work and that's what her colleagues focused on too.

"But when Jenna saw her former employer at an industry awards night, she believed she had no reason to fear for her safety. In fact, she felt more empowered than ever. She talked with the defendant. The conversation was pleasant. The defendant invited her to join him and others at a bar.

"She didn't see the harm. But that's not her fault. It was not her fault that to men like the defendant she was still considered prey.

"She didn't see the harm in being in a public bar with the defendant. There were plenty of other people there.

"She didn't see the harm in having a few drinks. The mood was great. Everyone was celebrating.

"She didn't see the harm in going into a karaoke booth to belt out a song or two. And she didn't go into that booth just with the defendant. She had a friend with her. Polly Gould.

"But the defendant knew the harm. He knew the dangers. He knew the evil he had planned.

"He knew he didn't have a chance to win Jenna Lewis's heart by respectful consensual courtship. She was out of his league. But he was determined to have her. He spiked her drink with GHB—a colorless, odorless drug that is highly favored by rapists. When Polly Gould left the karaoke booth to visit the bathroom, Jenna was already feeling groggy from the effects of the drug. It was then that the predator, Eddie Mawson, seized his chance.

"He was on top of her before she knew it and in her drug-affected state she was practically helpless, unable to find the strength, the wits and the wherewithal to resist, to fight back.

"Eddie Mawson put his hands all over Jenna's body. He groped her breasts and her buttocks, went under her dress and digitally raped her.

"Ladies and gentlemen of the jury, you will hear from a witness who saw this despicable act with his own eyes. You will hear from witnesses who will attest to the impact this attack has had on her. You will hear from the police who listened to Jenna's story and were compelled to arrest the defendant. You will hear from forensics experts who will confirm the presence of GHB in Jenna Lewis's bloodstream and you will hear from the police who questioned the defendant and who found him in possession of the date rape drug GHB.

"Now, I said when I began that Jenna Lewis was a brave young woman. She had the courage to pursue her dream job in the face of sustained and horrific abuse. And now she is displaying phenomenal courage to pursue justice for the crime that has been committed against her. Any rape survivor who comes this far to hold their attacker accountable does so at a very high price. This trial and the details that will be presented in this courtroom will make their way out to the general public. To find justice, Jenna Lewis will pay extra in terms of humiliation, public scrutiny of her personal life and unfair judgment.

"Most sexual assault cases never get this far, the victims opting to either not report the crimes committed against them or else withdraw their statements once the considerable pressure starts to bear down upon them."

"Make no mistake, Jenna Lewis is a victim. But she is not a victim who will stay silent. She is a survivor who has the courage to pursue justice at great personal cost.

"This case will be extremely tough going for all of you but I urge you to heed the story the evidence tells. Do that and you will be doing your job to ensure that justice will be done here in this courtroom.

"Thank you."

As Elliott gathered his things and stepped back to his desk, I watched the jury. He'd done a good job of setting the right tone. The sense of civic duty is strong in the vast majority of jurors. Some don't respect the role and they see it as nothing but an imposition. But I was sure everyone with that attitude had been flushed out during the selection process. I was confident that our twelve jurors wanted to be here. Before today they've been questioned by me and Elliott during voir dire, they've been advised by a judge—who bears an almost regal aura of authority—as to the fundamental importance and gravity of their role and now they were in the courtroom as active participants for the first time. This experience is almost always deeply moving for jurors. By that I mean they all tap into the depth of the responsibility of the task. Yes, some carry biases, but on the whole, jurors tend to feel proud that they represent the conscience of the community. Elliott's words would have done exactly what he wanted them to. He steered their solemn inclinations his way. Now it was my turn to steer them back.

I moved briskly to the lectern. It wasn't for effect, exactly. I was genuinely eager to get started. I didn't take my notes. I didn't need them. I began to speak as soon as I reached the lectern.

I don't know how to say this without coming across as conceited, but this was my wheelhouse. I guess if you hired a lawyer you'd want them to feel comfortable and confident addressing the court. That said, arrogance doesn't play well. If you're vain, pretentious or haughty, it doesn't matter what you're saying, all the jurors will be thinking is that you just expect them to follow your orders. And in this free country of ours, that will only make them recoil from you. They'll be convinced that you think you're better than them. And that can spell death for a trial lawyer. Because trials aren't about the black and white law. They'd about the impressions that you place in the hearts and minds of twelve flesh and blood human beings.

"Ladies and gentlemen of the jury, I too would like to thank you for your service. You've surely put on hold or found workarounds for some or all of the responsibilities that fall upon you outside of this courtroom. Your jobs. Your families. Your communities. Well, we are fortunate to have you here, and we are grateful. Because we have here an extremely serious matter for you to adjudicate. The fate of that young man over there, the defendant Eddie Mawson, is in your hands.

"Now from the outset, I have to tread extremely carefully because this is a sexual assault case and I agree that it takes a great deal of courage for a young woman to put herself through the rigors of a very public trial.

"What I will say, what I must say, is that this is an alleged crime. The fact that the defendant is here in court does not make him guilty. The fact that Jenna Lewis alleges that he raped her does not make him guilty. And when the time comes it will be you and you alone—collectively speaking—who will decide. But, and this is a big but, right at this very moment you must start with one absolutely crystal-clear notion in your head. The defendant, Eddie Mawson, my client, is innocent. He is an innocent man until it is proved here in this court and in your minds and hearts that he his irrefutably guilty.

"He is innocent until the prosecution can present to you evidence that wipes all reasonable doubt from your mind.

"Now that's a very, very high burden of proof and so it should be.

"The fact that a young woman alleges that the defendant raped her is not evidence that he did. The fact that the police filed charges does not make those charges true. The fact that he's sitting here being judged does not make him guilty. It makes him scared for his life but it does not make him guilty. No, it's up to you to decide. It's your call. And you can only deem him to be guilty if all reasonable doubt has been removed from your mind.

"So right now, I want you to look over there at the defendant. He is an innocent man. And innocent he must remain until you believe with all your heart that he is guilty.

"Now, you've already heard the prosecution make statements about the company that the defendant runs. He said that it was sexist and exploitative. Now I wouldn't stand here and condone such a workplace culture. But that's not what we're here to judge. We're not here to judge history. We're not here to judge the merits of how a business is run. We are dealing with something very specific. My client has been accused of a crime. So what evidence exists that he committed this particular crime?

"He was out on the town celebrating with past and present coworkers. Jenna Lewis and another woman, Polly Gould were drinking with the defendant. They were there of their own free will. They had other friends at the bar but they chose to stay and drink with Eddie.

"The three of them decided to sing some karaoke, so they moved into one of the booths with their drinks.

"Now what happened next is what's important and you'll hear two very different stories.

"Look, I'll say again that I know it takes untold courage for a woman to proceed all the way to court with rape allegations. The personal price of doing so is high. But I also am compelled to state that we are in the real world, and in the real world false rape allegations happen. Research shows that as many as one in ten rape allegations are false.

"Why would a woman do this? There are many reasons. It could be guilt for having engaged in sex that you regret. It could be revenge. It could be money.

"During this trial you will hear many statements in an effort to try and persuade you that Eddie Mawson is guilty.

"But you will not find one piece of evidence that proves he's guilty. This, ladies and gentlemen, is not an exercise in connecting the dots. You have to be presented with compelling evidence, that makes you believe there can be no other explanation for what happened.

"Eddie Mawson's life is in your hands. As this trial unfolds you will see that the so-called evidence falls far short of the need to dispel doubt from your minds. And you must then find him innocent.

"Again, I thank you for your contribution to finding true justice in this matter."

Chapter 24

All eyes watched Jenna Lewis approach the stand. She wore a blue jacket over a white blouse, a knee-length skirt and low-heeled shoes. I couldn't tell you the designer of her suit, but it was stylish and modest. It suggested that she hadn't wanted to overdo the formality of her court appearance. There was something honest about that. Her shoulders were stiff as she moved, and her head and eyes were aimed down. It was a difficult walk, clearly. Lewis was a very attractive girl with blue eyes, clear skin and dark brown hair that was parted in the middle and fell down to her shoulders. You didn't have to know her to know she looked tired. How could anyone in her shoes not be? Right at this moment, I didn't think she was a liar. I just thought there must be something more to her story. Hell, it could even be possible that she believed her accusations. Then again, I might have gotten it all wrong and perhaps my client really was a rapist.

The appearance of the bailiff beside Lewis broke my train of thought. The witness read the oath and then turned to face Goodwin.

"Miss Lewis, I just want to start by thanking you for your courage," Goodwin began. "So many sexual assault cases go unreported. Your testimony in this court is of vital importance. By taking this stance your voice will be heard far and wide."

I was half inclined to check Goodwin straight off the bat with an objection. This wasn't group therapy, it was a court of law and he was testifying. I let it go. There were bigger fish to fry. I had one eye on the jury. They wouldn't look too kindly upon an instant objection from me, no matter how right I was on the point of law. After Lewis nodded a graceful thank you to Goodwin, the prosecutor continued. He used a few questions to bring out Lewis's work and personal history. That done, he zeroed in on the events at hand.

"Miss Lewis, can you please tell the court what happened at the bar that night?"

"Yes, we'd all been to an awards night. It was an industry bash, and we all wanted to continue partying so we decided to go to Blackjacks."

"Who were you at Blackjacks with?"

"I was with people I work with now plus people from Adrenal, the company where I used to work."

"That's the company founded and owned by the defendant, correct?"

"Yes, that's right."

"How would you describe your relationship with the defendant?"

"Well, we're not exactly friends. We talk when we see each other socially. But he used to be my boss. I used to work for him, so he wasn't someone I'd hang around with."

"I see. When you worked for the defendant, did he ever make you feel uncomfortable?"

"Yes, he did."

The speed of Lewis's reply was disconcerting and Goodwin wasted no time honing in on her answer. Just, I take it, like he'd done during their pre-trial preparation. "Could you please tell the court how the defendant made you feel uncomfortable?"

"Well, I was aware that he had feelings for me."

"How did you know this?"

"He told other people, who told me."

"What did he tell them?"

"Objection, Your Honor. Hearsay."

"Sustained."

Goodwin coughed and smiled a little. "Miss Lewis what did these people tell you?"

"They told me he said he wanted to, um, have sex with me."

Lewis cast an uncomfortable glance around the courtroom, as if fearing a reprimand for being vulgar. But the gallery loved it. You could almost hear the delight in the murmur that rippled through the courtroom.

"I see," said Goodwin. "Was the attraction mutual?"

Lewis shook her head vigorously. "No."

"Did the defendant do anything to make you feel uncomfortable at his company when you worked there?"

Lewis nodded. "Yes. He would come up behind me at my desk and stand very close to me and put his hand on my shoulder."

"So he touched you?"

"Yes. With his hands and with his thigh."

"What did you do when he did this?"

"I shrugged his hand off as politely as I could. I didn't want to upset him. He was my boss."

"Is that why you left Adrenal?"

"It wasn't the only reason. It was partly because of that."

Goodwin pinched his chin and stepped to the side of the lectern. "Miss Lewis, back to the night at Blackjacks. Why were you drinking with the defendant if you were not fond of him?"

"I didn't hate him. I'd left Adrenal and I had another really good job at a place where I loved to work. And I kind of felt sorry for him."

"Why?"

"Because he never had a girlfriend, for one. And also a lot of people were only nice to him to his face because he was the boss, he had a lot of money and he would buy everyone drinks. And drugs. He was generous with his drugs."

"What kind of drugs?"

"Cocaine."

"Was he giving you cocaine at Blackjacks that night?"

Lewis nodded guiltily. "Yes, he was."

"Where were you ingesting the cocaine?"

"He'd give us his bag and we'd take it to the ladies' bathroom."

"I see. So you were drinking a lot and snorting cocaine. Then what happened?"

"We decided to do some karaoke. So the three of us took our drinks and went to one of the rooms that was free. We sat down and started going through the songs. I went first and then Polly. Then it was Eddie's turn."

"So you were having fun?"

"Yes."

"Then what happened?"

"I had to go to the bathroom, so I left Polly and Eddie there. Then I came back. I did another song but I had to sit down because I felt very drunk all of a sudden."

"Really? Why would that be?"

"I had no idea at the time. But I turned around to speak to Polly but she was gone."

"Gone where?"

"Again I didn't know. I assumed she needed to go to the bathroom like I did."

"I see, and then what happened?"

"I just remember slumping in the seat and suddenly Eddie was on top of me."

"What was he doing exactly?"

Lewis bowed her head. "He was trying to kiss me and he was touching my body."

"Where did he touch you?"

"He grabbed my breasts and then his hand started moving down. I tried to push him off but I was just so weak. It was like I was suddenly the drunkest I'd ever been. And then I was scared because I could feel what he was doing to me. I wanted to scream, but I couldn't. He kept putting his mouth over mine and then he got his hand under my dress and then he put his fingers inside me."

Again, the packed gallery behind me hummed as people couldn't help but comment. Goodwin paused while Judge Odell eyed everyone gathered in his court and quietened them down without having to say a word or even raise his gavel. Goodwin shook his head. "What did you do?"

"I kept moving my head to try and avoid him. And I kept saying, 'No.' Then somehow I managed to fling myself to the side and I fell to the floor. He bent down to pick me up but I got up myself. I don't know how. Then I went to the door."

"Did he try and stop you?"

"No. I think he kind of realized what he'd done. I don't know. He didn't follow me out."

"What did you do then?"

"I went to the bathroom. I felt so out of it I could barely cry. All I wanted to do was get out of there, so I called an Uber from the bathroom and left."

As Lewis continued her testimony, I noticed it was almost word for word what was on her statement to the police she'd given the day after the incident. And every member of the jury and the gallery was hanging on her every word. I made a few notes but I avoided speaking to Eddie. I was sure any exchange I had with my client would appear heartless and I couldn't afford to misstep here. Goodwin had the jury right where he wanted them. He had the upper hand, and for now there was nothing I could do about it except give Lewis my respectful attention. I didn't have to turn around to gauge the mood of the room. I heard every tut-tut, every muffled expression of outrage and affront.

Goodwin kept Lewis talking on the stand for as long as he could and when he was done it was no surprise that Judge Odell called it a day. For the first time that day, Goodwin looked at me. He couldn't help himself. His face was studiously dour but he allowed himself the hint of a smug smile. His strategy was going swimmingly. I bet he wanted the day to end at this point so the jury would be sleeping on the awfulness of Jenna Lewis's testimony. Her words would be ringing in each juror's head as they hit the pillow, the image of her so distraught and yet courageous still fresh in their minds. The opportunity for me to cast even the slightest bit of doubt was put on hold until the next day. This was a significant advantage to Goodwin. He knew it, and so did I.

The next morning, I found myself standing in front of Jenna Lewis, who waited for me to address her with her chin up and eyes on me. She appeared ready and willing to respond. I wouldn't say I had stage fright standing there at the lectern, but I did feel a high degree of unease. I had to tread very carefully. I had to be considerate and gentle, compassionate and patient with Lewis if I was to keep the jury onside. If I failed to handle her with due care then I'd come across as being callous and cruel, which would not serve Eddie Mawson well at all.

"Miss Lewis, you said that you were enjoying Eddie Mawson's company before the three of you entered the karaoke booth, isn't that right?"

"Ah, yes. I was. Like, we weren't buddies but we got along okay. The three of us."

"By the 'the three of us' you mean Eddie, Polly Gould and yourself?"

"Yes, of course."

"Did the three of you have a lot to drink?" I asked, careful not to make it just about Lewis. Part of the minefield through which I was walking was that I couldn't be seen as directing presumptuous blame at the victim of an alleged rape. In most circumstances, I wouldn't think twice about asking hard direct questions that made a prosecution witness uncomfortable. All the better that I unsettled and, yes, even intimidated them. If I believed their story was complete BS, sometimes it was best to try and strip it away ruthlessly to expose the lies. I was ambivalent about Jenna Lewis, I didn't know whether she was lying or telling the truth, or at least the truth as she recalled it, but for my client to be innocent—whether I believed that or not—there had to be a key flaw in her story.

"Yes, Eddie had an open tab at the bar. And he kept the drinks coming."

"What were you drinking?"

"Cosmopolitans."

"Do you know how many you had?"

Lewis shook her head. "I have no idea."

"Was it closer to four? Seven? Ten?"

"I don't know. Maybe six."

"And you were doing drugs?"

Lewis's eyes shot out to the gallery. I assumed she had her parents there. She bowed her head with shame. "Yes."

"What drugs were you taking?"

"Cocaine."

"Whose cocaine was it?"

"Eddie's."

"And how long were the three of you hanging out together at the bar?"

"A couple of hours, maybe."

"Now, you've said you and Eddie weren't really friends. You made it clear you weren't really fond of him. Why did you stay with him so long if you didn't like his company?"

"I don't know. We were just drinking and Polly and I are friends."

"So you don't really like the guy but you're getting free drinks and free coke. That was the situation. Am I right?"

Lewis had a deadpan expression on her face, like I'd cornily stated something obvious. In that moment, the jury got a glimpse of something to suggest that this was no innocent Bo

Peep on the stand. Not that this condemned her by any stretch, it was just a dose of reality—a glimpse of her authentic, as opposed to rehearsed, character. "Yes. As awful as it sounds, I was taking advantage of Eddie's generosity."

I shrugged. "I get it. To a lot of people your age, they'd be like, 'Who wouldn't?' Right?"

"Yes."

"But it's not like you couldn't afford your own cocaine, right? I mean you work as a designer for Ubivision. You earn a three-figure salary, don't you?"

"More or less."

"So you can afford to buy your own drugs, can't you?"

"Yes."

"Do you buy cocaine every now and then yourself?"

Again Lewis's eyes shot to the same spot in the gallery. "No."

"No? Okay, how often to you use cocaine then?"

"Hardly ever."

"I see. So you're saying you're not a habitual cocaine user, is that right?"

Lewis nodded her head sharply and kept her eyes on me to deliver her response with utmost earnestness. "No, I'm most certainly not."

"Okay," I said. "Now your blood test revealed that you had the drug GHB in your system. How do you explain that?"

"I can't explain it."

"You believe someone spiked your drink, don't you?"

"Yes, that's right."

"And you told the police that you thought it was Eddie who spiked your drink, didn't you?"

"Yes."

"Whose idea was it to go sing some karaoke?"

"It was mine."

"Really? You suggested that the three of you go and have some fun singing silly pop songs?"

"That's right."

I lowered my head before re-engaging the witness. "I don't understand. This is a guy you say you don't particularly like, yet you hang out with him for hours accepting his drinks and his coke."

"I wasn't really thinking about that."

"Miss Lewis, you told the court that you knew Eddie was attracted to you and that he gave you the creeps when you worked at Adrenal. Yet you were happy to hang out with him. Can I ask, did Eddie make a pass at you before you went to the karaoke booth?"

"No."

"Did he touch you at all?"

Lewis gave the question a few moments of thought before shaking her head. "No."

"Did he say anything to you that was unwelcome? Did he make any kind of sexually loaded comment?"

"Not that I can recall."

"If he did, though, it would have disgusted you, right?"

"Yes, most definitely."

"So it's fair to say that because you knew he was attracted to you, you'd have been unwilling to tolerate any sexually inappropriate behavior from him, right?"

"I guess so."

"Can I take that as a yes?"

"Yes. It's a yes. I mean, you know what I mean."

"I totally understand. So if Eddie didn't keep his hands to himself or if he said anything suggestive, you'd have been out of there, right?"

"Yes."

"No matter how much free coke and booze he sent your way, right?"

Lewis dropped her jaw and dead-stared me. "I wasn't using him," she said.

I raised my hands. "Sorry, I thought we'd established that you were."

"Objection," called Goodwin.

"On what grounds?" asked Judge Odell.

Goodwin was clearly unsure what to grab onto. "He's badgering the witness."

"Your Honor, I—"

"Overruled," said Judge Odell. "Please continue your cross-examination, Mr. Madison."

"Certainly, Your Honor. Miss Lewis, I won't ask you to go over all the details of what you allege to have occurred in the karaoke booth."

"Thank you."

"When you left the booth after the alleged attack, you went to the bathroom. When you came out of the bathroom, what did you do?"

"I wanted to go home. So that's what I did."

"Did you tell anyone that you'd been sexually assaulted?"

Lewis shook her head. "I was really out of it, on God knows what. I had no idea at the time that my drink had been spiked. I just felt so unsafe. I was a mess, and I was ashamed. So I left."

"You didn't try to find Polly to tell her you were leaving?"

"No. I just wanted to get home."

"You didn't feel the safest bet was to ask your friend to help you?"

"That may sound like a sensible idea now but in my state I wasn't able to use my best judgment."

"So you pulled out your phone and called for an Uber, right?"

"Yes."

"Where did you wait for the Uber?"

"I went outside and waited."

"Okay. The Uber app on your phone tells you where the car is, so you could have waited until the driver was outside before leaving the bar. Why did you wait outside?"

"I didn't want to stay in there," said Lewis, with some fire in her eyes. "I wanted to be as far away from that place as possible. I was a complete mess and I'd just been raped. Sorry if my decisions weren't the most logical."

I could feel the buzz of the gallery behind me as the onlookers were enervated by Lewis's emotional display. I knew I'd reached a point that had swung the sympathy back to her. I had to show that I was not trying to pick on her. I took a moment to check my notes.

"You did make a clear decision the following morning, right? That was when you went to the police. Did you struggle with whether or not to go to the police?"

My tone was conciliatory and Lewis breathed easier in response. "Yes, I did struggle. I wasn't sure what I should do, and whether I wanted to get the police involved."

"So you called the police when?"

"At about eleven the next morning."

"I see. Did you discuss what you should do with anyone before you made that call?"

"No."

"You didn't confide in anyone. You didn't consult anyone? You didn't call Polly, for instance?"

"No."

"Even though Polly called you several times during the night and left you messages?"

Lewis looked somewhat surprised that I knew Polly called her. It wouldn't have taken her long to realize that I, of course, had spoken directly to Polly. Plus, Lewis's phone records were in evidence.

"I couldn't bear to. I wanted to be alone."

"Yes, I see. But you didn't speak with anyone else on the phone after you left the bar?"

"No."

I then picked up a sheet of paper from the lectern. "Miss Lewis, I've got your phone records here. There's a record of you taking a call at one-fifteen in the morning. The call lasted for twenty-three minutes. Who were you talking to?"

"I don't remember speaking to anyone," said Lewis, looking confused.

I held the printout up and turned to Judge Odell. "Your Honor, may I approach the witness?"

"Yes," said Judge Odell.

I went and handed the sheet to Lewis. "It's this number here. I've highlighted it in yellow."

The confusion remained on Lewis's face as she studied the printout. She then shook her head. "I have no idea whose number that is. I can't remember speaking on the phone at all.

And I was in no condition to speak. Maybe I pocket dialed the number."

"Maybe," I said, returning to the lectern. "If it was a pocket dial that number would have to be on your Favorites list or else be used recently, wouldn't it?"

"I guess. But like I said, I have no recollection of talking to anyone."

"Okay. Do you have your phone on you now?"

Lewis's forehead knitted briefly as though I'd asked something random and odd. "Yes, I'm pretty sure I do. Yes, I switched it off though, for court."

"That's okay," I said. "Would you mind just switching your phone on?"

"Objection," cried Goodwin. "This is a courtroom not a game show. If Mr. Madison wants the witness to phone a friend then—"

I raised my hands as I cut Goodwin off. "Your Honor," I said over the prosecutor. "I'm just asking the witness to dial the number. She can just hit the call button then hang up. That action will prompt the phone to display the name of the person the number belongs to, if it's in her contacts, which we assume it is."

"Objection, Your Honor," said Goodwin. "What's the relevance here?"

I turned to Goodwin then back to Judge Odell.

"Your Honor, I think it's a simple matter of finding out who the witness spoke to. I know that she can't recall having a conversation but the memory of the person on the other end of the line, however, might be crystal clear. She may have confided in that person and the prosecution has no interest in what she might have said? It will take but a minute to find out. It's worth knowing, I believe, Your Honor."

"I agree," said Judge Odell. "Overruled. Miss Lewis, please do as Mr. Madison has requested."

Lewis nodded. "Yes, Your Honor," she said before turning her phone on. Everyone in the courtroom struggled to stay silent as the seconds passed. Lewis then referred to the sheet and tapped in the number. "No, it's no one I know."

"Your Honor, permission to approach the witness and check the phone?" I asked.

"Granted."

I stepped up to Lewis and she handed her phone to me. I compared the phone to the printout. "Ah, I said, you got a digit wrong. See?"

Lewis looked at the phone and rolled her eyes. "Sorry. I'm such an idiot. I'm so nervous I can't think straight."

"That's okay," I said. "It's an easy mistake to make at the best of times. Try again."

I handed the phone and printout back to Lewis. This time, after she had tapped the numbers, dialed and then hung up the call, her eyebrows leaped up in surprise. "It was Alex," she said, handing me her phone.

"Alex?" I said, taking the phone from her and looking at it. "Alex Herron?"

"Yes. He works at Adrenal. He was at the bar that night."

"Right," I said returning to the lectern. "Why was he calling you at that hour, Miss Lewis?"

"I have no idea. Maybe he knew I'd left the bar suddenly and was checking on me."

"Are the two of you good friends?"

"No, not particularly."
"Have you spoken with Alex since that night?"
"Yes, I have."
"And he never mentioned that he called you?"
"No, I guess that must sound strange but—"
"No biggie, Miss Lewis," I said. "But yes, it is a little strange."
I gathered up my papers.
"No further questions, Your Honor."

Chapter 25

Polly Gould just about strutted up to the stand, such was her air of purpose. She was wearing a similar outfit to what she wore when I first met her at the Adrenal office. Today her cardigan was pink mohair, her shirt a blue tartan and her pinned-back hair a bright shade of purple. I saw Judge Odell's eyes follow her to the stand, clearly not sure what to make of this curious creature. I bet he had a point or two of court dress etiquette on his mind that he may have been inclined to offer but he, like most of the people in the room, I'd wager, found Gould's buoyant presence an instant delight. After she took the oath, she sat and stared at us all through those Bill Gates glasses with her chin confidently jutted out.

Elliott Goodwin cleared his throat and began to introduce Gould to the courtroom by way of a few introductory questions, covering the fact that she had worked alongside Jenna Lewis at Adrenal, and that they hadn't seen much of each other since Lewis left to work for Ubivision. The post-awards night drinks at Blackjacks was a great chance for them to catch up.

"Miss Gould, how are female workers treated at the defendant's company, Adrenal?"

"It depends on who's doing the treating."

"Could you please elaborate for the court?"

"In short, women, girls, females, whatever term you prefer to use, we were treated anything but equally. About the only thing that was equal was the pay but we were mostly deemed to be inferiors by the guys there. I'm a programmer and I'd put my work up against any of them. But they just couldn't seem to get past the fact that I don't have the same anatomical hardware as they do. At times, it was like we girls were more or less aliens. They seriously struggled to relate to us and for many of them this deficiency caused frustration. And that in turn made them feel somewhat emasculated, which manifests as derision or even contempt. I'm speaking generally, of course but if you wanted me to recount in detail all the times I've been the subject of unwanted attention or disdain we'd be here all week."

"How do you manage to work in such a difficult environment?"

"For the most part, I can just shut it all out and just do my work. I put my headphones on, listen to my music and get lost in my own little world of code."

"So the workplace culture at Adrenal is sexist?"

"Worse. Misogynistic would be my word. It's not as bad as it used to be, but there are still guys who like to annoy you or bait you daily like it's some kind of sport."

"This is the culture over which the defendant presides?"

"Yes. But like I said, it used to be worse. That was a big part of why Jenna left. It got better after she'd gone, I have to admit."

"Did you ever see Eddie Mawson degrade his female employees?"

Gould shrugged her shoulders and looked at Mawson with a regretful downturn of her mouth. She then nodded. "Yes, I did.

I mean, it wasn't direct. I saw him laughing when one girl, who lasted two days at Adrenal, was being made fun of by the guys."

"How so?"

"This guy was dry humping her behind her back. She had no idea. Then Eddie and a couple of others started laughing. She turned around but missed what the guy was doing. Then I saw them do the blow-job thing when she spoke at a meeting. Again, he just seemed to find it amusing."

Gould lifted her hand beside her face to simulate the gesture but thought better of it.

"We know what you mean, Miss Gould. They were mimicking fellatio."

"Yes."

"And the defendant, the boss of these guys, was laughing?"

"Yes," said Gould. "But having said that—"

"Thank you, Miss Gould," said Goodwin, cutting her off. She got the message and left her sentence unfinished. She flicked an apologetic glance at Mawson. Clearly, it was not in Goodwin's interest to have Gould offer anything in Mawson's favor. I made a couple of notes as Goodwin continued.

"Miss Gould, when you, Miss Lewis and the defendant were drinking together at the bar—at Blackjacks—did Mr. Mawson make you feel uncomfortable?"

"I wouldn't say that but both Jenna and I knew what he was like, and we were a little wary of him."

"Why were you wary of him?"

"We knew he liked Jenna, and he had touched both of us at work once or twice which was not appropriate."

"He touched you at work?"

"Yes. A couple of times."

"How so?"

"He once came up behind me and put his hands on my shoulders to give me an impromptu massage."

"What did you do?"

"I just about jumped out of my chair and asked him not to do that. But another time we were in a meeting in the conference room, and as he was addressing everyone he walked around and then grabbed my shoulders again and squeezed them. I was about to say something but he let go and moved on."

"Miss Gould, when you left the defendant with Miss Lewis in the karaoke booth, didn't you think it might be unwise to leave her alone with him?"

"I have to say that I did, but I was very drunk by that stage and I was less inclined to worry about anything. I mean, we were in a public place. I didn't seriously think that Jenna needed to fear for her safety."

"But she did, didn't she?"

"Yes. She did, and I feel terrible about that. I should not have left her alone. I should have gone straight back to her after I'd been to the bathroom. I have to live with that."

The emotions got the better of Gould and she began to sob. She then quickly composed herself and wiped away the tears from her eyes. "I wasn't much of a friend to Jenna," she said.

"Nothing further, Your Honor," said Goodwin, who promptly gathered up his notes and vacated the lectern. When he took his place back at the prosecution desk, his colleagues bent in to offer him praise. So they should. He had done well. I didn't have to study the jury for long to know what they thought of my client.

I needed to steady the ship, quickly and emphatically.

"Miss Gould," I said when I took my place at the lectern. "Can I just go back a little to when you were discussing the goings-on at Adrenal?"

"Yes?"

"You said the defendant laughed at the girl being mocked, right?"

"Yes. Mandy was her name."

"Did Mandy stay at Adrenal?"

"No, she left pretty much the next day, as I recall."

"And was the workplace culture the same after she left?"

Gould shook her head with slow purpose, like she was compelled to do so out of fairness. In my opinion, she was aware that she might say something that wouldn't please Goodwin, who would have stressed to her that the best way to help Jenna Lewis was to stick to Eddie's unseemly, sexist behavior.

"Yes, it was the same. It was after Jenna left that things began to change."

"Can you elaborate, please?"

"Eddie began to show some leadership. He refused to laugh at the sexist juvenile humor and he admonished one guy in front of everyone."

"Admonished?"

"There was this guy who'd deliberately talk over any girl who spoke during meetings like they had nothing of value to say. Eddie cut him off told him not to do it again."

"And the culture changed?"

"Yes. It improved a little. Some of those guys will always still be dicks—pardon my French. But things became more tolerable, I have to say. I still shut myself off and get on with my job but the culture is better than it was. Put it that way."

"Miss Gould, I'd like to ask about your relationship with Jenna Lewis. To your knowledge she was happy working at Adrenal for the most part, is that right?"

"Yes. She wasn't too stoked with her job but the money was good."

"She stayed for the money?"

"That was a big part of it until she got a better offer over at Ubivision."

"Miss Gould, did Jenna Lewis ever ask to borrow money from you?"

Gould looked uncomfortable but she remained straight-backed and resolute. The jury was going to believe every word that came out of her mouth. "Yes, she did. Several times."

"Several times? How much did she ask to borrow?"

"It was usually a few hundred dollars but one time she asked to borrow five thousand dollars."

"She earned a great salary, didn't she?"

"Yes."

"Did she ever say why she needed to borrow money?"

Gould shook her head. "She said her family belonged to a very strict church and they had a lot of charity work they needed money for. And Jenna said sometimes she was just too generous and didn't have enough to cover her bills and expenses."

"I see. Did you lend her the money?"

"Yes. Always. She always paid me back when her next paycheck came."

I lowered my head and then looked at the jury for a moment before turning to face Gould. "Miss Gould, did you believe Miss Lewis's explanation for why she needed that money?"

Gould shifted in her seat. "I didn't know what to believe."

"So you didn't believe her?"

"No, if I'm being totally honest. I didn't."

"Did you suspect that Jenna Lewis had a drug problem?"

Once more, a ripple went through the courtroom. I was the most unpopular person in the room right now, that was for sure. Still, they all fell silent quickly, not wanting to miss a word of Gould's response.

Gould faltered. "I don't know."

"Okay, I'll put it another way. You've been out partying with Miss Lewis other than that night at Blackjacks, haven't you?"

"Yes."

"And did you often use cocaine with Miss Lewis?"

"Yes. She always seemed to have it."

"She always seemed to have it on her. Now that wasn't what she told the court yesterday."

"I don't know what to say," said Gould.

I let the silence fall for a few moments so that this would sink into the jury's collective mind. Lewis had lied about her drug use.

"Ms. Gould, that night at the awards show, did you do coke with Jenna before ending up at Blackjacks?"

"Yes, I did."

"Was it Jenna who had the coke or was it you?"

"It was Jenna."

"At Blackjacks whose coke were you and Jenna using?"

"Eddie's."

"Had Jenna run out?"

Gould shook her head. "No, she had plenty. I saw how much she had at the awards. It was a few grams. At Blackjacks, she just wanted to use Eddie's instead of hers."

"I see. Do you think that's the behavior of someone with a drug problem?"

Gould shrugged. "I honestly don't know. There's a lot about Jenna I don't know."

"Do you think that's why she had to ask you for money? Because she spent so much on drugs?"

"Objection," cried Goodwin. "Speculation."

"Sustained," said Judge Odell. "You don't have to answer that."

"Well, that's exactly what I thought," said Gould, who clearly didn't take kindly to being shut down.

"Order," said Judge Odell sternly. "Strike the witness's last comment. Ms. Gould—"

"Sorry, Your Honor," she said.

I wasn't sorry at all. The same couldn't be said for Goodwin, whose face was red with contained rage. The jury was getting an unfiltered look at Jenna Lewis and he didn't like it one bit.

"Thank you, Miss Gould," I said. "No more questions."

Chapter 26

Following Polly Gould's testimony, Judge Odell called a short recess. I had a few words with Eddie before excusing myself to go to the bathroom. Outside the courtroom, I found Donna Amerson standing there, waiting for me, apparently. I'd exchanged a few text messages with her in the lead-up to the trial, hoping that she would find the time to come. Although she wasn't Jenna Lewis's counselor or caseworker, I was hoping that if she attended the trial, she might see there were cracks in the story of this alleged rape. The sight of her now actually had me feeling optimistic that this was exactly what she wanted to express.

"Donna," I said with a smile. "I'm glad you came."

"Wouldn't miss it for the world, Brad."

She was clearly being sarcastic. I'm sure she had to put a mountain of work aside to leave her office for the day. But what she wasn't doing was smiling.

"Were you here yesterday?" I asked.

Amerson nodded. "Yes. I saw all of Jenna's testimony. And now Polly's. But I need to get back to work. I've seen enough for now."

There was a hint of disapproval in her tone.

"Okay. And?"

"And what, Brad? Do you think that after you've attacked this young woman that you've got me on your side? Is that what you think?"

"I didn't attack anyone in there, Donna."

"You practically slut-shamed Jenna Lewis. You've made her out to be a coke whore."

Amerson kept her voice down but her cheeks were flushed with rage.

"Whoa, wait a second now. I did no such thing. I was extremely careful about how I elicited certain facts that, while they might be unpleasant and embarrassing, were absolutely vital to getting to the truth about what happened between Eddie and Jenna. I'm defending a man who is accused of rape, Donna. If he's going to spend even one day in jail, I'm going to make sure it only comes after rock-solid proof is presented in this court. We can't put people in jail based on feelings. We have to judge with facts."

Amerson had her arms folded. It was clear the process had upset her. And who am I to say that she was wrong? Maybe a lot of other people in the court thought the same as she did. Maybe the whole jury did. I didn't know. But I did expect a jury, endowed as they were with a profound sense of duty and a conviction to appraise the case on evidence not emotion, to understand that what I was doing was trying to test the veracity of Jenna Lewis's accusations.

Okay, I admit it. I was trying to raise questions about her character. What else was I going to do?

"Look, Donna. I don't expect you to just agree with me but I was hoping you'd look at it with an open mind."

Amerson nodded. "I do have an open mind."

There was a pause as I wondered if her words were loaded. Did this mean she was possibly open to changing her mind as I hoped?

"Tell me you don't think there's something not right here," I said. "I mean, to me it sounds like this girl is under a lot of pressure. One part of it, clearly, is that she is deeply ashamed to have all this come out in public. The court just heard, or at least understood, the possibility that she lied about her drug use. I wonder how her parents are taking it, how they're treating her. Are they behind her, Donna?"

"I don't know."

"If they're not supporting her, who's she got?"

"I don't know that either. As you know, I'm not her counselor and I've been too busy to keep regular tabs on her."

"Would you have time to check in with her?"

"I am going to do that. I need to know that she's got the support she needs. Her counselor may only spend a couple of hours with her a week, and that's if Jenna goes to her."

"It would be great if you talked to her."

"Brad, I'm not going to be your spy."

I held up my hands. "I know. I know. Just talk to her. If there's anything I do need to know then... you understand that my client shouldn't be punished in this court for being a douche bag, right? The only thing that matters here is whether or not he committed rape."

Amerson dropped her arms and sighed. "Alright, alright. Get down off your high horse, will you? I've told you I'll see her. I don't know what will come of it. I'll see what I can do."

"Thanks, Donna."

"Don't mention it," Donna said with a huff before walking for the exit.

Chapter 27

Ocean's Eleven wardrobe. Perfectly cut for his ectomorph frame, the suit tapered from broad shoulders down to pointed black boots. When he sat himself down in the stand, he swept his hair back off his face, not that even a strand had been out of place. The women in the jury were practically swooning, the men diminished in unseen ways. I had no doubt Tirado was aware of the publicity this case was drawing and he'd be hoping to catch the eye of anyone in Hollywood on the lookout for talent. I also thought he'd be lapping up this opportunity to inject that legal thriller script of his with some first-hand experience. The way he read the oath I'd bet my house that he'd rehearsed like he would for a screen test in front of Quentin Tarantino himself. As Goodwin led Tirado through some establishment questions, I had my fears confirmed that the Tirado effect was going to be bad for my case. All I could do was sit and wait for my chance to get up and snap everyone out of his spell.

"Mr. Tirado, you were working at Blackjacks the night of the alleged attack, weren't you?"

"Yes, I was. I'm the head bartender at Blackjacks and I have a solid recollection of that night."

"Good then," said Goodwin. "And you remember seeing the defendant there?"

"Yes, I do. He asked me to open up a tab for him and I did so. He and his friends gave that credit card a pretty decent work out."

"Did you see the defendant sitting with Jenna Lewis and Polly Gould?"

"Yes, I did. They were at a table near the bar. He would come over whenever he wanted another round of Cosmopolitans."

"Cosmopolitans?"

"A Cosmopolitan is a cocktail. Vodka, cranberry juice and Cointreau served in a martini glass. It's popular with the ladies these days, but there was a time when it was considered a man's drink."

"Okay. But are they very high in alcohol?"

"They're as alcoholic as any cocktail—right about average. One will get you in the mood. Three will get you drunk. But that's exactly what they're for—to get you out of feeling sober real quick."

"Do you remember how many cocktails the defendant and his friends consumed?"

"I wasn't counting," said Tirado.

"Mr. Tirado, did you speak with the defendant?" Here we go, I thought. Goodwin couldn't wait to get to this part.

"Yes, I did. I felt I had to offer him a little advice."

"About what?"

"About women."

"Could you please elaborate for the court?"

"Sure. This guy Eddie was like a lot of guys who have plenty of money but no idea about how to behave appropriately. When he ordered a round of Cosmopolitans, he asked for 'three more leg-openers.' I said nothing then but after that he turned to one of his friends at the bar and said something about the girls he was with dying to, ah, jump in the sack with him. He said something along the lines of, 'They'll do anything for a few lines of blow.' That was when I thought I'd offer my two cents' worth. I told him his attitude was kind of lame and that if he wanted to stay single he was going about it the right way. He just looked at me, didn't reply and went off with his drinks."

"Do you think he took your advice to heart?"

Tirado shook his head. "No. It went in one ear and out the other. And look what happened."

"Objection," I called. "Speculation. The witness is testifying to something he did not see first-hand and has not been established as fact."

"Sustained," said Judge Odell. "Mr. Tirado, please limit your comments to what you saw and what you heard."

Tirado raised an apologetic hand. "Sorry, Judge. Won't happen again."

Goodwin wrapped up a few questions later and I wasted no time taking his place. Tirado looked at me and nodded a greeting, like we knew each other. I just stared straight back at him. "Mr. Tirado, how long have you been a bartender?"

"Four or five years," he said, rolling his eyes up to think. "Five."

"And how often have you had to throw a man out of Blackjacks?"

"That happens at least a couple of times a week."

"Because you've seen a lot of people get drunk there, obviously. And some of them just don't know when to stop, right?"

"That's right."

"But let me ask you this: have you ever heard other men speak disparagingly about women at your bar?"

"Yes, I have."

"I'm in no way condoning my client's language but I dare say you've heard a lot worse."

"You can say that again. I've heard stuff that would make your toes curl."

"Misogynistic remarks?"

"Yep. Real vile stuff that reflects the worst of the male side of our species. These guys come in. They've just been dumped. Rejected. Loudmouths with little petunias for egos. Saying the most heinous shit, I mean stuff."

"Did you offer those guys advice?"

"No point."

"And where would Eddie Mawson's comments sit on a scale of misogynistic vulgarity?"

"I'd put them towards the low range. One, because he was an idiot. He had the sexual wherewithal of an awkward teenager. I'm not saying what he said was nice. But if you ask me it looked like he didn't even believe it himself. He was doing what he thought men did—but he was clueless about it."

"So what you're saying is that while you're not excusing his disgusting remarks, you don't consider the defendant to be evil?"

"Couldn't have said it better myself," said Tirado, pointing at me with an impressed grin.

"No further questions," I said, and returned to Eddie Mawson's side.

"God, I'm such an asshole," Mawson said to me quietly, the shame weighing his shoulders down.

"Eddie, you acted like an asshole. Doesn't mean you're an asshole two-four-seven or will act like one forever. We all behave like assholes sometimes. Weed those lapses out of your life and you'll be a better man than most, I promise you."

"I'll take that on board," he said, looking at his fidgeting hands. I leaned over and gripped his shoulder. "Come on, Eddie. We're doing okay. We're really doing okay." But that's not what I really believed. We were on a knife's edge. We'd been hammered and we'd countered. But it was likely to get worse tomorrow. Oscar Guzman was up next. I had to make sure I had the perfect strategy to deal with whatever Guzman might throw at us. But first I needed to flesh something out with Eddie. Something was bugging me about Jenna Lewis's testimony earlier. Not for the first time, I was irritated to have to extract information out of my client. We needed to talk about Alex Herron.

Chapter 28

I wanted to get some distance from the courthouse before talking shop with Eddie. We passed through the scanners and took a crowded elevator down to the underground parking lot. As we walked to Eddie's car, I looked over my shoulder to make sure we were out of earshot of anyone else and grabbed Eddie's arm. He stopped in his tracks beside me.

"Eddie, I don't know how many times I've asked you to tell me everything. No detail is too small. Do you know why? Because it minimizes the chance of something taking me by complete surprise in the courtroom."

"What are you talking about, Brad? I've told you everything."

"Then why am I hearing in court that there's some relationship between Jenna Lewis and Alex Herron? She gets a call from him in the early hours of the morning and is on the phone for almost half an hour."

Eddie shook his head like it was going to help him come up with a good answer. "I don't know, Brad. I was as surprised as you that Alex called her."

"So they're not friends? Lovers? Exes?"

"Brad, as far as I know, they're not an item and never have been. Why don't you ask Alex?"

My eyes drilled into Eddie's. "I intend to. But I'm not happy that I'm finding this out now."

"Look, the only time I've ever seen them together was when Jenna was working at Adrenal. Their relationship was entirely professional, from what I could tell. It's not that big a surprise that he called her to check up on her, is it?"

"I don't know, Eddie. But the fact that I don't know about the phone call is kind of my point. We are now in the middle of a trial that has your future on the line. How many more things are going to crop up in court that you should have thought about telling me? We don't get two shots at this, Eddie. This is it. I'm trying to keep you out of prison and sometimes I feel like I'm fighting with one hand tied behind my back. Why is it that you don't seem to be willing or able or smart enough to think pro-actively yourself?"

"I understand, but I have put this trial above everything, including work. You do believe that, don't you?"

"Yes, I do, Eddie. But I have to tell you that I've struggled to believe in you, Eddie. I truly have. But I do believe you and I believe in your case. Yet when surprises like this come up in open court, it makes me wonder what the hell I'm fighting for."

Towards the end of my sermon, I'd raised the volume of my voice. I could see Eddie's eyes widening and his head tilting a little back as I continued. Then I noticed he was looking somewhat nervously over my right shoulder. I didn't have to wait too long to find out what had caught his attention.

"Having a lovers' quarrel, are we?" asked a voice from behind. It was Elliott Goodwin.

I turned around to see the prosecutor looking at me with smug satisfaction.

"Hell, Madison. We've only just gotten started. You should have saved yourself the stress by taking the plea. Too late now, though. Get some rest, boys. You're going to need it."

Goodwin was in his car before I could fire a shot back, but no comeback of mine was going to take that smile off his face. I wanted to bury him in court all the more.

"Brad," said Eddie. "Alex would tell me if there was something more between them. You're making too much of it."

"Let me be the judge of that."

It didn't seem to occur to Eddie that Alex had offered so little to the police and to me that he was not considered by either Goodwin or me as a useful material witness. That notion needed to be reconsidered. I needed to know what Alex knew about Jenna Lewis. There may well be something he knows that can help our case. And I needed to know why he hadn't volunteered this information already.

"Get your phone out, Eddie," I said. "Call Alex and tell him to get his ass to my office."

"I'm not sure—"

"For God's sake, Eddie. If Alex Herron isn't sitting in my office when we get back, there'll be hell to pay. I'll see you there."

I went to my car, put it in gear and hit the gas. The tires screamed as I steered the Mustang past Eddie, who held his phone to one ear and a finger in the other.

All the way to Santa Monica, the gloating voice of ADA Elliott Goodwin was ringing in my ears.

Chapter 29

Twenty-five minutes later I was sitting opposite Eddie and Alex Herron and I couldn't tell which of the two annoyed the hell out of me more. I set aside my frustration and tried to see if there was something in the Herron-Jenna Lewis relationship that we could use to our advantage.

"Alex, first up, thanks for getting here promptly."

"It sounded urgent."

"That's because it is."

"How can I help?"

"Well, you can start by telling me why you failed to mention to both me and the police that you called Jenna Lewis after she left Blackjacks."

"I just didn't think it mattered."

"It didn't matter that you called her in the middle of the night? It didn't matter that you had a twenty-three-minute conversation with her? It didn't matter that you were the only person she spoke to before she went to the cops the next day? Are you serious?"

Herron's brow contracted, lowering those arched eyebrows of his, supplanting his normal whimsical expression with one of genuine concern.

"We didn't have a conversation, Brad. Yes, I did call her. And she answered but we didn't talk."

"What?"

"There was no conversation. All I heard was her moving around and then slumping onto her bed. To me it sounded like she was home and was ready to sleep it off. I figured she had hit the answer button on her phone without meaning to. I mean, you don't have to be drunk to do that. Right?"

"No, you don't. But I still don't understand why you didn't tell me or the police about this. What you heard, or thought you heard, might tell us something about Jenna's state when she got home."

"From what I heard I couldn't tell anyone anything much. I couldn't tell whether she was drunk or tired. For the most part, all I heard was silence."

"If that's true why did the call last twenty minutes?"

Herron lowered his eyes. It was clear to me there was more to the story here.

"Alex," I continued. "If all you heard was Jenna Lewis flopping onto her bed, how come the call lasted so long?"

Herron's jaw had slackened, and his cheeks were flushed. Suddenly, he was the image of a guilty schoolboy. He said nothing.

"Alex?"

"It's embarrassing."

"What's embarrassing?"

"Why I stayed on the line."

"Why did you stay on the line, Alex?"

Herron sucked in and released a deep breath. "To hear her breathing."

Eddie was looking at Herron like he was speaking in tongues.

"You're saying you had a crush on Jenna Lewis?" I asked.

Herron nodded. "That's why I never mentioned the call to you or the cops. It was too embarrassing."

Eddie shook his head, clearly gob-smacked at what he was hearing. Herron turned to Eddie and shrugged. "I sure wasn't the only one who was attracted to her."

"Yeah, I'm getting the picture," I said, thinking how pretty Jenna Lewis had driven all those pent-up boys at Adrenal wild, not least the two clowns in front of me. "Okay, Alex, here's what we're going to do. I'm going to list you as a witness for the defense."

"What? No."

Herron looked consumed by fear.

"Yes. You're going to tell the court about that phone call."

"No, Mr. Madison. It's too embarrassing. Everyone will think I'm some kind of pervert."

I shook my head. "Relax, Alex. You don't need to tell the court that you were literally hanging on Jenna's every breath. Seems to me, you stayed on the line to make sure she was okay. Which is what you did, right?"

"Yeah, I guess," said Herron uncertainly, his apprehension far from abated.

"Alex, your friend Eddie here is fighting for his life. He needs help and you can help him. We need to focus on what you'll be able to tell the court about what you heard. And that's all you'll have to talk about."

"But I didn't hear anything."

"That's my point."

Herron shook his head. "I don't get it."

"Did you hear Jenna Lewis crying?"

"No."

"From what you heard, was there any sign that she was distraught?"

"I don't know."

"Okay. That's all we need to hear."

"But if I'm a witness, I'm going to get cross-examined. It's going to come out that I acted like a creep."

"No, it's not. That's not going to happen. And besides, I'm not going to just throw you to the wolves. You and I are going to spend some time together. We'll go through what you're going to say and we'll practice all the kinds of questions Elliott Goodwin will throw at you. Trust me, by the time we're done, you'll be more than able to answer him with your head held high."

"Who's Elliott Goodwin?" Herron asked.

Of course, Herron hadn't attended the trial. "He's the prosecutor. So, Alex. You'll do it? It'd be great for Eddie's case. I wouldn't ask you otherwise."

Herron looked sideways at his boss and tapped him lightly on the shoulder.

"Of course," he nodded. "I'll do it."

Chapter 30

The next morning, I laid eyes on the elusive Oscar Guzman at last. I didn't get much of a look at him until now as he disappeared up the back alley after I'd banged on his door. He did a quick scan of the courtroom and when his eyes fell on me I noticed a flicker of recognition. Yes, I was that guy you spotted through your peephole. I nodded at him. In a way, I was glad he'd fled because, no matter what Elliott Goodwin had warned him about me in trial prep, he didn't know what was about to hit him. I'd memorized his witness statement practically word for word so I was ready to seize on any discrepancy. Until then, I was going to enjoy observing Oscar Guzman and getting a feel for any character flaws I could exploit.

He'd run from me once. Now there was no escape. I had him right where I wanted him.

He'd arrived in a kind of flourish, slamming into the gate so that it flung wildly and noisily open. He took long strides and swung his arms as he approached the stand. He looked out of place, like he was setting off on a boardwalk jaunt rather than crossing a few feet of courtroom floor. He wore a gray polyester suit that was shiny and a cerise polyester shirt that was even shinier. The suit looked like it was having a hard time staying on his skinny frame. The fit was unconvincing—I couldn't tell if it was baggy by design or just too big. Guzman's hair was cropped short, as was the thin strip of hair above his upper lip. His mouth had a slight grin, giving the impression that he found everything he beheld pleasing to the eye. Somehow, I didn't think Guzman was quite that upbeat and untroubled.

There was confidence in his bearing. It seemed Oscar Guzman had it all figured out, and I for one couldn't wait to see how true that was.

As for ADA Goodwin, there was a distinct swag to his demeanor. He was clearly looking forward to seeing the impact his key eyewitness would have on the jury. He cleared his throat before speaking in a voice that was just a bit too loud at first and had to be dimmed in the space of a sentence.

"Mr. Guzman, you were working at Blackjacks the night of the alleged assault, weren't you?"

"Yes, I'm what they call a barback. I go around the bar, pick up empty glasses, wipe down tables—keep the place picked up and clean. That's my job."

"And part of that job means that you clean the karaoke booths too, right?"

"That's right. There are four karaoke booths in Blackjacks and when I do my rounds I check each one."

"Good. Mr. Guzman, can you please tell us what happened that night when you went to check on the booths."

"Well, the first one was empty and there was nothing to clean up and then I went to the next one. The door was shut so I thought someone was in there but you can never be sure. So I checked. I opened the door. And when I opened the door, I saw a man kissing a woman and, you know, feeling her body."

"I'm afraid I'm going to have to ask you to be specific, Mr. Gonzalez. What was he doing with his hands?"

"He had a hand up her dress."

"What was the young woman doing?"

"She didn't look like she was as, you know, into it as he was. She was just kind of dazed. Floppy. Out of it."

"Out of it. Do you mean drunk?"

"Yes. Very drunk."

"And what did you do?"

"I shut the door quietly and went on with my job."

The gallery murmured its disapproval. Guzman bowed his head, knowing that his words reflected poorly on himself.

"Mr. Guzman—"

"Look, I see that kind of thing just about every night. People come to the bar, they get drunk and they make out in the booths. That's what they do at Blackjacks."

"I understand, Mr. Guzman. If Jenna Lewis was being assaulted, why wasn't she screaming, fighting, or calling for help?"

"That's right. I only found out later she had been assaulted."

"Objection," I called out so loud Guzman almost jumped out of his seat. "The allegation that the defendant sexually assaulted Jenna Lewis has not yet been proved. Far from it."

"Sustained," said Judge Odell. Please strike that last comment by the witness. "Mr. Goodwin, please continue."

"Thank you, Your Honor," said Goodwin. "Mr. Guzman, now that you know Jenna Lewis has alleged that the defendant raped her. Does that accord with what you saw?"

"Does it what, sorry?"

"Jenna Lewis says the defendant raped her. Is that what you saw? A man putting his hand between her legs without consent?"

Guzman nodded. "Yes. She was unable to do anything to stop him. Maybe I should have asked if she was okay. But I felt like I shouldn't be in the room with them. I felt like a peeping Tom. I'm so sorry I did nothing to help her."

"No further questions, Your Honor."

With that Goodwin returned to his seat. I didn't get up right away. I made a few notes and then got to my feet. I kept my eyes on Guzman as I stepped up to the lectern.

"Hello, Mr. Guzman," I said. "Nice to see you again." In my peripheral vision I noticed Goodwin lift his head quickly to bore his eyes into Guzman. I took it that Guzman neglected to tell Goodwin about my surprise visit. Guzman lifted his chin and nodded.

"Now can I just start by asking how long were you working at Blackjacks?"

"About five years."

"Did you work other jobs?"

"No. Just Blackjacks."

"How many shifts a week?"

"Six."

"Six days a week for five years. But you would have had a few breaks. You know, some time off, right?"

Guzman shook his head. "No time off. Vacations are for wimps," he said, cracking a smile. Unfortunately, he didn't win many people in the courtroom over with his humor. Becoming self-conscious, he turned to the jury. Obviously, something that Goodwin must have told him hadn't sunk in. What the jury thinks about you matters. Big time. "That was a joke. I never took a break."

"Because earning money was more important, right?"

"Objection," Goodwin called. "What's the relevance here to the crime that we are dealing with?"

I turned to Judge Odell after a half glance at Goodwin over my shoulder. "Your Honor, establishment questions are not the sole privilege of the prosecution. I thought what we're doing here was obvious."

Judge Odell nodded. "Objection overruled," he said with a glare at Goodwin. "Please answer the question, Mr. Guzman."

"What was the question again?"

"I asked if the reason you never took a break from work was because you needed the money."

"That's right. I did okay with tips and I didn't want to give up my shifts."

"I understand," I said. "That makes perfect sense. So am I right in saying you no longer work at Blackjacks?"

"Yes, that's right. I got another job."

"What kind of job?"

"Objection," cried Goodwin again. "Relevance. Is the defense going to be asking about whether the witness is happy at his new job? Whether he's made friends there? We are way off track now, Your Honor."

"The relevance of this question, which I'd argue is little more than an establishment question anyway, will become clear very soon, Your Honor," I said.

"Overruled," said Judge Odell. "Please answer the question, Mr. Guzman."

"I got a construction job," said Guzman.

I nodded me head. "I see. Now, Mr. Guzman, when did you stop working at Blackjacks?"

"I'm not sure."

I wasn't about to let Goodwin cut in with another objection, so I went for the salient point I wanted to come out. I picked a document up off the lectern and raised it. "The employment records at Blackjacks state that your last shift was the night of the alleged assault. Why did you leave so suddenly?"

Guzman's eyes opened a little wider, as if to better help him see what was coming. That is, he looked very much like he'd have loved prior notice of my questions and a good few hours to process his responses to them. In other words, I was sure I was looking at a guy whose story was complete BS. I just had to let the jury see what I saw clear as day.

"I was upset by what happened. You know the cops interviewing me. The thought that I'd done nothing to help that girl. I felt bad. I didn't want to show my face there anymore."

"Are you saying you didn't go back because you were ashamed?"

"Yes, that's right."

"You left and never went back, is that right?"

"Yes."

"What did you do for money?"

"Like I said, I got another job. In construction, where I don't have to be dealing with drunk people."

"Good for you. Could you tell us the name of the company you're working for now?"

"I'm just working for a friend. He gave me a job."

"A friend? Really? And what's this friend's name?"

"Objection," called Goodwin. "Relevance."

VEIL OF JUSTICE

"What's it to you?" said Guzman indignantly. "Are you calling me a liar?"

"Overruled," said Judge Odell. "Mr. Guzman, it's the defense attorney's job to ask you questions. And they don't have to be questions that you like but you must answer them with civility."

"Pedro Sanchez," Guzman said to me. "Look him up."

"Thank you, Mr. Guzman. "One last question. At the bar that night, did you speak to anyone after you witnessed the incident?"

"No. Just the police."

"Were you aware at all that Jenna Lewis was in tears?"

"No."

"You didn't talk to anyone at the bar, not even Matt Tirado, the bartender?"

"No. I just did my job. I know how to do my job. He doesn't need to tell me."

"Fair enough. So you didn't speak to any staff after the incident?"

"No."

"Did you speak to any of the customers after the incident?"

"No."

"So you just clocked off and went home after your shift ended, right?"

"That's right."

"Did you go back to clean the booth where you saw the defendant and Jenna Lewis?"

"Yes."

"What did you find there?"

Guzman was frowning at me, his jaw set tight. "I found a leather jacket."

221

"This was the defendant's jacket, wasn't it?"

"I don't know."

"It was a man's jacket, right?"

"Yes."

"And the last time you looked, there was only one man in the booth, right?"

"Yes."

"So it most likely was the defendant's jacket, wasn't it?"

"Another guy could have been in there before."

"But you would have seen it when you did your job, which was to check and clean the booths after they'd been used, right?"

"Yes. I guess it probably was the defendant's."

"There's no mystery here, Mr. Guzman. You took it to the bar and the defendant claimed it when he left. But in doing that, you said nothing to the bartender, right?"

"What?"

"You told the court you didn't say another word to anyone else in the bar after the incident you witnessed. I asked you specifically."

"I didn't."

"So you didn't say to Mr. Tirado, 'Hey, I found this in booth number one, I think it belongs to that guy'?"

Guzman shrugged. "I probably did. What does it matter?"

"It matters a lot, Mr. Guzman. Being evasive apparently for no good reason suggests you've got something to hide."

"Objection," Goodwin cried. "Not only is Mr. Madison testifying, but he's also badgering the witness."

"Sustained," said Judge Odell while glaring at me. "On both counts. Watch yourself, counselor."

I raised my hands. "My apologies, Your Honor. I'm done with Mr. Guzman."

Yes, Judge Odell had my comment struck from the record but I'd made sure I'd called out Guzman to make a point that I hoped the jury absolutely concurred with—that the key witness for the prosecution was full of shit.

Chapter 31

The slab of transcripts was inches thick and it hit my desk with a loud thump. Tomorrow, Goodwin was putting a psychologist on the stand and I needed to do a few hours of prep. Before I got into that, though, there was the literal pile of paperwork in front of me. I called out to Megan, who I'd asked to stay late with me, and asked for coffee. The transcripts were the testimonies of Matt Tirado and Oscar Guzman. I picked up a yellow highlighter and got started.

I was grateful that Donna Amerson had taken an active interest in Eddie Mawson's case, and I was going to do everything in my power to make sure she stayed informed. She was understandably too busy to attend every day of the trial, so I was going to deliver it to her. To make things a little easier for her, I highlighted every section that if it didn't actually create doubt then it certainly posed a serious question.

Megan came in with a cup of coffee and placed it in front of me.

"I can do that if you like," she said. "You'll be here all night."

"Thank you, Megan. I know you can but I'd actually prefer to do it myself. Going over these transcripts might prompt me to think of a new lead or a fresh idea. I just don't feel like I've got an edge in this trial. As much as I hate to say it, I think Goodwin's got the upper hand."

"It's not over yet, Brad. Not by a long shot, and I'm sure you'll come up with something. You always do."

"I wish I knew what that something was now."

"I'll leave you to it. Let me know if you need anything."

"How about pizza in about an hour?"

"You got it. I'll have it here at seven."

"Great. If you want to go out and stretch your legs or do some shopping, by all means go for it."

"I think I might do that. See you in an hour."

"With pizza?"

"With pizza."

"Reggio's?"

"Where else?"

I didn't have to tell Megan what I wanted. She knew I was hooked on Reggio's wood-fired pepperoni pizza. It was a new place that had opened up a few months ago. I salivated just thinking about it.

"Oh, wait up," I said, getting to my feet and digging my wallet out of my back pocket. "Take this." I handed her my Visa card. "Get whatever you want."

Megan nodded with a smile, spun around and headed for the elevator.

Left alone, I began tackling the transcripts. Page after page, I grew more certain that Eddie Mawson was innocent. What I didn't know was why Jenna Lewis would put herself through this horrible experience. The testimony of Matt Tirado did portray Eddie Mawson as being insecure and sexually clueless. And yes, what Tirado overheard Eddie saying to his friend at the bar made him out to be a sexist jerk. If Eddie Mawson came out of this trial a free man, I was going to find him some kind of finishing school that could help him grow into a better person. Then again, if this trial didn't make him see the light nothing would. Eddie didn't have to tell me he craved genuine affection and intimacy. The guy reeked of loneliness. Hopefully, he'd begun to realize that being a douche would never help him get what he wanted, that it would only ensure he never did.

As I went through Oscar Guzman's testimony line by line, I kept thinking that surely this would raise alarm bells for Donna. On the stand, he hardly deviated from the statements he had given the police. He sounded rehearsed, scripted even. Now that can happen to any witness, so it could mean nothing. But my hunch was that it damn-well meant something. The guy was lying. But my conviction that he was lying didn't matter. I had no proof. I had no motivation to point to that would explain his lies. I had no idea why he ran away from me that day other than the fact that he didn't want to face me until he absolutely had to. And in my mind, that's what his court appearance was—a task he'd been assigned. A task that he must either have been paid to do or compelled to do. So someone, somewhere, had something on Oscar Guzman. Of that I was certain.

"Dinner is served."

Megan's voice took me by surprise. I was so deep in thought that I didn't hear her come in. I looked up and sighed, leaned back and placed my hands behind my head. "Smells so good," I said, as Megan placed the box on my desk. "What did you get?"

Megan shook her head. "Nothing. I'm good. I'll eat at home."

I opened the box. "Megan, come on. Here, grab some."

Megan smiled and relented, leaning forward to pick up a slice. She took a bite as she headed back to her desk. With a slice in one hand and the highlighter in the other, I got back to the transcripts.

Two hours later, I was done and I called Megan back in. I gathered up the pile and handed it over. Dozens of colored pieces of paper were sticking out from the edges. I'd made notes on each one, giving Donna a quick and easy reference. My hope was that if she had sufficient doubt then she might take a more active role. She'd told me herself that a false accusation would be a huge setback for the genuine cases she was struggling to bring to light.

Megan's arm sank with the weight of the papers. "It's probably better I run these over myself," she said.

"No, Megan. Get a courier. It'll be there in an hour. Donna's at home expecting the delivery and she wanted it by ten. We'll easily beat that time. So just package it up, call the courier and then you can go."

Megan walked out and I heard her pick up the phone and make the call. The courier guy arrived within fifteen minutes. After he left, Megan came back into my office. Well, she stood in the doorway saying nothing until I sensed she was there.

"What is it, Megan?" I asked. "Watching me work must be just about the most boring brand of entertainment."

"I was just thinking," Megan said in a way that suggested I needed to invite her to complete what she was saying. I knew that tone of voice. She was thinking of giving me some advice, woman to man.

"What were you just thinking?" I said, putting my pen down and resting my forearms on the desk.

"You're not going to like me saying it, but—"

"Come on, Megan. Out with it. As far as I'm concerned, you could never say anything I didn't need to hear."

Megan stepped forward and sat down. "I'll just come out and say it. What's going on with you and Abby? I don't get it. You shouldn't give up on her."

I laughed. This was not the only time Megan had asked about Abby and offered me some well-meaning advice. But while I'd intimated to Megan that Abby and I had had a falling out, I'd spared her the details.

I hadn't spoken with Abby since I'd delivered the news that one of her charity projects was being backed by a drug lord. I'll never forget the expression on her face as I told her how I'd come to know Cobus Lombard and how he was the point man for Darius Tucker. It was crystal clear that Lombard wouldn't have come within ten feet of Abby's fundraiser if not for me. The fact his goons had tailed Jack and I in San Fran made me think they'd been watching me for some time before and since. I wasn't about to deny anything to Abby. I felt sordid and stupid. I'd led them to Abby. I'd practically sent Tucker a written invitation.

Abby had turned positively ill when I advised her that there was absolutely nothing she could nor should do about it. If she contrived a way to exclude Tucker, it would fail. He'd see through it and she only risked pissing him off. Even though it was a trifling investment for him, he'd never allow himself to be backed out of a deal. Again, I insisted that Abby do nothing.

"What? Just continue on as though I haven't placed Camilla's project in the hands of a drug dealer?"

"You don't have a choice. There's nothing you can do about it. I'm sorry."

"Get out of my sight," she said, tears of disbelief and rage welling up in her eyes.

I didn't need to be told twice. I walked away vowing to approach Tucker myself.

On that front, I'd made no ground whatsoever. I'd called Cobus Lombard requesting a meeting with Tucker. He flatly rejected my request and made it plain that Tucker had no interest or time for me whatsoever unless I was stupid enough to get in his way.

I told Megan to forget it. I wouldn't be seeing Abby again.

What I didn't tell Megan was that I'd vowed to try and make things right. I had to find a way to get Tucker to let go. Exactly how I was going to do that, I had no idea. And if I did find a way, it was never going to get me back on Abby's good side. It would at least make living with myself a bit easier, if not exactly a breeze.

Megan listened with a slack jaw.

"Talk about screwing the pooch," she said when I'd finished. "That's a hell of a self-sabotage act, Brad. Almost Shakespearean."

"Thanks, Megan. I think you can see now that the good ship Abby has not so much sailed as rocketed off into the sunset. She's a disappearing speck on the horizon with her foot on the afterburners."

On that note, Megan went home, knowing full well there was no way she could put a positive spin on what she'd been told. After she'd gone, I poured myself a scotch and began to prepare for the following day's witness.

Just after midnight, when I was about to leave for home, I got an email from Donna Amerson.

"Thanks for the homework," she wrote. "I'm not prepared to say anything other than I consider this to be very much an open case. I want to speak with Jenna. I'll try to get some time with her soon. I'll need to tread very carefully and there's no guarantee she'll be willing to see me."

I was heartened to know that Donna was not ruling anything out about Jenna Lewis's case, but that was not the entirety of Amerson's message.

"Just so you know, Anna Shand is not known for her impartiality."

Dr. Anna Shand was the witness I was preparing for. Elliott Goodwin was putting her on the stand in the morning. From my research I'd already formed an impression of what to expect from her expert testimony. But what Donna wrote next really took me by surprise.

"Anna and Goodwin are pretty tight. She did the victim assessment report for Doris Goodwin, Elliott's mother."

Chapter 32

I was grateful to live so close to my office because Donna Amerson's email prompted me to work almost through the night. Although I'd done my research on Dr. Anna Shand, the fact that she'd conducted the evaluation of Elliott Goodwin's mother some twenty years earlier had somehow eluded me. At the time of Doris Goodwin's assault, Dr. Shand was beginning to make a name for herself in the field of rape trauma. I knew from previous research that she'd almost become a fixture of Los Angeles rape trials, where her evaluations and expert opinion had helped the State secure more than a dozen convictions. One of those cases involved Doris Goodwin. I found it particularly interesting that Donna would point out her track record. By the time I left the office I had pages of notes on Goodwin's next witness.

I'd taken a nap in my chair before leaving just as the sun was coming up. I went home, showered and shaved, did fifty push-ups and fifty sit-ups, put on a clean shirt and freshly dry-cleaned suit and made coffee. I resisted the temptation to put my head down, or to even close my eyes for long. I had to break my body out of its normal sleep pattern. I stayed on my feet and kept moving, pacing around my apartment, looking over my notes and watching the morning news.

It seemed to take an eternity for eight o'clock to come around but by then I had the car started and was off to court. I wouldn't say I was feeling refreshed but I was eager to get started.

Forensic psychologist Dr. Anna Shand had a composed, dignified bearing. That, combined with a long list of academic qualifications and accomplishments, was enough to cement in the jury's mind that she was someone not only to be listened to but trusted. Purely from a biased professional standpoint, I didn't care much for the woman. She was supremely well positioned to drive nails into my case and I didn't care if she was Mother Teresa herself, as a witness for the prosecution, I had to find a way to undercut her presumed virtue. For now, though, ADA Elliott Goodwin had the floor, and he intended to milk it for all it was worth.

The good doctor was sixty-five if she was a day but she kept her shoulder-length hair dyed platinum blond. Circular framed glasses gave her an intellectual look and her faint smile showed, perhaps, a slight condescension, as though we should be grateful to have her in our presence. Maybe I was reading too much into it with my own prejudices. Okay I was, because while I saw a rather smug looking academic convinced of the worth of her every word, the jury saw someone successful, clever, a high-achiever and someone with sass and smarts who was as impartial as Mother Nature herself.

First impressions. Perhaps nowhere more than in a courtroom do they count for more.

His ode to Dr. Shand's brilliance completed, Goodwin moved on from establishment questions to the case at hand.

"Dr. Shand, could you please explain the role of a forensic psychologist in a case such as this?"

"Certainly," Dr. Shand replied, tilting her head to the side, just enough for her hair to swing away from her face ever so slightly. The minor movement, along with the squint of her eyes, told the court that her worthy mind was sharply engaged on the matter. "The role of the forensic psychologist in a sexual assault case, put simply, is to examine all the forensic evidence obtained by the authorities and to assess the survivor."

"So you looked at all the evidence and you spent a long time interviewing Jenna Lewis?"

"Yes, I did. I spent four hours with her, which was enough time for me to form an expert opinion on her condition."

"Before we get to that expert opinion, could you tell the jury about the other forensic evidence you examined?"

"Yes, of course. There were traces of the defendant's DNA on Jenna's body. There were clear signs of injury to her vagina and slight bruising of her breasts."

"I see."

"And the blood test results indicated she had GHB in her system. There was also a not insignificant level of alcohol in her blood, not to mention cocaine, but since the samples were taken the following day, they were obviously reduced."

"Was forensics able to gauge how much alcohol Jenna Lewis had in her system at the time of the alleged attack?"

"Yes. And Jenna herself, as well as others, stated she'd had enough alcohol to get very drunk. The stimulation she got from the cocaine she took would have countered her drunkenness somewhat. Not that it affected her blood-alcohol level. But she reported feeling very drunk, very quickly. At the time of the alleged assault, she was almost paralytic."

"By that you mean blind drunk? So drunk she could barely stand?"

"This is not something we can describe scientifically but yes—blind drunk is a fair illustration of her degree of inebriation. But it is her contention, and mine, that her physically compromised state was brought upon by the GHB in her system."

"Dr. Shand, would you please take a moment to tell the jury what GHB is and what its effects are?"

Before Dr. Shand could open her mouth to reply, I was on my feet.

"Objection. The witness is a psychologist. She is not a doctor of pharmacology nor a doctor of biomedicine. The court should not merely assume that the effect of drugs on the human body is in her professional wheelhouse."

Dr. Shand looked at me with mild offense. She was about to answer for herself when she was beaten to the punch by an even more offended Elliott Goodwin.

"Your Honor, the witness is an expert in the field of sexual assault. She is more than qualified to provide a highly informed opinion of how alcohol and drugs affected a victim. The defense is simply being obstructive."

Judge Odell's eyes had been locked on me from the moment I'd objected, and they hadn't left since. "I agree. Overruled. You may answer the question."

"Thank you," Dr. Shand said to Judge Odell before returning her attention to Goodwin. "Now, the drug gamma hydroxybutyrate is better known as GHB. It serves to depress or sedate the central nervous system. It is an odorless and colorless liquid, and as such it's the most common date-rape drug. I couldn't count the number of rape victims I've seen who have had their drinks spiked with GHB."

"So Jenna Lewis attributes her extremely intoxicated state to this drug as opposed to alcohol?"

"Yes."

"And she did not take it voluntarily."

"She maintains that her drink was spiked, and I believe her."

"Dr. Shand, you produced a detailed report on this case. Could you please outline your findings?"

"Certainly. Over the course of several interviews I was able to assess Jenna's mental and behavioral reactions to her ordeal. The effects took the form of flashbacks, during which Jenna relived the horror of the moment, trying to escape her attacker but being unable to. As she told me, it was like one of those dreams we are all familiar with where you want to run for your life but your body won't move, but worse. During these flashbacks, it's hard for the victim to distinguish the episode from reality."

"So Jenna Lewis experienced horrific flashbacks?"

"Yes. On three occasions at least."

With further questioning, Dr. Shand testified that Lewis displayed or reported clear signs of rape trauma. She said she'd evaluated hundreds of victims over her career and what she observed and heard from Jenna Lewis left her with no doubt that her subject was a bona fide case of rape. With such a resounding summary of his case, Elliott Goodwin concluded his direct examination.

When Judge Odell invited me to cross-examine the witness, I made my way over to the lectern and greeted Dr. Shand. I wasted no time getting started.

"Dr. Shand, I just want to be clear. You testified that Jenna Lewis had flashbacks."

"No, I—"

"I'm afraid you did. You were very clear. Mr. Goodwin asked of you, 'So Jenna Lewis experienced horrific flashbacks?' and you replied, 'Yes.' Did you witness Ms. Lewis having a flashback at any time?"

"No. She reported to me that she experienced flashbacks."

"So you are testifying that Jenna Lewis had flashbacks based on second-hand information. Isn't that correct?"

"Yes. It was certainly not my intention to confuse the jury."

"I'm sure it wasn't but, to play devil's advocate, Jenna Lewis could have told you anything, isn't that right?"

"I can't deny that that's a possibility. But I think you're making too much of this aspect of her suffering. My evaluation of her trauma was built on more than her telling me she had flashbacks."

"So we have a young woman who was drunk and taking drugs being taken advantage of, isn't that right?"

"Yes."

"Yet there were no signs of injury on my client when he joined his friends at the bar after the alleged attack. Jenna Lewis didn't leave a mark on him. And she didn't make a sound trying to get him off her. How do you explain that?"

"Mr. Madison, I don't mean to be rude but you are peddling common misconceptions about rape. You think that the victim must have done this or said that. She must have scratched and bitten her attacker. She must have screamed at the top of her lungs in a desperate attempt to get help. But these are what I call rape myths. This is not, in the vast majority of cases, what victims do."

"What do they do then?"

"They kick, mostly. But as you know, the victim was heavily sedated by the GHB in her system."

"I see. And do you know the exact time Jenna Lewis ingested the GHB?"

"No. Of course not but—"

"No one knows, Dr. Shand. No one can say with utmost certainty that the drug was even ingested at the bar. Isn't that right?"

"I get your point."

"Yet you took her word for it with no scrutiny at all."

"I'm there to evaluate the impact of a traumatic event. I'm not a crime-scene detective."

"But you are here to tell the jury that Jenna Lewis isn't lying about being sexually assaulted, isn't that right?"

"I'm here to present my findings and my conclusion was that she was raped. Of that I have little doubt whatsoever."

"I suppose you were just as certain that Jasmine Tan was telling the truth, weren't you?"

"Who?"

"Jasmine Tan. Eleven years ago, you testified that she was a genuine rape victim and yet three years ago, the man you helped convict was released from prison. And he was released from prison because Jasmine Tan was found to have falsely accused him of raping her."

"Ah, yes. That was unfortunate."

"Unfortunate? An innocent man spending eight years of his life in prison is unfortunate, is it?"

"I think—"

"What is that, Dr. Shand? Is it just the collateral damage of your expert testimony?"

"No. That's not how I look at it."

"Okay, we'll have to agree to disagree on that point. But tell me this: can you look the jury in the eye and tell them there is no way on this God-given earth that Jenna Lewis could be lying about being raped?"

"I made an evaluation based on decades of experience and it is my sincere belief, my expert conviction, that Jenna Lewis did not fake her rape trauma."

"There's no way?"

Dr. Shand shook her head.

"No."

"We set a very high bar in court about pronouncing guilt, Dr. Shand, as I'm sure you know. So you feel the jury should entertain not even a bit of doubt? You're telling them, I swear to you that Jenna Lewis is telling the truth?"

"I'm here to offer my expert opinion and my expert opinion is that Jenna wasn't lying. I'm not sure how else to say it."

"You're certain she's telling the truth, are you?"

"Yes. I'm certain she's telling the truth."

"That's exactly what you said about Jasmine Tan. Pretty much word for word. And look how that turned out."

There was a moment's pause as Dr. Shand went to answer but held her tongue.

"Nothing further, Your Honor."

Chapter 33

Goodwin followed up Dr. Shand with a couple more expert witnesses. I challenged them every way I could. I exposed the flaws in their methods and their backgrounds. In short, by discrediting them, I conducted a harm reduction campaign for the sake of my client. By day's end, I'd tested Judge Odell's patience, and I could see the jury had grown weary. I wasn't sure to what extent me and my objections were to blame but they looked genuinely fatigued. The day-in, day-out grind of the trial was getting to them. We were about a week in, right about the time that jury members start to pine for their old familiar routines free from the obligations of the court. This meant the stakes between Elliott Goodwin and me only rose higher. If I didn't come out with a decisive blow, I felt sure the jury was inclined to convict Eddie.

Every spare minute of the day, I had my mind on the case, looking over the evidence again and again hoping I would see something in a new light, hoping a new lead would appear. But I had no fresh leads, no new angles, no new witnesses to throw at the case.

Back in my office the effects of having next to no sleep the night before began to take hold. As I sat in my chair I had the compelling urge just to close my eyes and drift off. I shook my head to rid myself of that temptation and leaned forward once more over my desk. In front of me were all the documents I had relating to the next witness for the State. Marty Cosgrove.

For better or worse, I envisioned Marty being on the stand as my chance to bring in the bigger picture I wanted the jury to see. I needed him to discuss how he went about his business. I knew I was not going to get away with just grilling him about how he conducted business. Goodwin would object and Judge Odell would sustain. But if Goodwin fished around how Marty came to know Eddie then this would open the subject up to me to explore. I was sure Goodwin knew little about Beacon Capital and how they had preyed on up-and-coming tech companies. He'd just want to establish the fundamentals of their relationship before proceeding to use Marty to throw shade on my client.

My thoughts didn't just circle around trial strategy. The prospect of facing Marty triggered some powerful emotions. I still suspected he'd played a hand in Claire's accident. No, I couldn't prove it, but no one else was going to, least of all the cops. They went off on the wrong track to begin with, never deviated, and had now lost interest. Everyone, Claire included, was prepared to accept that it was a hit and run that would remain unsolved. Claire's recovery was the end of it. Jack and I were the only people convinced that the car accident was an act of foul play. There was no reason anyone would want to kill Claire. But Marty was hitting Claire up for money before the crash, and through Eddie's case I'd come to regard him as a man who'd sell his mother if it meant winning a deal. If it was an attempt on Claire's life, who else but Marty Cosgrove had the motive, the means and the character to carry it out?

I had to put these thoughts aside. If I carried them into the courtroom, the temptation to apply the blowtorch to Marty Cosgrove could easily result in me overcooking things. I had to stay calm and focused to achieve my goal, which was to have Marty make it clear that Eddie was a victim of a ruthless business world. That he had been preyed upon by men who wanted to take what he had grown, and who wanted to get it as cheaply as possible by disgracing him publicly. Through him I could show that there had been a precedent, an almost exact replica of events in San Francisco involving Beacon and its rival company Crestway. Sure, Marty could help the jury see all of these things. But he wasn't going to do so willingly.

All I needed was for Elliott Goodwin to give me an in. If he delved into the business relationship between Eddie and Marty then it was on. He couldn't object to me exploring that in cross.

I managed to get a couple of hours' sleep before rising at dawn and getting more prep work done at home.

"You look tired," said Eddie when I saw him in court. He didn't look full of pep himself. He gave me a half smile and turned to face the bench. I noticed his hands were shaking and I put a hand on his shoulder. Although my job gave me a front-row view of trials, I could still only imagine the grave and dreadful uncertainty of having your fate in the hands of strangers. Not only that, but to have someone stand up and try their best to convince a jury that you are evil and should be sent to prison.

"Hang in there, Eddie," I said. "Just a couple more prosecution witnesses and then we get to call ours. The trial is going well and I've got plenty more doubt to seed in the jury's mind."

Eddie watched the jury file in. "They don't like me," he said. "They think I'm guilty. I know they do."

I leaned over to him. "That's not the vibe I'm getting, Eddie. Not at all. Don't presume that they want to put you away. They know the responsibility they have and they will use their good conscience. All they need is doubt. I've given them some already and I've got plenty more in store. Trust me."

Those last two words were out before I knew I'd said them. Normally, I wouldn't express confidence in winning. To get ahead of yourself only courted disaster. Every lawyer knows that trials are a gamble. Uncertainty is their core trait. Beyond expense, the main reason trials were avoided was because neither side knew which way the jury would go.

Trust me. I leaned back in my chair and hoped I wouldn't come to regret those words.

When Goodwin called Marty to the stand I turned around. The first surprise was how full the gallery was. I hadn't noticed it build behind me as I tried to lift Eddie's spirits. The second surprise was the sight of Claire. She was seated next to Marty and they kissed before he stood up and made his way through the gate. For a second, I caught Claire's eye. I wouldn't say her face was filled with contempt. More like staunch reserve. She looked at me like she didn't know me and didn't want to. I felt a pang of guilt. It was a reflex action. Then I reminded myself that it wasn't me who put Marty on the stand. It was Goodwin. Maybe Claire sensed I was relishing the opportunity to take

Marty down publicly. And as much as I hate to admit it, she was right, as usual.

Marty took the oath and sat with confident expectation, waiting for Goodwin to begin. The prosecutor got the background questions underway and quickly moved into how Marty and Eddie had become acquainted. Marty gave some detail about his job and Beacon. Goodwin, for the benefit of the jury, asked him to explain the basics of venture capitalism and how he'd proposed to help Adrenal grow.

I could have thanked him out loud.

"Would you say a great deal of trust is needed between the two parties in a business deal like this?" asked Goodwin.

"Absolutely. It's crucial. We were putting a lot of money on the table. We analyzed the business, of course, but we need to know we can work closely and productively with a prospective partner. When a company like ours gets involved, the company we've decided to partner with hits a higher gear real fast. We're like jet fuel to the process. Eddie had to expand his company to get his next game to market in the quickest possible timeframe. Without us it would take him three-to-five years. Our involvement cuts that down to twelve months, tops."

"Were you confident that you'd be partnering with the defendant?"

"Objection," I called. "Relevance."

Goodwin turned to Judge Odell and held out his hands in a preacher-like manner. "Your Honor, I'm establishing the relationship between the witness and the defendant."

"I thought we'd covered that in the previous forty minutes," I said. "I'd suggest we should be focusing on what light the witness can shed on the events we're here to consider."

"Your Honor—"

Judge Odell cut Goodwin off while looking dead at me. "Overruled."

I sat back down and Marty took his cue to continue. "I was more than confident that we'd be partners. He gave me his word."

"It was a done deal?"

"Yes. We had the paperwork ready and all the issues ironed out. The only thing missing was the sign-off. It was a done deal. Until suddenly it wasn't."

"What do you mean?"

"The defendant went with another investor. It was a total blindside. So much for his word."

Goodwin shook his head and paused while Marty's words lingered in the jury's mind.

"So I take it the deal was still on the table on the night of the alleged rape?"

"Yes, it was. Eddie had told me they were out celebrating and I thought I'd go and have a drink with my future partner."

"And did you?"

"No. I mean, I went to Blackjacks and said hello to Eddie but he was very drunk and rather messed up, so I didn't stay long. I just chatted with a couple of other people and then left."

"How do you know he was very drunk?"

"As I was coming in, he came out of the karaoke booth. He was staggering as he made his way back to the bar."

"Did you speak with the defendant?"

"Only briefly."

"What did he say to you?"

Marty paused. "He said to me, 'I hope you get your dick sucked by some bitch tonight because I'm not.'"

Goodwin again let Marty's words hang out there, no doubt enjoying the ripple of muttering behind him in the gallery.

"Could we just unpack that a little?" asked Goodwin, turning to the jury. "We've already established that the defendant waited in the karaoke booth alone after Jenna Lewis had left, after allegedly being raped by the defendant. Then you arrive and he effectively complains that he didn't get, um, his dick sucked?"

"That's right."

"Mr. Cosgrove, did you see Jenna leave the karaoke booth?"

"No. No, I didn't see her inside the bar at all."

When Marty said these words, he turned his eyes to me. This struck me as odd only because it was the first time he'd looked in the direction of the defense table. But if I wasn't mistaken, he seemed to be wondering if I was paying close attention to what was being said. I added his last statement to my notes.

"What did you do after the defendant spoke to you?"

"I followed him to the bar but I didn't stay with him. I spoke briefly with some other people and then left."

"Thank you," Mr. Cosgrove. "No further questions."

When I replaced Goodwin at the lectern, I placed my notes on the top and looked at them for a moment. I didn't feel as I'd anticipated. By that I mean I wasn't savoring the opportunity to tear Marty Cosgrove down. In the back of my mind, a degree of caution had crept in. I decided to alter my strategy and tone down my adversarial instincts.

"Mr. Cosgrove, you told the court the defendant effectively ditched you for another company. Is that right?"

"That's a fair way to put it."

"He behaved ruthlessly and you didn't like it, and you wanted the court to see that side of him, isn't that right?"

"I don't aim to have him seen in any particular way. I just told the court what happened."

"Doesn't Beacon, the company you represent, have a reputation for being ruthless?"

"There's no place for sentimentality in the world of venture capital."

"I see. But beyond ruthless, isn't your company renowned for being outright predatory?"

"Objection," called Goodwin. "Relevance. This is not a trial of Mr. Cosgrove's business activities."

"Your Honor, the prosecution saw fit to explore the business relationship between the witness and the defendant. I should be free to do the same. This is the foundation of their relationship."

"I agree," said Judge Odell. "Overruled. Please answer the question."

"Some people may say so."

"So being ruthless is a badge of honor in your world, wouldn't you say, Mr. Cosgrove?"

Marty nodded. "That's a fair comment."

"So when the defendant ruthlessly 'dumped you,' as you say, wasn't he just being a good businessman?"

"Ruthlessness and deception are not the same thing."

"Mr. Cosgrove, when did you agree to become a witness for the prosecution, which is another way of saying supporting the case against the defendant?"

"I don't remember the exact date."

"I do. It was immediately after the defendant dumped you, wasn't it?"

"That sounds about right."

"And did you approach Assistant District Attorney Elliott Goodwin or did he approach you?"

"I approached him."

"So it's fair to say that you taking the stand against the defendant today is purely an act of spite, isn't it?"

I heard the gallery behind me stir and saw the eyes of the jury lock on Marty.

"I can see why you would think that, but it's not true."

"Mr. Cosgrove, your job is essentially to buy a significant, if not majority, share of a promising company, right?"

"On a very elemental level, that's correct."

"And you want to buy it as cheaply as possible?"

"Naturally."

"Tell me, if the owner of a company you're targeting is accused of rape, that dramatically reduces the value of his company, does it not?"

"I know what you're getting at. And the answer is yes."

"The offer you made Adrenal went down significantly after Eddie Mawson was charged with sexual assault, didn't it?"

Marty's jaw tightened. "That's true but, as we discussed earlier, business is not sentimental."

"Fair enough. But the thing is you've been in the exact same situation before, haven't you?"

Marty looked at Goodwin. I guess he was expecting Goodwin to jump in but I heard nothing from the prosecution desk. I was sure Goodwin was itching to object but he'd opened the door on business deals.

"You mean Aldoron?"

"Yes. Exactly Aldoron. Aldoron was a gaming company in San Francisco that you wanted to buy, wasn't it?"

"Yes."

"And while you were negotiating the terms with Aldoron's owner—a young man named Aldo Roche—he was hit with sexual assault charges, right?"

"Yes."

"And because of that, the value of his company dropped, right?"

"Yes."

"Well, isn't that a coincidence?"

"I'd have to say it is."

"A coincidence, Mr. Cosgrove, or a business tactic?"

Marty laughed and shook his head. "If it was a tactic, we failed miserably. In both cases, we lost out to another buyer."

"Would it be fair to say, though, that you had a lot riding on winning Eddie Mawson's business?"

This was a question Marty clearly saw coming. He tried to hide his irritation but was not entirely successful. "Yes, it was critical. Both for me and for Beacon Capital."

"It was a deal you could not afford to lose, is that right?"

"The company was on a knife edge financially, as was I. Are you going to come out and suggest that we set Eddie Mawson up to exploit his vulnerability?"

"I have no idea to what lengths you will go to get your way, Mr. Cosgrove. But, as you say, you lost out to another perhaps more ruthless company."

"Perhaps? You think?" Marty straightened in his chair and looked at me like he expected better of me. My line of questioning was obviously becoming tiresome. "Do you want to ask me about the other company, Crestway? The one that stole two deals from under our nose?"

I held up a palm. "No. Let's move on. Mr. Cosgrove, something you said earlier caught my attention."

"What was that?"

"You said, now what was it?" I ran my eyes over my notes. "Ah yes, you said that you didn't see Jenna Lewis *inside* the bar at all."

"Yes. That's what I said."

"Does that mean you saw her outside the bar that night?"

Suddenly, Marty seemed to look more comfortable. "Yes. I did."

I heard Goodwin stir behind me. This was news to him, obviously.

"Can you tell the jury what you saw Jenna Lewis doing outside the bar?"

"She was getting into what I presume was an Uber."

"Were you able to see whether she was upset or not?"

"She didn't look happy but I wouldn't say she looked particularly upset."

Elliott Goodwin let out a loud, sharp cough. It was all he had at his disposal to stop his own witness in his tracks.

"Really? She didn't appear to be upset?"

"No."

There was a moment's pause as I regarded Marty Cosgrove with a combination of surprise and suspicion. On face value, the way he was talking, it seemed clear that Marty was open to me questioning him freely, as though he were my witness and not Goodwin's. Apparent as this was, I was uneasy. A man I'd expected to be treating as a hostile witness now appeared to be obliging. If I didn't know better, I'd think Marty Cosgrove was trying to help me.

Or was it a trap? I had to tread carefully.

"If she was getting into the car, how could you see whether she was upset or not?"

"Because the car door stayed open for a moment."

Goodwin coughed loudly again, and I didn't have to turn around to know that he was glaring at Marty.

"I see. And she wasn't crying?"

"No."

"She wasn't in obvious distress or anguish?"

"No."

"She just looked rather unhappy? What, glum?"

"Yes. Disgruntled more than anything."

"So you're saying that Jenna Lewis, who has alleged that just a few moments earlier she was raped, was showing no sign of trauma?"

"That's right."

Judge Odell stared down the gallery to silence its murmuring. The attendees fell silent without him having to raise his gavel.

"And then she shut the door, I presume?"

"No, someone else did. He was holding the door."

"Who was?"

"Alex Herron."

"Alex Herron? The person who is Eddie's second-in-command at Adrenal?"

"He's at Adrenal? Okay. I'm not sure what his role is."

There was a pause as I struggled to process what I was seeing and hearing. The mention of Alex Herron's name was jarring. It seemed like such a non sequitur, it messed with my brain.

Last time I talked with Herron, he was all bashful about calling Jenna to see if she was okay. He was too embarrassed to tell anyone about it, he said, because they'd think he was a creep. Now he was putting Jenna in an Uber? And he's decided to keep that to himself? What else hadn't he told me?

I'd convinced Herron to testify in support or Eddie, and suddenly putting him on the stand seemed to be highly risky. God only knows what else he'd been keeping to himself.

I didn't know exactly where to go now with Marty. The temptation was asking him to flesh this scene out and find out what else Alex Herron hadn't told me. But that was the problem—if I asked open-ended questions then I might not like the answers and where they took me.

I had to focus on what Marty could tell me about Jenna. That was it. I had to pretend for now that I wasn't interested in Alex at all.

"Were you close enough to hear the tone of their conversation?"

"No. It was all very quick. He opened the door for her, and when she got in he handed her something."

I paused, wondering whether to ask the next question only to find the answer weakened my case. Was that where Marty was leading me? Had he set me up for a fall?

I had to take the risk and ask.

"Did you see what he gave her?"

Marty shook his head. "No, it was something small that Jenna held in the palm of her hand. Then she put in her purse."

"Is that right?" I asked, wondering what the hell Marty Cosgrove was up to. And I was damn sure Elliott Goodwin was wondering the exact same thing.

And as for Alex Herron, I couldn't wait to give that twerp a piece of my mind. If I didn't know any better, I'd think Eddie Mawson and Alex Herron were conspiring to ruin my case.

I took a few deep breaths and reminded myself that these computer nerds were like a different species. I thought I'd made it clear to them that they had to get their heads out of virtual reality and deal with the nuts and bolts of the real world.

Somehow, though, I doubted my message would ever sink in. And maybe that meant I shouldn't risk putting Alex Herron on the stand. But I was in no position to drop a witness. I needed to get Herron to fly straight pronto or else his colleague was going to spend most of his thirties behind bars.

Chapter 34

After I finished my cross-examination, I returned to my desk. Marty left the stand to return to the gallery but as he reached the gate, Goodwin stopped him. I watched as the prosecutor did his level best to keep his voice down and his temperament cool. He pretended to be having a quiet chat but I could see the indignation in his eyes from where I was sitting. I could just imagine what he was telling his witness. Marty was a wild card, no two ways about it. Instead of sticking to the script, he'd strayed and, unwittingly or not, had diluted Goodwin's case and perhaps bolstered mine. The way Marty responded, it was clear he wasn't about to be admonished for speaking the truth.

Yet again, I found my logic at odds with my eyes. Was I reading this right? Was Marty intent on helping me, or was this some kind of trick to defeat me? Why on earth would Marty take my side now, if not to hurt me later? I found it difficult to accept that his cooperation was out of the goodness of his own heart.

Marty calmly fended Goodwin off, pushed the gate open and went to Claire.

I turned back to my desk and rearranged my files, not sure what to make of it all.

Goodwin then got to his feet and addressed Judge Odell.

"The State rests, Your Honor," he said.

Judge Odell took the opportunity to call it a day, saying he had to excuse himself as he was feeling unwell. Court would resume in the morning. Both Goodwin and I wished him the best before packing up.

A new sense of urgency overcame me. Elliott Goodwin had played all his witnesses. Now it was my turn. And there was one witness I needed a word with, as soon as humanly possible.

I was on the phone to Alex Herron as soon as I left court, hitting his number again and again. I left a brief message at first asking that he get back to me urgently. Thirty minutes later, I did the same thing. Having gotten no response, I drove straight to the Adrenal office to corner him there but was told he hadn't been there at all that day.

Cursing his name, I moved onto the next item on my urgent to-do list. I needed to find out what the hell Marty Cosgrove was playing at. When I called him, he told me, in a brief and officious conversation, that he would see me but wouldn't be free until 9:30pm. He had to make up for the lost time he'd spent in court.

I arrived at Beacon Capital on time and was greeted by the blond receptionist.

"You can go through, Mr. Madison," she said before I even reached her desk. I thanked her and made my way to Marty's office. The door was ajar and though it I could see Marty tapping away at his computer, his salmon-colored buttoned shirt rolled up to his elbows and his suit jacket hanging on the back of his chair. He heard my footsteps and called me in and offered me a seat while he tapped away with his eyes on the screen. He finally hit the enter button of his keyboard and from my seat I could see a progress bar appear on his screen as the computer began saving what must have been a large file. Satisfied his laptop was doing its job, he spun his chair around and faced me with a guarded smile.

"Thanks for seeing me, Marty."

"No problem. What can I do for you?"

"Well, Marty, I'm struggling to figure out what happened back there in court today. What was that all about?"

Marty lifted his eyebrows a touch. "I did what I thought was right. That's what happened."

"Goodwin put you on the stand to bury my client but you ended up doing the exact opposite. You helped me, Marty, and I'll be straight with you, I don't know how to take it. My instinct is to take your testimony on face value and to be grateful, but to be honest, in the back of my mind I'm wondering what the hell you're up to."

Marty jabbed a finger at me lightly. "That's on you, Brad. I know what you think I've done."

"I'm sorry, Marty. There were a bunch of things that added up to fuel my suspicions. Now, I honestly don't know what to think. And that's why I'm here. I want to apologize to you and to listen to whatever you want to say to me."

Nothing about Marty's countenance was defensive. He was at ease and centered in the manner of a man who'd done some reflection. He reached down to a drawer and produced a bottle of Highland Park whiskey followed by two tumblers. He turned and pulled out the stopper and held the bottle poised over a glass, checking to see if I was in the mood to indulge. When I nodded, he poured and pushed a glass my way. He took a sip before speaking.

"Yes, Goodwin wanted me to help crucify Eddie. Of course he did. And to be honest, that's precisely why I went to him in the first place. Just like you said in court. I was pissed at Eddie. He played me for a fool and ran off with Crestway."

"I get it," I said. "My understanding is that you were on the brink financially and that deal was going to keep you afloat."

"Yes and no. We were in a tight spot but we didn't have everything riding on the Eddie deal. I had a couple of other irons in the fire. Well, I worked my ass off ensuring that we weren't putting all our money on the one horse, if you know what I mean."

"I do. I guess that's why you were hard pressed to be at the hospital with Claire?"

"Yes. I'd been burned in San Fran and I needed a few options to hedge my bets. So I had three projects in the works. And if I failed with all three then, yeah, I was totally screwed. I'd have lost my job and I couldn't tell you what I'd be doing now."

"So the other projects worked out, obviously?"

"They did. But not overnight. Eddie's desertion left a black hole that was going to take some filling. But I was so angry, I went and offered my services to Elliott. We ran through what I could testify to and I was initially happy to be a weapon for Elliott to wield against you and Eddie. But as the weeks went on, and our business fortunes turned, I became less angry and more concerned with right and wrong."

"Your conscience got the better of you?"

"You could say that. I mean, I had a bone to pick with Eddie and he could be a real dickhead sometimes but by and large I thought he was pretty harmless. I didn't believe he was a rapist."

"I find myself thinking, why didn't you come to me? But I can imagine you thought that would be futile."

"That's exactly right. You made it very clear what you thought of me."

I bowed my head, thinking about how I'd raged against Marty, and the scene I made at the hospital.

The shame that gripped me was potent but it was checked somewhat by the fact I wasn't the only one who believed Marty was up to no good.

"If I can offer not an excuse but a perspective," I said. "From where I stood, Beacon Capital and Crestway were two of a kind. Two companies that were prepared to go to criminal lengths to get what they wanted. I still think Eddie was set up precisely to slash the market value of his company."

"I agree that that's a possibility, but it wasn't us."

I looked firmly at Marty. "It's still not beyond the realm of possibility that you're playing me now. You could be opening up to me like this with one purpose in mind—to get me off your tail and have me hang all my suspicion on Crestway."

I laid out some more detail, such as the information we got from Aldo Roche about money laundering. Marty's response was that most venture capital companies knew that in-game purchases could wield huge profits. He said the virtual economy of a video game was a legitimate and highly profitable revenue stream. He said it was no surprise that criminals had found a way to exploit it. Beacon Capital, he assured me, had no ill-gotten gains to launder and they had no criminal affiliations.

Marty took a sip and cupped his glass in both hands. "Jesus, Brad. Are you really so blinded by your feelings for Claire? Do you seriously think I'm playing you on the Eddie case?"

I shook my head. "No. Not anymore."

I left it as understood that my reply was in answer to both Marty's questions.

"But you think I tried to kill Claire, don't you?"

I put my drink down and leaned forward. "Okay, Marty. Tell me this—do you think that crash was an accident?"

Marty was staring into the table. He shook his head.

"Nope."

For a few moments there were no words because I had none.

"Are you serious? You're telling me that all this time you've been happy to let the police drop their investigation while you thought it was attempted murder?"

Marty leveled his eyes at me. "I don't think it was attempted murder. I know it was."

"What?"

As I processed the implications of his words, Marty picked up his phone and began scrolling through it.

"You agree that it was no accident?"

He didn't take his eyes off his phone. "Yes. That's right."

Once he'd found what he was after, Marty reached out to show me his phone. "When Claire was in the hospital, I got this."

I took the phone and read the text message displayed on the screen.

"HOWS YR WIFE? NEXT TIME U WONT BE SO LUCKY"

I fell back in my chair. "They were after you, not Claire."

Marty nodded.

"So it was a botched hit?"

"Yes."

"I guess there are no prizes for guessing who was behind it," I said.

"Crestway, obviously. The sender's number is blocked, and even if it was traced I'm sure it would turn out to be a burner. But it's Crestway, for sure."

"So why haven't they come back to finish the job?"

"Because I'm no longer a threat, I guess. I lost Adrenal. They won. You were right about this being a ruthless business but even I was shocked by what Crestway was prepared to do."

There was no way Marty was playing me now, I was sure of it.

"What I don't understand is why they needed to go that far," he said.

"What are you talking about?"

"They didn't have to kill me to get Adrenal. Taking over Eddie's company was a done deal the minute they entered the picture. Here I was, I'd spotted Adrenal's potential from a mile away. I did the legwork, got to know Eddie, won his trust. And everything we did was super confidential—at least it was on my side. I couldn't say the same about Eddie's. Crestway didn't just sweep in out of the blue—they were invited in by someone."

"Who? Eddie?"

Marty shrugged. "I've got no idea. I put it to Eddie that someone had leaked our deal to Crestway but he denied it. They knew I was negotiating with Eddie, I'm sure of it."

"Marty, do you actually know who's behind Crestway?"

"I have my theories but that's all they are—theories."

That Marty still didn't know who was running Crestway didn't surprise me given how long it had taken Jack to find out.

"Well, I've got more than a theory, Marty."

"Is that so?"

"Yes," I said, pushing my empty glass back to him. "Pour another one. You're going to need it when I tell you."

Chapter 35

I went to sleep thinking about Alex Herron and woke up doing the same. It wasn't just a matter of wondering where he was or how much time I'd have to review his testimony or how well I could restrain myself from giving the guy a serve. I was wondering whether or not to pull the trigger on seeking a continuance. If Judge Odell was like most judges, he'd want to hear a damned good reason before he granted a delay to a trial that had been scheduled and agreed to by all parties. And I knew without a shadow of a doubt that Elliott Goodwin would object his blessed heart out. But of all the reasons for seeking a continuance, an AWOL witness that was key to the defense's argument was a pretty good one. The first witness I was planning to call was actually Dr. Ed Stanovich. The guy was just about the most credentialed medical toxicology expert on the planet. He had almost a paragraph's worth of academic letters after his name and he kept himself busy in a variety of positions. He headed up the toxicology division at the USC, he conducted highly acclaimed research into emergency medicine and he had countless papers published in esteemed medical journals. If you wanted to know the precise effects of any drug you might put into your system, Dr. Ed Stanovich was your man.

During the course of the trial I'd made notes on everything about Jenna Lewis's movements and actions at Blackjacks. From her accounts and those of others I was able to detail when she arrived, how much alcohol she'd consumed and how much cocaine she'd snorted. Then there was the level of GHB that was detected in her system the following day. I'd fed that information to Dr. Stanovich, and he'd sent me back a report that would form the basis of his testimony. I was confident this testimony would be compelling. When we'd first met a few weeks ago, he was champing at the bit to be involved. He'd served as an expert witness in dozens of cases ranging from traffic accidents, medical malpractice, worker's comp and DUIs. In Ed I had a true toxicology expert, unlike the good Dr. Anna Shand, the forensic psychologist Elliott Goodwin, had put on the stand to give her two cents' worth on the drugs in Jenna Lewis's system. Dr. Stanovich was the real deal. And in the report he sent me, he said there was no way of telling when Jenna Lewis had ingested the drug GHB. From the concentrations found in her blood, Lewis could have had the drug any time in the previous thirty-six hours. What was unknown and unknowable was how much GHB she took, unknowingly or otherwise. Was it a small amount closer to the time of her blood test or a large amount thirty hours prior? There was no way to tell. Hence we would be left with the irrefutable fact that, if we accepted that her drink was spiked, there was nothing to prove that it was spiked at Blackjacks. This was reasonable doubt in a nutshell, all wrapped up in a bow, and I very much looked forward to presenting it to the jury. I checked my watch. Six-fifteen. Megan wasn't due in for at least another half an hour.

My mind got pulled back to Alex Herron. I'd give him until seven to get back to me before I started calling him again and asking Jack to go find him. I didn't want to seek a continuance. I had momentum from Marty's testimony and I wanted to keep it going. I was itching to put Dr. Stanovich on the stand and have him blast Dr. Shand's phony drug expertise out of the water. The jury would see there was no evidence that Jenna Lewis was anything other than drunk in that booth. No one had to help her in. No one had to help her out. She went in and out on her own two feet and although she was drunk, she was clearly able to function. Compounding this absence of certainty was that for all the prosecution's full-blooded assertions to the contrary, there was a high degree of ambiguity surrounding the discovery of a vial of GHB in Eddie's jacket. A jacket he left in the karaoke booth. A jacket that Oscar Guzman found and handled. A jacket that was set aside in a public bar. A jacket, in other words, that was not in the sole possession of its owner. No speculation on this. Pure fact. The defendant's jacket had a life of its own that night. I'd somehow drifted into closing argument mode in my mind, standing before the jury and driving home the irrefutable power of Dr. Stanovich's evidence. The vision was potent—my blood was pumping, my body charged. I was psyched. I wanted to get into court then and there.

"Good morning, Brad."

Megan's cheerful voice snapped me out of my Atticus Finch daydream. She was standing at her desk outside my office, putting away her purse and coat.

"Hey, Megan," I said. "When you're ready come in here for a sec, will you?"

"Sure."

Within ten seconds she was through the door. "You didn't pull an all-nighter, did you?" she asked.

I shook my head. "Nope, but I've been losing sleep, figuratively speaking, over a witness."

"Dr. Stanovich?"

"No. Alex Herron. He's dropped off the radar."

"Really? Has he got cold feet?"

"I think it's something like that. He was mentioned in yesterday's testimony. Marty Cosgrove said Herron put Jenna Lewis in an Uber outside the bar and handed her something. And guess what? Herron never mentioned this to me. So either Marty Cosgrove was lying in court—which he wasn't—or Herron chose to keep that rather highly relevant part of his actions that night to himself."

"Why would he do that?"

"No idea. He's either hiding something or it's just another example of his social defects. I mean, the guy was nervous as hell about admitting to the court he had a crush on Jenna Lewis, which between you and me could well be in creepy stalker territory. So maybe it's like that. Maybe it's not. But I won't know until I speak with that idiot."

"What can I do?"

I sighed. I looked at my watch again. Seven o'clock on the button. "Nothing, thanks, Megan. Damn him. What a fool. I can't just wing it and hope Herron will turn up today. And I don't want him on the stand unrehearsed. I need to prep him—again—before putting him on the stand. I'm going to seek a continuance. I'll hit the judge up for it first thing. Yep. That's what I'm going to do. File a motion for continuance."

"You want me to do it?"

"That'd be great. The witness I want to present today is absent. The witness is vital to the case for the defense. Request a day or two to locate him and ensure that he's brought to court."

"Got it. How many days exactly?"

"Better make it three. That will push it out to the weekend. Goodwin's going to object like crazy and Judge Odell won't be too jazzed by it either. So let's aim high."

"I'll get on it."

As Megan left my office, I picked up my phone and called Eddie. He answered brightly, like he'd been awake for hours. He told me he had no idea where Alex Herron was. Eddie said he spoke to him early the previous morning and that he'd called a couple of times later in the day but hadn't heard back. I asked him if that was unusual for second-in-command, the guy he'd entrusted his multi-million-dollar enterprise with, to be unreachable. I didn't even try to hide the sarcasm. Deadpan, Eddie said, yes he did think it was odd but he was sure Herron hadn't run out on me. As I face palmed, I told Eddie I didn't share his confidence. At the end of the call, I was reminded of what cell phones have cruelly stolen from us—the satisfaction of slamming the phone down.

After Eddie, I tried Herron again. No luck. My next call was to Jack Briggs. He answered smug and easy, sounding sun-lounge comfortable as always.

"Shouldn't you be preparing for court, you know, standing in front of the mirror and trying to sound impressive?"

"Yes, but there's been a change of plans. Are you free or are you getting your nails done?"

"What's going on?"

"A witness has dropped off the radar. I wanted him on the stand as soon as today but he may well be a no-show and I can't let that happen. I don't know if he's gotten nervous or what but I need to speak to him ASAP. I'm going to seek a continuance but I need you to pick this guy up and bring him to me."

"And if he doesn't want to come?"

"Don't give him an option. Hear what I'm saying? I don't care if you have to hogtie the fuckwit. I'll send you his work address and number. It's in Santa Monica. I want you on him as of now. His home address is in Pacific Palisades. I'm sending you that too. Start there. How soon can you get there?"

"Forty minutes."

"Okay."

"What's the bet he calls you the minute I reach his door?"

"Fine with me. Just so long as he shows his face before we're back in court. I've just about had it with these guys, Jack. They live in another dimension. Einstein's in virtual reality, Neanderthals when it comes to real-world social IQ."

Jack sighed. "You want to keep bitching or do you want me to get on the road?"

"Go already."

After the call, I sat at my desk and spun things around in my head. It was then that I had a thought that turned my blood cold.

What if Herron had not dropped off the map willingly? What if someone didn't want him helping Eddie to beat the charges against him? What if that someone was Darius Tucker? Was Alex Herron the next Aldo Roche?

Chapter 36

"All rise, the Honorable Sean Odell presiding."

The bailiff's voice rang through a mostly empty courtroom. There was Eddie, me, Goodwin and his team, the bailiffs and just a handful of people in the gallery. The jury had yet to be called in. Whether or not they would make an appearance at all today hinged on the success of my motion for continuance. If Judge Odell denied it, we'd have to continue with the trial immediately. The jury would be called in and, since the prosecution had finished presenting evidence, it was my turn to put witnesses on the stand. To that end, one of the few people taking up bench space in the gallery was Dr. Stanovich, who I'd already greeted and was seated right behind me.

"Thanks everyone, and good morning," said Judge Odell, who got settled into his chair and began perusing the documents placed in front of him. He then read the case before picking up a sheet of white paper to peruse.

"Okay, up first, the court will take up the defense's motion for continuance," he said. "Mr. Madison, are you ready to proceed?"

"I am, Your Honor," I said.

"Mr. Goodwin, are you ready to proceed?"

"Yes, Your Honor."

"Mr. Madison, you're the movant. Let's hear from you."

With that I got to my feet. I told the judge that, as the motion stated, a key witness I was due to put on the stand as early as today had gone missing. I stated that Alex Herron was an important eyewitness to the events at Blackjacks and that he was a work colleague of the defendant. I said that while I wasn't quite ready to place a missing persons call to the LAPD, I wasn't sure what had become of my witness and how long it would take to find him. I certainly hoped to find Herron as early as today but it was not something I could guarantee the court. That was why I requested a three-day postponement.

Judge Odell didn't look up once as I spoke and he didn't grant my adversary that courtesy either when he addressed him.

"What's your response, Mr. Elliott?"

Goodwin snapped to his feet. "Your Honor, the document filed by the movant does not show sufficient cause for the motion. The movant is stalling for time. This trial was scheduled months ago, its date agreed to by all parties. The fact that he's let a witness slip through his fingers only shows that he has not adequately prepared for the case. I contend that it is not the court's job to compensate for his lack of diligence."

I cleared my throat.

"Your Honor," I said. "ADA Goodwin may like to keep his witnesses in a cage in his basement. I, on the other hand, am inclined to leave them to roam the face of this earth as freely as the Constitution of the United States allows. And, correct me if I'm wrong, stuff happens. Life happens.

"In Mr. Goodwin's perfect world, there's no such thing as a bad cop or a good defense lawyer. The only diligence I've failed to apply in this matter is not polishing my crystal ball harder. This is an unforeseeable event and I'm making every effort to find my witness.

"At this very moment, my private investigator, Jack Briggs, is on the streets trying to track him down. We will find him. It's just a matter of time."

As I said this, a horrible thought forced itself into my mind—that I'd soon be receiving a photo of Alex Herron's bloodied and brutalized corpse.

"Fair enough, Mr. Madison," said Judge Odell. "But three days is a reach. You've got twenty-four hours."

"Your Honor," I said. "Given that I need to—"

"Twenty-four hours, Mr. Madison. It's either that or I can deny the motion, we get the jury in here and start hearing from your first witness. I'm not delaying this trial for three days because one of your witnesses got the jitters."

"A day would be greatly appreciated, Your Honor. Thank you."

I headed for the exit with Dr. Stanovich by my side. I apologized for putting him out, and said he'd be on the stand this time tomorrow: rain, hail or shine.

Goodwin was on my heels as I reached the lobby and stopped to take my phone out. It had buzzed inside the courtroom. I felt nauseous as I raised the screen into my eyeline. I was relieved to see it was a call from Jack that I had missed. As I tapped his number, Goodwin brushed past me.

"See you bright and early tomorrow, Madison."

Asshole.

"Jack," I said as he picked up. "You called."

"Yeah," he said. I could hear he was driving. "I checked out Herron's place."

"Any sign of him?"

"Nope. He's been there recently if the pizza boxes are anything to go by."

"You went through his trash?"

"No. I went through his house."

"*Broke into* his house, you mean? I didn't ask you to do that but—"

"I know. Bonus points for initiative, right? I'll take mine in cash, thanks."

"Did you find anything interesting?"

"Nothing. The only thing that stood out was that his car was there. He's got a Silverado locked away in his garage."

"How do you know it's his?"

"Because there's a photo of him tailgating at Levi's Stadium."

"Really?"

"Geeks are football fans too, Brad."

"So that's it? What are you doing now?"

"I'm on my way to Adrenal to see if anyone there has a lead."

"Good. I told Eddie to let his staff to expect you and to, you know, give you everything your heart desires."

"So Eddie hasn't heard from Herron?"

"No. He's getting a little anxious. Not out of concern for his friend but due to the fact that he needs to find someone else to take charge at his office. Keep me posted. But…"

"But what?"

"Jack, I think we need to consider that Herron may not just be gun-shy about testifying."

"What do you mean?"

"I mean, a part of me is worried that—"

"He'll end up like Aldo Roche?"

"Exactly. I'm sure now that Crestway is behind this whole thing. Tucker's got his hands on Adrenal, and he got it for a song once Eddie was charged. My guess is that Tucker wants Eddie alive for now so he can tap into his knowledge, but a conviction will see Eddie lose all claims on the business."

"I have to admit, that crossed my mind," said Jack. "And before you say it, I'm proceeding very carefully."

"Good," I said. "Later."

It appalled me to think that Eddie was just a doomed pawn in Tucker's game, and for no other reason than having the smarts and gumption to launch a successful company that caught Tucker's eye.

As I drove back to Santa Monica, I racked my brain for something I could offer Tucker to change his brutal course.

I came up with nothing and put that mission on hold.

Back at my desk, I got my mind back on my top priority—clearing Eddie Mason's name.

I had my head buried in case files when I heard voices outside my door. My ears pricked up, listening for a male voice in the hope that Herron had at last shown his face. All I heard were female voices, though. Megan was no doubt explaining to the visitor that I was too busy to take a walk-in. A few seconds later, though, there was a knock on my door.

"Yes, Megan. Who's—"

Megan slipped into my office quickly and shut the door behind her with discreet purpose. She then stepped forward with that really-hate-to-break-that-do-not-disturb-rule contrition.

"Brad. Someone's here to see you. I told her this wasn't a good time and that you were in the middle of a trial but she said it was urgent and that you'd want to see her."

"Did she now?"

"Yes. And she said her purpose did have something to do with the trial."

"Who the hell is it?"

"Her name's Donna Amerson. Like I said, she insists on seeing you. And—"

"And what?"

"She's got company."

Chapter 37

"You can't be here," I said to Jenna Lewis, who stood as soon as she saw me appear. I was trying to be nice but it was clear to one and all that I wasn't pleased about this particular surprise visit. "I mean, you shouldn't be here."

Donna Amerson stepped over to Lewis and put an arm around her.

There had been seconds of silence by now, so I came out with the obvious.

"Okay. Someone needs to tell me what's going on."

"It was my idea," said Donna.

"I kind of had that already figured out."

"Jenna's going to need a lawyer, Brad."

"Well, I'm kind of in the middle of something. Up to my eyeballs defending the man who Jenna says raped her."

"She's going to need a defense lawyer. Look, can we take this into your office? You wanted me to look into Jenna's case and I did. We have a situation."

Donna spoke slowly to make it clear that I'd be a fool to refuse her. Not that I was going to. Donna's words had certainly gotten my attention.

"Come in. Can we get you coffee?"

Lewis shook her head and walked past me with rounded shoulders.

"I've drunk a pot already but I'll take another," said Donna. "Black, please."

I nodded to Megan to count me in. I shut the door behind Donna, pulled a second chair from the corner of my office and motioned for them to sit.

Sitting forward in my seat, I looked over at Donna. "Okay, what's the situation?"

Donna glanced at Jenna before speaking. "Brad, we've been up most of the night. What we're here to tell is not going to please you but at the same time it means you win."

"Win what? The trial?"

Donna nodded. "Yes. Brad, I'm afraid it's a false accusation. Now before—"

"Damn it. I knew it," I said, turning to Lewis. "Do you have any idea what you've put Eddie Mawson through, Jenna?"

With bowed head, Lewis stared back at me with sorrow and remorse. Or if she was putting it on, she was doing a damned good job. Shocked as I was by the news, the urge to air both my vindication and indignation was strong. I was ready to punish Lewis like an outraged headmaster, ready to wag a finger in her face and give her the "look here, young lady" this and that. A gently raised palm from Donna stopped me in my tracks.

"I suggest you listen first, Brad," she said. "This is going to take some unpacking."

"Okay," I said, taking a deep breath to calm myself back down. "The floor's yours."

"Jenna was blackmailed into making those accusations. She—"

Lewis reached over to touch Donna's arm.

"It's probably better coming from me," Lewis said, before lifting her chin and steeling herself to address me. "About a year ago, I got into a bad relationship. I was doing a lot of coke. It went from being just a part of my life to a way of life for me. By that, I mean I became an addict. Not that I'd have ever admitted it to myself or anyone back then. But I was burning through a lot of money to keep myself in coke. And there was one guy who I bought off the most. We worked together at Adrenal. That's where I met him. You know him. At least I'm sure you know of him. Alex."

"Alex Herron?" I said, stunned but also somewhat relieved she didn't say Eddie Mawson.

"Yes. He always had coke and had a side hustle dealing. But he was discreet about it. He didn't sell to anyone at work."

"Not to Eddie?"

"No, Eddie had no idea Alex was dealing coke. But Alex didn't want anyone at work knowing he sold drugs. He was above the street dealers and would sell to them. He had quite a few guys in various bars that would buy off him."

I rubbed my eyes, thinking about my two withholding morons Eddie and Alex and how completely over them I was. "Alex Herron is a drug dealer?" I asked with a degree of fatigue, which must have confused my present company.

"Do you want me to go on?" asked Lewis sheepishly.

"Yes. Please continue. Hang on. Before you do, you said he sold to bars. Was he connected to Oscar Guzman at Blackjacks?"

Lewis nodded. "Yes. Oscar bought off Alex and sold bags at Blackjacks to customers on the sly."

"I see," I said. "Please, go on."

It was at that moment that Megan returned with the coffees. She handed them out and asked if I wanted her to do anything. I asked her to shut the door and hold all my calls. Once she'd left, I invited Lewis to continue.

"Anyway, at one point I went to bed with Alex. I mean, I wasn't that attracted to him. I never was attracted to him at all."

"But you liked the fact that he had coke on tap and that he was generous with it," I surmised.

"Yes. I regretted sleeping with him. But it was the one and only time that we had sex. I felt slutty and the shame of it kind of snapped me out of it. I backed off the drugs and stopped hanging out with him. But that's when I found out I was addicted. I went back to Alex but just for the drugs, not sex. I insisted on paying for my coke. I felt like that was one last virtue I had—that I was just a customer and not a slut. No one had any idea this was going on. We were very discreet. Like I said, Alex wasn't selling to anyone at work but me. Eddie would not have liked that but he would have freaked if he knew Alex and I had slept together. We both knew he had a crush on me. Alex told me Eddie wouldn't hesitate to fire him if he found out we'd, you know, had sex."

"Okay," I said. "After you left Eddie's company, did you keep buying coke from Alex?"

"That's one of the main reasons I left Adrenal. Yes, there was toxic masculinity there but I could work around it or ignore it most times. No, I left because I wanted to get away from Alex and the hold he had over me. But it turned out that I couldn't."

"Why the hell not? The drugs?"

Lewis bowed her head and pressed her brow with her fingers. She began sobbing and once she'd started, her sorrow flooded out. Donna comforted her but I knew what I was seeing. Jenna Lewis was inconsolable. All that indignation I'd felt previously blew away. I felt so sorry for the girl. A moment later, Lewis steeled herself to continue her story.

"The reason I couldn't break Alex's hold on me wasn't the drugs. After I started at Ubivision, I went for weeks without cocaine. I felt like I had beaten my addiction. But Alex still had a hold of me."

"How?"

"He'd made a sex tape without me knowing," Lewis said, wiping her eyes before sitting up straighter with newfound strength. "He'd hidden two cameras in his room and made a clip from the footage. I hadn't seen him in weeks and out of the blue he sent me an edited video. There's me snorting lines, going down on him and taking him from behind. All in HD.

"I can't tell you how mortified I was. He assured me that only the two of us had seen it. He told me not to worry. He said no one else ever needed to see it but he needed to see me to discuss what we were going to do about our 'situation.' I was so angry at him I could have killed him. But I met up with him. I had no idea what he wanted. I thought he was going to try and force me into more sex but that wasn't it. He said he was helping out a friend in a business deal and that Eddie Mawson was in the way somehow. He didn't give me any details about this deal, but the gist of it was he wanted me to help frame Eddie. Alex had a plan for making a rape claim against him. He told me Eddie would never be prosecuted, he'd never go to jail. He'd just be out of the picture as far as this deal went."

I believed every word Jenna Lewis spoke. The connections were all starting to become clear. I was beginning to think

I'd critically underestimated Alex Herron. And so had Eddie Mawson.

"Did Alex mention Beacon Capitol or Marty Cosgrove at all?" Lewis shook her head. "No."

"Crestway? Cobus Lombard? Darius Tucker?"

Lewis's puzzled expression only firmed. "No. He mentioned no names at all. Like I said, I was completely in the dark about that side of things."

"So he blackmailed you to go along with his plan?"

"Yes. He told me if I didn't do what he said he'd make sure everyone in the industry saw what a 'coke whore' I was. His words. And he was going to make sure my parents found out."

At this point, Donna chipped in. "Jenna comes from a very conservative, very religious family. She's been somewhat estranged from them in recent years. Her court appearance and her testimony were scandalous enough as far as her family is concerned but a sex tape is next level. They would be devastated and their standing in the church community would be destroyed."

I remembered Lewis being in the stand, so ashamed she could barely lay eyes on her parents in the gallery.

"So you agreed to do what Alex said?"

Lewis nodded. "Yes. I felt I didn't have a choice. Well, I did. I just chose what was best for myself and what was worst for Eddie. I never thought I'd have to go to trial. Alex said it would never get that far. He promised."

"How could it not? You went to the cops."

"I couldn't see how it would play out. I didn't think that far ahead. I just wanted to keep Alex at bay, so I kept doing what he told me to do. Eddie's going to be fine, he'd say."

"So how did it go down in Blackjacks? You all get high then at some point during the karaoke you plant the vial of GHB in Eddie's jacket."

Lewis nodded.

"And then Alex gave you another vial outside the bar. That's what Marty saw, right?"

"Yes."

"So you took the GHB when you got home, knowing they'd blood test you after you went to the cops?"

Again, she nodded.

"His DNA just got on you accidentally."

Lewis's eyes shifted to the side, showing the discomfort of her conscience. "No. We passed the bags of coke between us under the table, and whenever Eddie handed it to me I rubbed the bag on my inner thigh."

I exhaled sharply and shook my head at Donna before addressing Lewis.

"Well, Jenna, I'm not sure what to say right this moment. But yes, you are going to need a lawyer. However, I am not your lawyer and so none of this conversation we've had here is privileged. You understand that, right? I can walk out of here and go to the cops and tell them everything you told me. Eddie's case will be thrown out, which is a plus from our end. But you will be in yet another, much bigger mess. You'll be facing a raft of charges, and I'm not sure how you'll get through it all without time served. Donna?"

Donna nodded. "I've been through all of that with her, Brad. She knows where this road leads. But there's something that I hope will work in her favor."

"You mean mitigation?"

"Yes. Jenna thinks Alex has done something else that's particularly bad and he's gotten away with it."

I raised my eyebrows at Donna. "What, something that trumps drug trafficking, sextortion, aiding and abetting in the commission of a felony, and conspiracy?"

"Yes," said Lewis. "I think he killed someone."

The next words that came out of Jenna Lewis's mouth shocked me. When she had finished speaking, I picked up the phone.

"Jack," I said when the call was answered. "Turn around. I need you to go back to Alex Herron's place. Now."

Chapter 38

I saw Donna and Jenna out but not before telling Jenna that, once the dust all settled, I'd be happy to represent her. I called Eddie and told him to meet me at Adrenal. He asked why. I said I had some good news and some bad.

"Which do you want first?" I asked.

"Always start with the bad."

"Okay. The guy that you trusted to run your business while you're on trial for rape is out to destroy you."

"Alex? What are you talking about?"

"He framed you, Eddie. He blackmailed Jenna Lewis into making those claims against you. I'll explain when I see you."

"What the actual...? Okay, so what's the good news?"

"Well, the good news is that your rape charges are going to be thrown out and your case will be dropped cold."

Eddie let out a brief laugh of disbelief. "What? Are you sure?"

"Jenna Lewis is going to retract her allegations. But not just yet. We need to keep a lid on this for now. If you speak to Alex, nothing has changed. You understand me? For the moment, your trial will resume tomorrow and we're expecting Alex to take the stand. If he does contact you, tell him I need to speak to him as a matter of urgency."

"Got it."

"Like I said, I'll run you through everything at the office. Which you're on your way to as we speak, right?"

I heard Eddie exert himself, like he'd sprung himself out of his chair. "Yes, I'm on my way."

Twenty minutes later, we were in the Adrenal conference room with Eddie listening dumbfounded as I relayed what Jenna Lewis had told me.

"Why would Alex do that?"

"Right now, I've only got theories to go on. But look at the situation right now. With you sidelined he's got the run of Adrenal. So it suits him from that end. Either he's doing it out of pure ambition and jealousy over what you've achieved. Or maybe he's doing Crestway's bidding. With you locked up he'd most likely get the keys to Adrenal."

"So Cobus Lombard is involved?"

I shook my head ruefully. "Up until recently I would have thought Marty was involved somehow but he's not. For one, there's only one upside for him—to punish you for screwing him out of your agreed deal. No, if there's someone else involved it would have to be Darius Tucker."

I tapped my hand on the table. "Eddie, I want you to be straight with me on something. You kept Alex out of Marty's deal, right?"

"Right. It was just between me and Marty. We both wanted it to be totally under wraps until we'd worked it out. I only ever spoke to him on the phone in private. And when we met face-to-face, it was never in an office, neither his nor mine."

"So how did Darius Tucker find out something was on? He didn't just send his lawyer, Cobus Lombard, to lean on you out of the blue. He knew something was going on. Tell me this, did you ever do coke with Alex?"

A flicker of discomfort appeared on Eddie's face. "Occasionally. You know, when we had something to celebrate."

"Cocaine and secrets don't go together well, Eddie. Are you sure you were never tempted to brag or share your excitement about a prospective deal with Alex? Might you have let it slip that you were looking at bringing Beacon Capital on board?"

Eddie looked sheepish. "Now that you mention it, I may have mentioned something about the Beacon deal. But that was the kind of thing you always talk about in this industry. Pretty much everyone who launches a start-up dreams it will blow up. And you can't help but imagine how that would actually work. You talk about the what-ifs all the time. Alex knew that. He'd been in that position before."

"The what-ifs being if you hit the lottery and your product takes off?"

"Exactly. God, I'm such an idiot." Eddie's mood had turned a little bleak, as it began to dawn on him that a few careless words might have led to his life being taken to the brink of ruin. "I'm actually pretty sure I said something along the lines that a big play was in the works."

"You said that to Alex?"

Eddie nodded. "Yes."

I leaned forward and clasped my hands together and said nothing while my brain went to work. I wondered if Alex Herron had an existing connection with Darius Tucker that pre-dated his time at Adrenal. There was a good chance he was moving Tucker's coke. Still, there was no way a small-time dealer like him would have a direct line to the boss. But Herron was nothing if not resourceful. Maybe he found a way. Maybe he dug up the name Cobus Lombard and approached him. It was not beyond the realm of possibility.

"Eddie, I'm going to go out on a limb here and say it's almost certain you gave Alex a hint and that's all he needed. Suddenly, he's got an idea for how he can win brownie points with a very powerful man, and reap the rewards of running a high-growth tech company. Does that sound far-fetched to you?"

Eddie shook his head ruefully. "I gave him a job. I paid him well. I trusted that son-of-a-bitch. And this is how he paid me back? The guy's a psychopath. He totally screwed me. I mean, to set me up as a rapist and watch me go to jail? I can't understand why he hates me so much."

"Maybe it's not personal. I mean, what if it's not about you specifically?"

"What do you mean?"

"I mean, someone else got screwed in all this—Marty. So, what's the connection between Marty and Alex. They never met through you or your company, right?"

"When you were shooting your mouth off on coke, did you ever mention Marty by name?"

"Not that I can remember but, jeez, I guess it could have slipped out. But as far as I could tell you, those guys never laid eyes on each other."

"Yet in court Marty said he saw Alex outside the bar with Jenna. So he knew who Alex was. When he said it, I just presumed that it was through you. But then Marty was actually surprised to learn that Alex worked at Adrenal. His exact words were, I looked up the transcript, 'He's at Adrenal? I'm not sure what his role is.'"

Eddie shrugged. "The gaming industry's not a big world. They could have just met at the awards night before Blackjacks."

I shook my head. "True. But I doubt it. Marty would network the shit out of that kind of thing. He wouldn't talk shop with anyone without trading cards, getting names and numbers. His job is to hustle up deals. If he'd met Alex that night, he'd know a lot about him and he'd know for sure which company Alex worked for. No, that's not how they know each other. Where was Alex working before you took him on?"

"He came to LA from San Francisco. He said he'd had his own start-up that didn't work out, so he came to try his hand in Silicon Beach."

Eddie's words prompted me to remember that when I first met Alex Herron, he told me that he understood Eddie's position, that running your own gaming company was tough. The tailgating photo Jack reported seeing in Herron's house was not a holiday photo. That's where he lived.

"Eddie, what was the name of Alex's company?"

"I can't remember," Eddie shrugged and began tapping at his phone. "I can find out, though."

Within a few seconds, Eddie had it.

"Here it is. Keyko. That's right. He told me he came up with the name by cutting it out of Donkey Kong."

"What happened to it?" I asked, though I was beginning to think I knew the answer.

"Don't know," said Eddie, frowning at his screen.

"Okay. We need to find out if there's a connection between Alex's company and Beacon Capital."

Both Eddie's thumbs got busy as he searched. He stopped, tapped on a link and then scrutinized the page.

"Here's something," he said, handing me the phone. It was a tech news article that detailed Beacon's churn and burn spree targeting Silicon Valley minnows. Mentioned in the article was one sorry casualty that had been bought and sold for parts, wiped from existence almost overnight—Keyko.

That's how they knew each other: Marty Cosgrove had taken Alex Herron's dream and ripped it to shreds.

"I need to run this past Marty," I said, looking up my contacts. "See if he can add anything."

My call went straight through to Marty's voicemail. I left a message and gave it a few minutes. Eddie got some coffee brought in and we brought some of his staff members in to help search for any trail that Herron might have left. They'd check his emails, chat rooms, and they'd try locating his phone. I called Marty again and got the same result. I put a call through to Beacon Capitol and spoke to one of the receptionists. She recognized me and told me that Marty was out of the office all day and that to keep trying his cell was the best option.

"Look," I said. "I don't want to sound dramatic but it's very important that I reach him as soon as possible. Did he say where he was going?"

"He said he had a meeting with Adrenal. That's all I can tell you, Mr. Madison."

"Thank you," I said and hung up.

"What did they say?" asked Eddie.

I leveled my gaze at him, still trying to make sense of it. "She said that Marty went to see you."

"What?" said Eddie, puzzled. "Marty hates me for what I did to him."

"Well. That's what he told her. That had a meeting with Adrenal," I repeated. "I've got no idea what to make of it. Unless…"

"Unless what?"

"Unless by Adrenal he means Alex."

"What the hell?"

"Maybe Alex is going to try and pitch him a deal. Who knows?"

My phone vibrated with an incoming text message. I thought it might be Marty getting back to me but it was Jack.

I opened it to see a photo of what I presumed was Alex's car. The front end was all smashed in. Another photo followed. It was a close-up of the damage. The black paint of Herron's Silverado was streaked with paint that was the color of Claire's car.

"Jesus Christ," I said. "He's not going to pitch Marty a deal. He's going to kill him."

Chapter 39

With Adrenal staff members trying to track Herron's phone, I asked Eddie if there was a way we could track Marty's. He said there were a few methods to track someone's phone without their knowledge and consent. They typically entailed sending a text message but this would only reveal the location of the device at the time the message was received. It was no good for a moving target. Eddie said for real-time tracking, the best way was to go through someone close to Marty, a contact he would have added to his device finding app.

"Has he got a wife? Kids?"

I looked at Eddie. Obviously, the fact that I'd told him Marty was married to my ex-wife had slipped his mind.

"Yes, Eddie. He's married to my ex-wife. Remember? And he lives under the same roof as my daughter."

"Oh, yeah. That's right. Well, give her a call then. Ask her if she's been added to his tracking app."

Eddie had clearly given no thought whatsoever to the life of the man who had been devoting most of his waking hours to keeping him out of jail. I wasn't hurt so much as baffled by the degree of his disconnection.

I grabbed my phone and pulled up Claire in my contacts. Poised to make the call, the feeling of apprehension stirring around in my stomach was not unfamiliar. Over the years it had made itself felt on numerous occasions, like when I'd just gotten her number and was steeling myself to ask her out on a date, like when on numerous occasions during our marriage I had to cancel something we'd planned—such as a rare night out, or a birthday party for Bella—because of work. And now here it was again as I wondered how she was going to react to me trying to find Marty, and whether I could get what I needed to get done without freaking her out.

"Hi Brad," she said. "What's up?"

Her tone was not unfriendly, which was good. The Bella pickups and drop-offs over the past few months since our hospital showdown had taken much of the heat out of all that. Still, that look she gave me in court could have frozen the seven seas. For the most part, our relationship had operated in a businesslike, functional way, with the smallest dash of cordiality. I felt I was only ever one wrong word away from relighting the old fuse.

"Listen, Claire, I'm trying to track down Marty. I'm with Eddie Mawson and we really need to speak with him."

"Okay. Did you try calling him?"

"Yes, that's the thing. He's not answering. But we were thinking maybe you're listed on his phone's finding app. You know, that would mean you'd be able to see his real-time location."

"What the hell's going on, Brad?" Her voice was icy seven seas cold.

"Claire. I need to find him. I think he might be in danger."

"Now you're freaking me out. Is this another one of your crazy imaginings? Not long ago you thought he was out to kill me. Now you're saying this… Can you please tell me what's going on?"

"Claire, can I explain later? Please. We're wasting time. I really need to find Marty. Can you just check the finding app on your phone? Please."

"I know exactly where his phone is, Brad. I'm looking at it." I could hear contained rage in Claire's voice. Whatever patience she had for me had dried up.

"What? His office told he was out for a meeting. I didn't know he was home, obviously."

"It's true. He did have a meeting and for privacy he came home to prepare for it."

"That's good. Can you put him on?"

"He's just stepped out."

"For how long?"

"I don't know. He's gone for that meeting and he didn't want any interruptions, so he left his phone here. Marty's not far away and no one's bashing our door in with an ax. So I think you can stand down, Brad. I'll get him to call you when he gets back. Okay?"

"No, Claire. It's not okay," I half shouted. "If you love your husband, you need to take me seriously. He's in danger. Tell me where he went."

"He said they were just going to walk the canals."

I was on my feet and exited the conference room while beckoning Eddie to follow. "What exactly did he tell you?"

Claire fumbled a little before her memory kicked in. "He was excited. He just said something about a deal being back in play."

"Shit. When did he leave?"

"It was about fifteen minutes ago. Brad? Who's he meeting?"

I couldn't tell Claire that Marty was possibly meeting the man who had put her into a coma, the man who'd botched his first attempt on her husband's life, the man who was now, in all likelihood, intending to finish the job.

"No time to explain. I'm coming over."

I hung up and pocketed my phone as I ran through the Adrenal office. When I reached the lobby I turned to Eddie as he caught up.

"Your car's here, right?"

"Yes."

"Give me the keys."

"But—"

"Give me the damned keys, Eddie. I'm driving."

Eddie led me outside to the lot next to his building. When we reached his car, I realized why he was reluctant to hand over the keys. I'd just commandeered a canary yellow 2015 Porsche 911 GTS.

I tapped on my phone, got behind the wheel and passed the phone to Eddie. I flicked the key to the right and, with a press of my foot, the engine came to life with a predatory roar.

"That's Jack's number there," I said to Eddie. "Call him and tell him to get to Claire's house immediately."

I took the Porsche to the lot exit then hit the gas, pulling out into the traffic with the rear end fishtailing, the wheels screeching and the engine snarling with ravenous glee. With the lights going our way and 430 horsepower, we could be at Claire's house in just over five minutes.

Chapter 40

I parked the car across Claire's double garage and I ran along the side of her house to the Grand Canal. Over the hedge I saw Claire standing on her lawn with her arms folded, looking up and down the Grand Canal. At the sight of me, she stepped through the small gate and held out a phone.

"He got this text just before he left."

"HERE WITH COFFEE"

The number of the sender was blocked.

"They could be anywhere," I said.

The Venice Beach canal network wasn't expansive. There were only six in total—the main canal that ran past Claire's house and south into Marina Del Ray, a shorter canal at the western end and four quarter-mile canals linking them to form a grid. Not big in terms of Los Angeles' suburbs but it added up to a couple of miles of walkways. A hell of a lot to cover on foot. I tried to think of what landmarks there were in the area that would be possible meeting points. The only thing I could come up with was the park on Dell Avenue.

Getting to the park I'd have to cross three of the four link canals. At the bridges of each cross canal I could stop and scan the entire length of each waterway for any sign of Marty.

Without saying a word, I broke into a run and bounded over the arched footbridge in front of Claire's house. As I turned left, I heard Eddie's heavy footsteps behind me. I'd almost forgotten he was there. I stopped.

"Follow the Grand Canal up that way," I said to him, point northward. "Keep your eyes peeled and at the end make your way to Dell Avenue."

"Okay," he said. We were about to go our separate ways when I checked myself. "Hang on. My phone."

I hadn't gotten it back from him after the drive to Claire's. He thrust it at me.

"Call me if you see anything," I said.

Phone in hand, I took off on the walkway that ran along one of the link canals. As I ran, I called Jack. And when he answered, I told him to come into the canals from the west side via Ocean Avenue. I didn't ask how long he'd be. I didn't wait for a response. I just hung up and kept running.

There were very few people about. Normally, there was a steady flow of tourists and power-walkers making their way around one of Los Angeles' most picturesque and highly sought-after precincts. By the time I reached Dell Avenue, I'd settled into my fastest middle-distance stride. I couldn't afford to sprint—I'd run myself out too fast. I knew I could hold this pace for at least half an hour.

At Dell Avenue, I ran up and crossed over the road bridge. The park was about five hundred yards dead ahead. Between me and it were two more canal bridges. I saw a car up ahead traveling north but otherwise the place was almost empty of people, which seemed so at odds with being part of the mass of cars and people that was the city of LA.

As I ran, I wondered what Alex had planned for Marty. Could he actually be thinking of committing murder in broad daylight? Was he going to turn up with a gun and shoot Marty on sight? I instantly put my ears on heightened alert for any telling sound. Had he brought a knife with him? And why did Marty agree to meet him? Wouldn't he know that Alex Herron wasn't his biggest fan? But maybe that had been set aside. Maybe Herron had downplayed his enmity. Maybe he'd proposed a deal they could both benefit from. Who knew? All I knew was that Marty seemed to be buying what Herron was selling.

I reached the next canal and stopped. I checked one way and then the other. No sign of them, so I pressed on. At the next canal I did the same. Nothing.

The park was on the other side of the third bridge, and I reached it to find a few people there but no sign of Marty. My wild guess that they'd arranged to meet there was probably wrong. Now I felt absolutely clueless about where they might be. They might not have stayed in the canal precinct at all. Herron might have had a car parked nearby and lured Marty away. Conceivably, they could be anywhere in a twenty-mile radius.

I pushed that thought out of my head and continued on Dell Avenue until I reached the last canal. Again, no sign of them.

By now I had scanned most of the canal network, but Marty and Herron could well have just rounded a corner somewhere and so remained out of sight. They could also be in a spot that I had already checked. I'd heard nothing from Eddie.

At the last bridge I saw nothing of interest. I ran down to the walkway and followed the canal west. Up ahead, I saw an elderly couple in matching tracksuits and headbands approaching. Both were carrying light hand-weights.

"Excuse me," I said. "I'm looking for two guys. One's about my height with glasses. The other shorter with blond hair. Have you seen them?"

"Were they drinking?" asked the man.

"We did see two gentlemen," said the woman. "One was so loaded he could hardly walk. Both of them could have been drunk, though."

"We stood aside to let them pass," said the man.

"Where was this?" I asked.

Both of them turned around and pointed west. "Down there and around."

"When did you pass them?"

They looked at each other. "Five minutes ago, I'd say," said the man, and the woman nodded.

"Thanks," I said and continued running in the same direction. As I came to the corner and turned right I looked down along that canal as far as I could see. What grabbed my eye first was the arched footbridges with white wooden rails. Then, my gaze was drawn to something beyond the bridge, something floating in the water. The Venice Beach canals were lined with boats and jet skis and canoes. I could tell immediately that this was not some kind of watercraft. It was a dark mass half submerged in the water.

"Marty!" I shouted, and sprinted for the bridge.

I bounded over the arch and continued along the waterfront, my eyes fixed on the shape in the water. Whatever it was, the shape hadn't moved at all since I'd spotted it.

As I got closer, I saw that the shape was a body, lying motionless and face down.

I took a running jump into the water and landed next to it. To my surprise, my feet hit the bottom quickly, so I found myself standing in chest-high water.

I grabbed the body and turned it over to confirm what I already knew. It was Marty, his face white and his flesh cold.

I stepped around, and took his head in my hands. Holding his chin up with my left hand and pushing his forehead back with my right, I leaned over and put my ear to his mouth. Ten seconds went by slowly without me detecting even the faintest breath. I put my face over his and put five breaths into him. Then I dragged him to the edge of the water and managed to get myself up and out without letting his head sink. I got my arms under his armpits and pulled. I had his torso out of the water when Eddie arrived. He jumped in and together we lifted Marty up onto the walkway.

Marty was now stretched out on dry land but still as lifeless as when I found him. I put two more breaths into him and then stuck my fingers into the side of his neck in search of a pulse. I could feel none.

"Call 911," I said to Eddie, who thankfully had the foresight to leave his phone on the bank before entering the water. As he placed the call, I knelt over Marty and did thirty compressions on his chest. Then two more breaths. Then another thirty compressions. Then a breath and pulse check.

"Come on, Marty. Hang in there." I shouted.

I don't know how long this cycle went on for exactly but at some point I heard sirens and then the voices of the paramedics as they arrived, having been directed in by Eddie.

I stood up and watched them take over. In a matter of seconds, they had an oxygen mask on Marty and defibrillator pads poised above his chest. I could barely blink as I watched, trying to detect any signs-of-life movement in Marty's chest or face. Nothing.

I felt a hand on my shoulder and turned around to see Jack. He'd obviously seen no sign of Herron.

"Can I borrow your phone?" I said, drained of emotion. "I need to call Claire."

Jack handed me his cell. I found Claire in his contacts and held the tip of my finger over her name. That dread I'd had in the past about calling her was nothing like this. My stomach was achingly hollow. I held off making the call, watching the paramedics and hoping that a second from now they'd have a breakthrough. There was nothing, though, apart from their own paramedic chatter as they went about their work methodically.

I turned and walked away from the scene and tapped on Claire's name.

"Hello? Jack?" she answered before her phone had even completed a ring.

"Claire, it's me." I know how I sounded. It wasn't how I wanted to sound at all. I felt sick to my stomach. How was I going to tell her Marty was clinically dead and that the paramedics were fighting to get his heart going again so they could load him into the ambulance? I fully expected their next moves to be a grave shake of the head and a cover pulled over Marty's face.

"Where's Marty? Did you find him?"

I found it hard to say anything.

"Brad?"

"Yes, we found him, Claire. But he's been in the water. The paramedics are working on him."

"What? Are you saying he drowned?"

Behind me, I heard the paramedics' voices rise in volume. They were exchanging phrases of action and command. I turned around to see them lift Marty onto a gurney. Jack was looking at me, mouthing words silently and clearly.

"There's a pulse," he said.

"Brad? Are you there?"

Claire was in tears, trying to fend off her worst fear yet bracing to hear it.

"Yes, I'm here," I said. "They're just getting him into the ambulance. He'll be okay, Claire. He'll be okay."

Maybe I shouldn't have said that but for the life of me I couldn't bring myself to say anything else.

Chapter 41

Claire answered the door almost as soon as I rang the bell. She was expecting me and, as usual, I was punctual. I heard Bella in the background shooting the breeze with Tyson. Claire stepped back and made way for me to enter.

"Come in," she said, holding the door open. She had a handbag over her shoulder and her car keys dangling from her hand.

As I walked in, Bella came up to me and wrapped her arms around my waist. I bent down to hug her and kiss the top of her head before greeting Tyson.

"I've got to get going," said Claire, watching on with a faint smile. "I need to grab some things before I go to the hospital." She then tilted her head in the direction of her garage. "Walk me to my car?"

"Sure thing," I said, releasing Bella.

I followed Claire as she walked down a hall that led to the street end of the house. At the end was a door that opened onto the garage. Figuring Claire wanted our conversation to be private I shut the door behind me while Claire activated the garage door.

As she waited for the noise to stop, Claire looked like she'd prepared something to say to me, but the thought of it was upsetting her. When she tried to speak, she struggled. When she put her hand to her mouth I could see her fingers were shaking. She then squeezed her eyes shut to quell the surging emotions. The tears would not be stopped, though. She bent her head and sobbed before steeling herself and taking a deep intake of breath.

"I'm sorry," she said.

"It's okay," I said and held out a handkerchief. "Here. It's clean."

"Thanks," she said, and began dabbing her eyes.

"How's he doing?"

"He's fine, Brad. He's more than fine. He'll be out in a day or two."

"That's great to hear."

"He wants to thank you."

"Claire, there's really no need. He's already texted. I mean—"

I was about to say that I felt that I was partly responsible for Marty's plight, because it had to be Marty's testimony that triggered Herron into coming after him again. I believe Herron thought Marty had turned the suspicion on him. He was sure he was going to be outed, and once more he had Marty to blame for ruining his plans.

"He wants to thank you in person. Can you just let him, please?"

"Let's just wait till he gets home. I'm glad he's on the mend."

Claire gave me a look of mild admonishment at my understatement. Of course, she'd gone to thank the paramedics personally for saving his life and they'd told her Marty was clinically dead when I got to him. And they also let on that she had me to thank more than them. And she'd done that. She'd thanked me with such deep, tearful gratitude that I could never again doubt what Marty meant to her, and her to him. I did have the urge to point out to Claire that Jack and I were half right, that her crash was no accident. And that it was just the culprit part that I'd gotten spectacularly wrong. But I kept these thoughts to myself.

"He wouldn't be here if it weren't for you, Brad."

"Yeah, well don't make me regret it," I said, trying to lighten the mood.

"I'm not going to let you forget it, Brad. I won't. Nor will Marty."

"Has he spoken to the cops yet?"

"He gave a statement yesterday. They have the whole story. Marty was led to believe that there was a chance he could still get in on a deal with Adrenal. This Alex guy said he could give him some inside help to divert the Crestway deal and usher Beacon back in."

"And Herron put GHB in his coffee, right?"

"You know about that?"

"Yep. The cops came to me for a statement yesterday. With the amount Herron had put in his coffee, Marty was literally a pushover to get into the water. He couldn't have saved himself."

Claire reached out and touched my forearm, her eyes swimming in tears. "But you did. Thank God you were there."

"I'm really happy that it's all turned out well, Claire. I'm happy for you both. I mean that."

"Thank you. That means a lot to me."

I looked out at the street. "Well, you'd best be hitting the road, huh?"

Claire nodded but didn't move.

"Brad, I'm sorry about what I said in the hospital that day."

I shook my head. "Hey, that's ancient history. Our emotions were running high and I was way out of line. I know that now. It should be me apologizing, not you. I'm sorry."

"Look, what I said about Marty getting equal custody of Bella wasn't true. I was just trying to say something hurtful. But I don't want to do anything to keep her from you. And that's why I wanted to talk to you in private now."

"You want to talk about Bella?"

"Yes. Let's come to a new arrangement, all three of us together. If she's happy with a fifty-fifty split and it's what you want and if it works for you, then let's make those changes. Okay?"

"That'd be awesome, Claire."

She smiled, wiped her eyes again and gave my handkerchief back. "Well, that's it then. You'll—"

"I'll drop her back tomorrow like normal. Let's keep things as they are until you've got the headspace to deal with it. There's no rush."

"Okay. See you tomorrow."

After Claire drove off, I shut the garage door and made my way inside to pick up Bella. She was coming with me to the office for a few hours before we filled in the afternoon doing whatever the hell we wanted. I had some paperwork to do on the Jenna Lewis case that couldn't wait.

Given Jenna Lewis's retraction, all charges against Eddie Mawson were dropped. ADA Elliott Goodwin was not happy at all. He felt as if a glorious triumph had been snatched from him. At first, he insisted that I'd strong-armed Jenna Lewis somehow but Judge Odell was having none of it. Goodwin wasted no time in filing a perjury charge against her and he was most displeased to learn I'd be defending her. The fact that Lewis could prove she'd been blackmailed into making a false rape allegation and committing perjury was definitely going to work in her favor.

The cops had pulled Herron out from under his bed at his mother's San Francisco residence and introduced him to a bunk in LA's Men's Central Jail. He had pleaded not guilty to a string of charges, including two attempts at murder, so Lewis would surely be a key witness for Goodwin at trial.

Even if Herron ended up taking a deal, I'd remind Goodwin in the strongest terms that without Lewis's voluntary assistance Marty Cosgrove would be dead. All considered, I was highly confident that I could get a result for Jenna Lewis that meant no time served.

Bella took a seat in reception while I went into my office.

My phone vibrated and I took it out of my pocket. It was a message from Cobus Lombard.

I'd been pushing him to pass on an offer to Darius Tucker. I'd hoped that he wouldn't be too attached to the project that he'd backed at Abby's fundraiser. I'd offered to buy him out at a fifty percent premium. I held no hope of patching things up with Abby, but at least she could move forward knowing that her cherished project was no longer tied to a criminal enterprise.

"The answer is no," Lombard's message read. "That is final. Bring it up again and it will be dealt with as a hostile provocation."

My charm had its limits, obviously.

I wasn't kidding myself that Abby would be thrilled if Tucker accepted my offer. To her, lawyer money was probably no better than drug money.

There was no way I could make it right.

Some things you just can't fix.

THE END

AFTERWORD

Thanks so much for reading *Veil of Justice*. I really hope you enjoyed the ride. Could I ask you to do a couple of things to help the book's prospects? First, please write a positive review on Amazon. Second, please recommend the book to fellow readers. Such support means a great deal to an independent writer like me.

All the best,

J.J.

Books by J.J. Miller

BRAD MADISON SERIES

Force of Justice

Divine Justice

Game of Justice

Blood and Justice

Veil of Justice

CADENCE ELLIOTT SERIES

I Swear To Tell

The Lawyer's Truth

Printed in Great Britain
by Amazon